FUTURE IMPERFECT

Carmen Capuano

Carmen Capuano Productions

Copyright © 2023 Carmen Capuano

All rights reserved

The characters and events portrayed in this book are fictitious. Any similarity to real persons, living or dead, is coincidental and not intended by the author.

No part of this book may be reproduced, or stored in a retrieval system, or transmitted in any form or by any means, electronic, mechanical, photocopying, recording, or otherwise, without express written permission of the publisher.

ISBN-13: 978-1-9168771-7-7

Cover design by: Ruan Human

CHAPTER 1

The dining hall seems busier than usual this morning. Or perhaps just louder. Each sound, however quietly made, however softly intended, seems an affront to my heart.

Is Greyson already here? I purposely don't turn my head towards his family's assigned table – I'm not sure if I will relax if I see him there, or be relieved if I don't. So I don't dare look.

Instead I keep my gaze fixed on the electronic reader which bleeps quietly as it scans my wrist, deciphering my level of essential nutrients, oxygen saturation, body mass - figuring out if I've been a good girl. Or not.

I am rewarded by a little door in the wall sliding open. I reach in and retrieve my plate. Hot waffles and syrup; I can only imagine that ELSA is satisfied that I am in optimum physical health.

Lucky me.

But the scanner can't see inside my head, can't sense the sharpening malaise that festers there.

"Thank you for my treat, ELSA," I

say, deadpan. If the Enhanced Living System Autonomy senses my sarcasm, it either chooses to take no notice, or a withering response is beyond its capabilities. I prefer to believe the latter, that ELSA is *just* a machine, devoid of personality, incapable of malice.

Clutching my warm plate, I cast my gaze around for an empty seat. Everyone sits at the same place for every meal, but unless I sit with Greyson and his family, I'm forced to constantly change places. Because unlike every other living soul, I have no place of my own.

Still, I don't look for him. There are days and weeks ahead when I will be more than happy to consider our wedding. But not today. Today I just want to be me – or as much 'me' as being an individual in the dome is allowed.

All I want, is to sit quietly and watch. Not that there is ever very much to see.

Sometimes I wonder what it is that I expect to find that's any different; parents sit with children, husbands sit with wives, all is as it should be and as it ever was. Apart from me.

I am an outcast, a social misfit. I have no husband and therefore no children. Nor do I have parents or siblings. Unique within the Dome, I alone, *am* alone. Truly.

It is perhaps that exact reason which makes me choose to sit next to an unknown family. Part of them by sheer proximity, I am necessarily separate by the circumstances of my birth, giving me a safe emotional distance from which to observe their breakfast repast. With them and yet not.

The parents and children, a boy of about ten and a girl who looks about seven, look at me as I sit down with them. I don't bother to smile or to make their acquaintance. Our fleeting connection is for the duration of this meal only. Unless I choose to sit with Grey's family, next meal there will be another table for me, another family. Different and yet the same.

I keep my gaze focused on my food, away from them, away from their boring, common, *wonderful* normality.

"ELSA wouldn't let me have waffles today." The little girl says to me, her gaze fixed woefully on my food. I nod slowly as if that answers her comment and return my gaze to the safety of my plate.

"I only ever had waffles twice before... but they were so good that I almost wanted to sick them up, just so I could eat them all over again."

It so innocently revolting, that despite myself, I bark out a laugh. Surprised into an involuntary response, I wonder what I can say that won't encourage further conversation.

"I'm sure she has a reason," I say stealing a glance towards her.

She looks at me so disparagingly, as perhaps

only a seven year old can, that I'm forced to continue with the regulatory wisdom. "ELSA knows what your body needs, not what it wants."

I shift my attention back to my food but her silence is so profound and protracted, that even though it's what I crave, I feel my eyes drawn unwillingly back to her face.

Her stare is wounded, her face a crumpled mess that makes me want to laugh and cry simultaneously. This is not the peace and solitude I wanted, that I had sought. But perhaps these circumstances will better alleviate my mood than solitude would have done? Perhaps chatting with the little girl will soothe me in a way that Grey's family with all their *knowing*, jovial chatter, can't.

I try to smile. I feel it tug at the corners of my mouth but it fades away before it reaches my eyes and I'm left feeling as hollow as before. Maybe tomorrow and all the other days I'll feel better, I'll smile for real. Maybe. But today, it's a struggle. I let my mouth form the flat line it desires.

"I'm Fortitude Smith. But most people call me Tudie. What's your name?"

"Willow," she says simply.

She smiles and unlike mine, her smile seems to reach each part of her face, transforming every plane and curvature, elevating it from merely beautiful to something more, something less easily definable.

I'm so taken aback that I almost gasp. I am

mistaken, I must be. All Alphas are beautiful, that's just how we are. There is surely nothing any different about this girl, no extra radiance, no indefinable essence of something extra-special... or is there? I'm no longer sure of my own perceptions.

I cut into one of my waffles. "Willow, that's a lovely name." The conversation might easily be concluded now without offence, but her smile lingers in my memory. She has touched me in some way that I don't just want to dismiss.

I glance briefly at her family, but no one is watching us, none of them listening. They're talking about the day ahead as if it's not going to be like every other day in the dome. On and on, from birth until death.

What I am about to do could end in me being punished by ELSA, but I know with absolute certainty that I will take the risk, that it's worth a week of porridge for every meal.

"It's the name of a *tree*," she volunteers, watching my knife moving backwards and forwards, sawing the waffles into pieces; and in that one word, 'tree' there is such longing in her voice it breaks my heart.

I nod. "So it is. And to grow straight and tall, trees need lots of good things."

I have seen real live trees only a handful of times in my life. And Willow - she who bears the name of one - has this child *ever* seen a tree? Ever touched the rough wood of a trunk, felt the soft crush of leaves within her palm? I doubt it.

I keep my voice even, bland and without emphasis, but I transfer a pyramid of bite-sized pieces of syrup-enrobed waffle onto her plate. It looks incongruous sitting there next to the kale and broccoli omelette, which looks like it's been produced with a whole forest of greenery and a scarcity of egg.

Willow's eyes are huge and instantly I am concerned. Will the child give me away? Will she exclaim loudly and alert her parents, attract ELSA's attention?

One heartbeat folds itself across time as I consider what my punishment might be. Just the porridge? Or solitary confinement? Certainly there will be no more waffles and syrup. And maybe not just for me. Maybe Grey will be punished too. For a computer, ELSA isn't always that rational.

But the girl makes no noise to alert anyone to what I've done. Instead she sits silently eyeing up the treat, as if afraid that if she raises cutlery to it, it will fade into nonexistence.

Before someone notices something amiss, I hiss through a false smile, "Bend over your plate, Willow! And eat it! Quickly!"

She doesn't need to be told a second time. By the time my words have faded into the air, the waffle pieces are gone, the last tiny globs of syrup scraped onto the green gloop and dissected into bite sized chunks. Reluctantly, she forces one of these into her mouth, nose wrinkling at either the taste or the smell. From experience I'd guess that it was a combination of the two.

"I know ELSA was designed to keep us fit and healthy," I lower my voice a little, "but sometimes I think she tries too hard. Don't you?"

Willow nods but otherwise ignores my question and looks around. "Where's your family?"

I take my time in answering and settle on the simplest thing I can say. "I don't have one."

Her face is incredulous, as if I have grown horns and fangs in an instant; as if my aloneness makes me a monster. "*Everyone* has family!"

I know she doesn't mean it to be hurtful, that she's only a little girl, but her words and tone of voice sting me like nothing else could have done. Greenery hangs from the fork suspended halfway to her mouth and I'm aware that we are starting to attract attention from her mother.

"Not me." I'm determined to keep it brief. It was a mistake to have chosen to sit here. To have let someone even a *little way* into my heart. I should have known better, me of all people.

I should have looked for Greyson after all, sat with his family, smiled vacantly when they talked about the wedding and just pretended to be okay about everything. But I couldn't. Not today. Not on this, the first anniversary of my father's death.

My heart hammers painfully in double time. I will eat quickly and leave. Walk away from this table, this unusual child.

"Why not?" The gloop finally makes its way to her mouth and her mother turns her attention back to the rest of the family. I carefully let my breath out.

"It's a long story," I say eager for this to be over, yet unable to ignore her question. "You'll be late for schooling."

She looks at me with a candour that's older than her years.

"I start today. My 'sessment is at ten am." She tries to affect a carefree attitude. It doesn't work and serves only to jangle my frayed nerves.

"Assessment," I correct automatically. "Anyway I have work," I fob her off.

"You're here now," she says. "Tell me."

I sigh. I could refuse and leave, but the pain when I think of my father is so raw, so excruciatingly intense that I want to scream. If I have to keep this inside me the whole day, I think that I might die too. In fact, dying might be the preferable option...

"My dad died last year. A year ago today, actually." Even though it doesn't feel like a year. It feels like only yesterday. Fresh and vivid and unaccepted.

She blinks, long lashes framing eyes that are

riveted on me, latched onto my pain. "Why'd he die? Didn't ESLA look after him?"

It's a conversation I don't want to have, but I tell myself that if I leave now, if I upset the girl, there is always the chance that she will tell about the waffle. Even though I did it for her.

I know I'm lying to myself, that I'm letting her pull this out of me, letting her pick the scab of my deepest wound. It will hurt, there's little doubt of that, but maybe, just maybe, it will also stop the suppuration from the cut, allow it finally to start to heal. And maybe then I can allow myself to accept that he's gone, forever.

"He wasn't ill. There was an accident. It was no one's fault really, but he was killed."

There's a lump in my throat, tightening it to a slit too narrow to even swallow my own saliva. But ELSA doesn't tolerate food to be left-over. Or anything really. Like what we eat, what we do is not our choice in the dome.

I cram the remaining bits of waffle into my mouth and force them down my gullet. The syrup, once invitingly sweet, now seems cloying, thick and heavily scented. I want to heave but I hold it down. The remembered expressed sentiment of Willow wanting to, 'sick it up so she could re-eat it', haunts me nauseatingly.

"Oh. That's terrible!" She clearly doesn't know what to say for a moment. Then her face brightens, "But you could sit with your mum and brother or sister."

"I don't have any other family." I hope I sound matter-of-fact, not self-pitying. But the sorrow and confusion in her eyes, informs me otherwise. Once again I am forced to explain.

"My mum died when I was born. I was the first child," I nod across the table, "like your brother was in your family. So with my mum dead, there could be no more children. It was just me and my dad." I force the lump down again. "Until he died too. Then it was just me."

"But everyone has to have two children!" she says, as if this is news to me. I say nothing.

Her gaze flits across the table. "I've got a brother but he doesn't like me. I don't much like him either." Her nose wrinkles in distaste once more. "So maybe you could be my sister? I know it wouldn't be real, but if we both tried, thought of each other like that, then it would be more real than me and him are."

Her words strike a chord with me. If a bond can be forged in marriage, why can't it be forged in other mutually agreed ways? Why must ELSA be allowed to dictate who we love?

Willow's eyes are honest, innocent and too hopeful for me to dash the dreams which reside there.

"I'd be honoured," I say. And I am. I'm genuinely touched by her kindness. It can't undo the pain of my missing father but it's something to cling to, a bond that is beyond ELSA's control. I reach across and squeeze her hand. "Sisters," I say.

"Sisters," she repeats after me, eyes shining. I wonder if I look as happy to her, even fleetingly, as she does to me.

"Look, I have to go to work now, but I'll come see you later. You can tell me about your day, okay?"

She nods.

"Okay then." I smile completely genuinely, for the first time today. "Good luck with your 'sessment," I grin, making it our private joke. "I'm sure ELSA will place you in the highest set!" I grab my plate and dash, before I'm late for work.

I feel her eyes watching me all the way to the disposal units, where I hold my wrist up once more to the reader. One of the many doors in the wall slides open and I deposit my plate inside, where it too is scanned.

Have a good day, Fortitude Smith, comes up on the digital readout and as my spirits have been slightly elevated, I can't resist answering back, giving the computer something to think about.

"I'll try, ELSA," I say, "but I'm making no promises."

The readout changes immediately. *A promise – a declaration or assurance that one will do something or that a particular thing will happen.*

As the future is unknown, promises cannot with any accuracy be made, Fortitude Smith, ELSA informs me.

I want to bite back but I refrain.

Your brain waves are displaying unusual and shifting patterns, Fortitude Smith. I also detect chemical changes in your physiology. This will be righted in your next meal with the correct balance of nutrients.

I don't enlighten ELSA that an axe in my hands and her torn and mangled electrical wiring at my feet, are one of the few things that could make me feel better. I turn away before I do something I will regret.

Bad timing means that Greyson arrives at the exit at the same time as me. He tries not to look hurt that I have clearly avoided him. I wonder if he has been watching me with Willow. And what he might have made of the fact that I'd avoided him.

"I thought you'd skipped breakfast," he says lightly, not betraying whether or not he'd known exactly where I was.

"Like ELSA would allow that," I joke equally lightly, unwilling somehow to share with him how I'm feeling, even though he knows why today is so hard for me. Maybe that's actually the reason. He knows as little as I do about that day last year. Nothing can be gained by us going over and over those sparse facts.

Luckily he adopts my pretended mood.

"Well in your case, she might make an

exception, seeing as how she wouldn't want you to get fat!" He slaps me playfully on the rump, making me jump. "Can't have an overweight Alpha. You'd have to go live with the Deltas," he jokes.

It's a thin attempt to take my mind off my troubles but since I've been avoiding him, I latch onto it. Upsetting and alienating Grey won't bring my father back.

"Hey, there's nothing fat about me!" I sidle up to him, allowing my chest to rub lightly along the side of his arm. "You on the other hand, well I think ELSA has a programming error over you. You're looking a bit padded-out these days!" I sprint lightly away, knowing that he will chase after me, needing suddenly the normality of our relationship more than anything else. Whilst marriage is part of ELSA's regulations, I've chosen Grey over all the other available Alpha males, so it almost feels like a victory. Almost.

I keep just ahead of him in the wide corridor, dashing through and around other workers on their way to and from work. But as I reach my section door I pause, letting him catch me up before I go in.

His lips brush mine briefly. Neither of us are breathless from the chase. Nor is there a breathlessness caused by passion. But there is love evident in the kiss, sweet and forgiving.

"I missed you at breakfast. So did everyone

else," he says and waits for a response. Maybe an apology.

I nod quietly, disinclined to admit where I had sat and why. For now I am still me, Fortitude Smith. Unmarried, unanswerable to anyone.

"You know you won't be allowed to keep running away from me once we are married." Something in his tone makes me aware that this is a serious concern for him. I raise my eyes and lips to his, once more, hoping that a kiss will prevent the need for explanation.

But before our lips touch, he places his hands on my arms and holds me slightly away from him. "You do know that, don't you, Tudie? That once we are wed you will have to be with me? That this thing you have about being different will end?"

I'm a little annoyed that he says it like I relish my differentness. I'm different because I was born that way. It was never a choice.

He is holding me so firmly I can't pull away, so instead I shift my gaze, waiting for the burst of anger I feel to recede. No part of my situation is Grey's fault. But neither is it mine.

Other Alphas pass us by, all strong, all beautiful, and I wonder how many of them ever stop to think about life, how fortunate and privileged they are, *we* are.

"You are the handsomest man I have ever seen." I don't mean it as a distraction from the previous conversation, merely as an honest remark and a way to move us back into being us.

One of his hands moves to my face, forcing my eyes to meet his. Cobalt irises look back at me from features that should only grace a God, fine chiselled cheekbones sitting either side of a nose that is both elegant and perfectly proportioned. His lips, full and wide, are drawn across bright white teeth in a smile.

"And you are the most beautiful girl in Alpha Class, Tudie. We will make beautiful children together!"

An involuntary fear strikes at my heart with his words but I dare not voice it. Instead I speak other truths, avoiding the things I don't want to face today. "I love you so much -"

He cuts me off, "And I love you too. So will you stop running away from me?"

I deliberately misunderstand. "I was letting you chase me until you caught me." I smile sweetly.

"That's not what I meant." He runs a hand down my cheek. "Let's have dinner outside tonight. We'll have a picnic somewhere pretty."

"But ELSA won't-" I protest.

"Let me sort ELSA," he says. "I'll send a request for fresh air and a little space for us. It will be approved," he assures me. "Like you said, ELSA has a blip in her programming when it comes to me." He winks theatrically. "Now get to work!"

Gallantly he holds the door open for me and

I reluctantly enter my work place. He is gone, but not before I have turned around to watch him striding up the corridor towards his own section, back strong and straight, hands once more at his sides.

And then the door begins to fall back into place, cutting off my view, making me wonder if he would *ever* have turned around to find me watching him, ever have needed one final glance of me, as I did of him.

With a *thunk*, the door closes and its latch engages. For some inexplicable reason it's the most ominous sound I have ever heard.

CHAPTER 2

I pore over the coming month's weather conditions in Delta Sector 9, and compare them to charts of previous years, that I pull out of the gap between my workstation and the wall. I'm supposed to dispose of the old charts, recycling them in the relevant bins, but I never do. It's not like I'm hiding them, because it's ELSA who produces them for me to use, but although I can't explain it, I choose not to publicise the fact that I keep them.

There's a strange beauty to be found in the flowing lines of the charts, whether sharply angled across the page, or curving smoothly, and I like to gaze at them, trace them with my finger. They are our history, our lives lived totally under cover of the dome, without chance to sample the strange and quickly changing weather conditions outside. For that reason alone, I feel they ought to survive, to be testament to the fact that we are not the centre of our own universe.

And the charts tell their own story - there are differences across the years, shown by a fluctuating line. Especially in the last few years, where conditions for growing and maintaining crops have become ever more erratic.

But this year's chart is even more striking than its predecessors. Filled with contrasting spikes and troughs, it reminds me of pictures of mountains and valleys, highs and lows which are all the more dramatic by their juxtaposition.

Luckily, the Deltas have me on their side, sending them ELSA's interpretations of the graphs. Telling them when to plant and shelter the various crops, when to give additional nutrients and finally when to harvest.

What any of those things actually entail is beyond my limited knowledge but that's of no consequence. I am merely the human interface between our arable farming sectors and ELSA. It's not something I chose. Like everything else in life, it's just my assigned role. But it's this which keeps our supply of food constant and of the highest quality.

Joy wanders over to my workstation just as I finish typing information into the monitor which will be relayed to the Deltas. I press 'send'.

"Greyson was looking for you this morning," she informs me, placing a cup of water on the edge of my desk.

I slurp at the drink, taking my time, choosing how best to respond. "The wedding is in a few months, there's a lot to sort out."

"Yes I know. Remember?" She flashes her own engagement ring at me, a huge diamond that someone in Kappa Class probably broke his back to extract from the mines. "Only a few weeks until I get married. And then I start my own family," her smile is rapturous.

The water in my mouth tastes suddenly rank, like sludge water, drained from a field. There's a sinking feeling in the pit of my stomach and I can't stop the words which tumble from my mouth. "Aren't you even a little afraid, Joy?" I ask.

Of having a baby? Of living your whole life just within these walls? Or never even trying to find out what else you could be? What else you could do? Of never, ever, being just you? I want to add all of these things but don't.

"Of marrying Brent?" she asks, looking surprised at the idea. Then she sees the look on my face. Interprets it in the only way she knows how. She pulls up a chair and sits down next to me.

"Look, Tudie, what happened to your mum was a terrible accident. ELSA has been improved since then. Births are so much more monitored and controlled now, than they were back then."

And she's right. But for me, that doesn't change anything. I don't feel inclined to mince my words. "She bled to death, Joy."

Part of me is ashamed of the fear and pain I am trying to offload onto her, as if the sharing of it will lessen its impact upon me, lessen my guilt at having survived at my mother's expense.

"She died giving birth to me!" I don't know whether I am more ashamed of this fact, or terrified about what it might mean for my own future. For my ability to keep on living, breathing in and out; of one day giving life to children of my own.

With long blonde hair which swishes delicately around an elfin face, Joy is too full of light and far too beautiful to look troubled. On her, the look is almost haughty, as if she is beyond earthly woes.

The monitor in front of me has gone black and into standby and in its dark mirror I see our joint reflection. Even on the screen she seems to shine, whilst my dark hair disappears, so that all that is revealed of me, are troubled eyes set within a pale haunted expression.

"It wasn't your fault!" she says, wrapping an arm around me, "And it won't happen to you. I promise."

I am reminded of ELSA's response to my own use of a promise earlier on. It seems fateful to say the least.

"You don't know what might happen, no one does!"

Joy doesn't reply. Perhaps she no longer knows what to say to alleviate my fears. Or perhaps I have sowed a seed of doubt in her head too! I am ashamed that I have blighted the day she is so looking forward to.

"Look, I'm just a little crazy today. What with it being the anniversary -"

"Of your dad's death," she finishes for me. "I get it, Tudie, I completely do! You've had the worst luck ever, but that's going to change, now you have Greyson."

I find myself smiling sadly, but there is a hope which is trying to spring up in my heart at her words. If I let it, if I nourish it there, then maybe I will find some peace. I think too about Willow and her offer of sisterhood. I have no real family and yet there are people who love me, people who *want* to be my family. Surely that has to count for something?

"Don't you have a job to get on with?" I say lightly. If we continue to talk like this, I think I might cry. And if I allow those tears to be unleashed, will I ever contain them again?

"I think the Gamma Sectors can do without my information just a little longer," she says. "I don't think food production will grind to a halt if we talk for a few minutes."

"I'm fine, honestly," I assure her. "I just need to get through today." I think about my fiancé's idea. "Greyson said we should go for a picnic tonight. Outside." I shrug, "The weather's going to be good."

Joy laughs, "Well you should know." She

stands, ready to move away, back to her own workstation. "If ELSA allows it, you should go. It would do wonders for your complexion."

I force a laugh. "First he implies I have to watch my weight, now you're saying I look pasty!" I expect her to laugh too, but she doesn't.

She stops pushing her chair back to its original position and favours me with her full gaze. "You are far from overweight, Tudie. In fact, if anything, you could do with gaining a few pounds. And you are still beautiful. That goes without saying. But in all honestly, you *have* been looking a little pale lately. Maybe the change would do you good."

Am I pasty after all? I think once more of our faces reflected on the dark monitor and pull a small mirror out of my desk drawer. My eyes are the same mid-brown they always are but there are dark smudges under them that I don't remember noticing before. My long brown hair, pulled back in a tight chignon is a little lack-lustre compared to memories of how it used to shine, and there is a slight furrowed line between my eyebrows that I'm sure didn't exist before my dad died.

I press my finger gently into the fold of skin between my brows. The crease isn't deep but it has a feeling of permanence, as if it's here to stay. I push the mirror back into the drawer, letting it fall wherever it may, amongst the other paraphernalia there.

"Will Grey still love me if I look old and haggard?" I don't mean to ask the question out loud, but it comes out nonetheless. I almost hold my breath, waiting for Joy's answer to the unintended question.

She seems surprised again and I'm forced to wonder why these thoughts that circulate in my head, seem not to bother anyone else. Is it really just the circumstance of my birth that makes me so different to everyone here? Or is it some other less definable thing?

"Grey? You really have to ask that question? Fortitude Smith that boy loves you more than anything in this world or the next!" She laughs, a light tinkling sound, as if my question is the most ridiculous thing she's ever heard.

"Grey couldn't fall out of love with you, if you sprouted horns and green teeth!"

It's so close to an image I had thought earlier, when talking to Willow, that once more there seems to be a significance to the day that I just can't shake. "I suppose," I say quietly, not really convinced.

She snorts derisively. "You *suppose*! Oh Tudie, you really are funny! How could any Alpha ever be ugly? It's just not possible."

I don't know if she's right or not. But then I'm used to not understanding much about my own life, *all* of our lives here in the dome. About our purpose; about why ELSA guards us so intently from the world outside.

"Joy, why do you think we give ELSA's orders and information to other sectors, when she could send it to them herself?"

If anyone knows the answer to this it's Joy; her father is one of the team of people who work on the computer system's mainframe.

"People with lesser intelligence don't respond well to being told what to do," she answers easily, "unless it's by another human. Certainly not by a machine."

I'm a little annoyed by this suggestion which seems just a little too glib. After all, the information I send is electronically relayed, it's not like I'm speaking to them in person.

"That can't be right. I mean they know the information is coming from ELSA anyway, and it's all for the greater good…"

For the first time I see what looks like a scathing expression settle on her face. Embarrassed, I turn away from her, pretending to study my screen for a moment. I press a button and the display lights up once more. I fix my gaze on it intently.

"Tudie, I'm really surprised at you. You know that Alphas are the only people who can understand ELSA's perfect reasoning. The other classes are less intelligent and therefore more emotionally driven. Who can really know what goes on in their tiny brains? So that's why Alphas marry Alphas, Betas marry Betas, and so on and everyone sticks to their own class."

There's something very *wrong* about the way she says 'their own class' as if she is talking about a different species. I feel my head snap back in her direction.

"Don't Alphas marry Alphas because they never come into contact with any other class or sector? Isn't that the reason?" My voice is sharp, shrill even; I no longer know if I'm asking her, or both of us. But what I do know, is that neither of us are really qualified to be debating this. I wonder how many times ELSA has allowed Joy out of the dome? More than that, I wonder how few times Joy has *desired* to be outside, where not everything is as beautiful and perfect and sterile as it is here, inside the dome.

She shrugs, almost reads my mind. "Don't you think there's a reason why all the classes live in their own territories, Tudie? And why the classes live so far apart from one another? Surely it's so that we don't come into contact by accident?"

I refuse to answer. Because my answer might really infuriate her. *Why would that be so bad?* I want to ask, but don't.

"Then of course there's not only the issue of intelligence which would make us so incompatible with other classes, but levels of attractiveness too."

Now she has my full attention. "What do you mean?"

She looks at me like I'm unbelievably stupid. "Come on, you have to be kidding me!"

"Tell me what you mean," I insist.

"Have you ever seen an Alpha who is just *pretty*, who isn't particularly beautiful in some outstanding way? Figure? Eyes? Hair?" she stands, hands on hips, daring me.

"Humans are an attractive species." I hunt around in my memory of schooling for a good example, "like leopards all have spots and are sleek and fast."

"Trust me, humans aren't *all* naturally attractive," she says as if she's an authority on the matter.

I have no experience with which to refute her words, having never seen anyone but Alphas my entire life.

"You don't know that!" I hate the fact that I sound dumb and more than a little unsure of myself. I try to be rational. "Okay, even if you are right, even if the other classes aren't *as* attractive as Alphas –"

"Tudie, my dad has seen the people in other sectors. Did you know that? He had to go out there long ago, when they tried to extend ELSA across the territories."

No, I hadn't known. Not that Joy's father had been so far outside the dome, or that there had been plans to extend ELSA's reach. I am silent, letting her continue in her own time whilst I mull those things over.

"He said a lot of the people were misshapen because of the work they did and many were pocked with disease and infection. But even those who weren't, even the ones who were strong and disease free, they were all ugly in some way."

"Why didn't ELSA get extended?" I ask, no longer interested in the attractiveness or not of the entirety of the human race.

"I don't really know. Something to do with the other classes' lack of intelligence and the fact that they seemed to be afraid of ELSA."

It strikes me that maybe their 'lack of intelligence' had stood them in good stead if that really was the case. For there is no denying that even though ELSA means well, her control of everything and everyone inside the dome is complete.

Unaware of the tangent my thoughts have taken, Joy trills a little laugh. "So Gammas marry Gammas, Kappas marry Kappas, and they all produce ugly, lower-intelligence children." She shudders as if the thought of such children walking the earth is repugnant. "And Alphas marry other Alphas and produce beautiful, intelligent offspring. It's how it's always been, since the dome. How it's *meant* to be."

She turns towards me, bestowing on me the

full beauty that is Joy. "And you will do the exact same thing, Fortitude Smith. You will marry Greyson and have the most adorable two children Alpha Class has ever seen."

Somewhere in the very pit of my stomach, something coils and uncoils.

CHAPTER 3

I spend the rest of the workday totally immersed in charts of wind direction and temperature fluctuations, working bent over my desk as if there was nothing more important whizzing around my head than numbers and co-ordinates. By the time Grey arrives, I am in such inner turmoil that I think I might explode if I have to stay inside much longer.

His face is carefree, happy, but this changes as soon as he sees me, picking up easily on what I have tried so hard to hide. "What's wrong?" he asks.

I shake my head. *Not here. Not now.* "It's just today – you know…" Even I don't know if that's the full answer, or just the easy one. The day has been full of strange twists and turns, and even stranger conversations. If I have to tell him exactly how I feel, I'm not sure where I should start. Today? A year ago? Longer than that?

He folds his arms around me, forcing him to place the bag he's brought with him, on the floor. The top gapes open a little and I see chunks of pie and packaged salad leaves. Food and comfort, that's what he's offering me. And what more could I really need? I wind my arms around his waist and draw us closer together, nuzzling my face into his neck.

"You got permission then?" I ask, my lips against the hot warmth of his skin there, not really aware until now of how much I had doubted he would.

I feel his head nod up and down. "I told ELSA that under the circumstances you needed to get away for a few hours. She totally agreed."

"But ELSA's a machine, Grey," I argue. "It can't possibly understand feelings. Not like that anyway."

He purses his lips and unwraps me from his embrace. "She might be a machine, but she's a pretty sophisticated one!" he counters.

I prod him lightly in the stomach, fingers encountering only muscle beneath his light top. "'Sophisticated' is 'she' now? And 'pretty' as well? I think you work with her components too closely for my liking!"

I'm aware that I'm only half teasing. Everyone refers to ELSA as a she, because of the acronym of the computer's title, although a machine can clearly be neither male nor female. And yet... sometimes I think that Grey admires the system just a little too much.

He laughs and picks up the bag of food. "Oh

jealously!" He bends to give me a light kiss on the nose. "Well I can't say I'm averse to two females fighting over me," he grins, "even if one of them is a computer!"

I laugh with him at the silly image he's conjured in my head of ELSA and I, each of us holding fast to one of his arms and tugging him in opposite directions.

"That's better," he says. "At least you're smiling again. Just remember it's you I'm taking on the picnic, not her." He grabs my arm, waves to Joy who is still working at her desk, and we are off.

My pace down the long corridor is almost a sprint and I am a little out of breath with anticipation by the time we reach the dome's main entrance. Floor to ceiling steel walls serve as doors, which pull back as soon as we scan our wrists.

Behind us, people stop dead in their tracks, watching to see who has been granted rare permission to go outside.

Enjoy your picnic, Greyson Ford and Fortitude Smith, the readout displays. *Please be aware that the outside temperature is currently 17 degrees centigrade and that air pollution from pollen is high.*

"Thank you ELSA," Grey says, then adds mischievously in a sing-song, "I'll miss you."

Before I have a chance to say anything, ELSA's readout changes.

I hope you find the time outside beneficial to

your well-being, Fortitude Smith.

It's so unexpected, and almost human, that I actually laugh. "Did you do this?" I ask Grey as we step through the doorway, leaving everyone staring wistfully in our wake.

"Absolutely not," he says and then when I continue to stare at him, hands on my hips, he gives in. "Well, I might have had a little something to do with the ever-so-slight tweaking of her programme…"

I laugh again at his rueful expression but it makes me think. Almost unconsciously, I make a half-turn back towards the people in the dome. Standing as I am, I could almost reach back and touch them if I chose.

No one has moved. It's like they are frozen there, rooted to the spot, against their wishes. It's almost creepy, as if they have no will of their own. My stomach coils once more, and I force myself to turn away from their faces, and back to the wonder of the outside. Out of sight, out of mind. Hopefully.

Behind me, the dome's doors shut almost silently with only the slightest hiss of hydraulics. Even though I don't watch the slow progress of those heavy sheets of steel, I *feel* them close, feel a weight shift from my shoulders, float upwards in the warm air and just dissipate. The effect this has on me is immediate.

With my back to the colossal structure which

serves as our cocoon, I can almost make-believe that we lead our lives out here, amongst the long grasses and the wild animals, unprotected and uncontrolled the way I've heard people used to be.

Without moving, I close my eyes and slowly reopen them. I'm standing on the very rim of my world, a flat piece of metal that serves as a kind of doorstep, but before I take one step onto that verdant carpet of wild grass, I remove my shoes.

"Take yours off too," I tell Grey.

He smiles and unfastens his shoes, casting them aside and stepping beside me onto the flat meadow. I pull him forward, needing to walk as far as it takes before I can no longer see the dome just by turning around.

Birds sing sweetly and it's such a strange sound to my ears that I find I am almost mesmerised by their haunting melodies, falling into an easy walking pace in time to their rhythm.

There is so much I want to talk about, so much to say - and yet I don't want to spoil the idyll of this moment by sullying it with worries. I reach for Grey's hand.

After over an hour of walking, we come upon a copse of trees. Not quite extensive or dense enough to be called a forest, they are still adequate cover from the immense structure, so that when I chance to look behind me, I can't actually see where we work and eat and sleep and spend every second of every minute, every day of our lives.

A little beyond the trees, a stream winds its way to whatever destination it seeks. Sunlight, dappled through the branches, hits the water here and there, making of the almost flat surface a jewelled floor glistening with bright diamonds.

"Here," I say, plonking myself down onto a shaded patch of grass. "Let's eat here."

Grey looks around him. "It's beautiful." He bends to pick a small flower from the grass and twines it around a loose strand of my hair. His hand lingers on me and I sense that he too, is holding something back.

I watch him lay out the food. As well as the salad and slices of pie I'd seen earlier, there's also fresh fruit and bread, slices of cheese and cold meats. Whatever he's said or done to ELSA has provided excellent results.

"This was such a good idea of yours," I say, picking at a slice of dry bread and popping some into my mouth. "I wish we could do this all the time."

"We probably wouldn't enjoy it as much if we did it all the time," he says. "And besides we have work to do."

Even though I don't want to ruin the day, I can't stop myself from thinking about everyone we've left behind at the dome. About the people who looked as if they longed to step over the doorway with us, but didn't. Because they had no permission to do so from ELSA.

"Why aren't we allowed out?"

"What do you mean? We're out now."

"That's *exactly* what I mean Grey. To come outside we have to have permission. Why is it like that? Why can't we just come and go as we please? All of us, not just you and me, today."

He looks at me like no one has ever asked that before. Maybe he's right, maybe no one has.

"It's ELSA's job to look after us."

"It's a *machine*." I smile so he doesn't take offense. "Surely it's good for us to be out in the fresh air?"

"ELSA was established to look after us, Tudie, you know that."

I'm suddenly angry with him for refusing to see my point. "ELSA is a machine, Grey, nothing more. We shouldn't have to ask its permission to do something so natural as go outside!"

He refutes my logic with some of my own. "Granted it's beautiful out here, Tudie. But there are pollutants we can't even see. Inside the dome we are protected. Air quality is monitored, germs and bacteria are destroyed, and we live at the optimum temperature for our organs to work perfectly. And all of that is ELSA's doing."

I can't disagree with him but the grass feels so good under my feet that I don't even try to resist curling my toes around the long blades. I watch him choose a slice of cheese and a crusty piece of bread whilst I think about his answer because I'm not willing to give up my point yet.

"Some of the other classes live outside, the farmers and the miners for example."

He nods. "They all do. Only Alphas live in a protected environment."

This is news to me. "Only Alphas live in domes?"

He nods again, mouth working on finishing off his bread and cheese. "The Dome," he says finally.

"What do you mean?" I ask before he can take another mouthful.

"There's only one dome, Tudie. But there are lots of Deltas and Kappas and so on, in lots of other sectors."

"Only one dome?" I'd always assumed that there were others somewhere, although now that I come to think of it, I've never heard anyone mention another dome. "Only us?"

Again he nods.

"Why?" I ask and when he doesn't answer, I continue, "Why are we the only Alphas?"

"I guess because we live by rules within the dome, two children per couple, we keep the population steady but the other sectors don't."

"But that doesn't explain why there is only one dome, one set of Alphas," I say.

"Does it matter?" he asks, his voice a little peeved as if I am ruining his grand gesture.

And perhaps I am. I try to change the subject a little. "Joy said that only Alphas are attractive." I wonder what he will say to this idea. "I mean we are taught in schooling that Alphas are the *most* attractive but she says that the other classes aren't attractive at all."

He shrugs. "I don't know. It's possible. They are subject to pollution and disease in a way that we aren't."

"She also said that they were less intelligent."

"Tudie, you *know* that. And doesn't that stand to reason? I mean if they were intelligent they'd be Alphas, and then they'd be with us in the dome." He doesn't finish his food. Instead he puts the remaining morsels on a plate, as if he's lost his appetite.

"What's all this about? Why are you so discontented today? Is it just because of your dad? Or is it something else? Something to do with us?"

His expression is so wounded that it pains me to see it. I can't explain what's wrong with me, other than that nothing seems or feels right. Is it just because it's the anniversary of my dad's death, or is it something more?

"I don't know. All I do know is that whatever it is, it's nothing to do with us." But the vague explanation isn't enough to set his mind at ease, I can see it in his face. With a mighty push I force all my worries to the very back of my head. There will be time tomorrow to examine them more fully, if I can, but for now I should be enjoying this wonderful thing Grey has done for me.

I smile as genuinely as I can. "I can't think of anyone I'd rather spend every minute of my life with, than you. We are perfect for each other." And I mean every word, so when he drops his face to mine, I pull him close, kissing every gorgeous inch of it.

I'm a little hungry. But not for food. It's affection I crave, the warmth that suffuses me whenever I am in his arms. But Grey is picking once more at the food. I settle for shuffling closer to him.

The ground beneath me is warm and I relax onto it, lying back and letting my gaze drift upwards to the treetops and the blue sky beyond. "The world must be such a big place," I comment.

If he shrugs again, I can't tell. "This is the nicest part of it though, where we are."

I look at him, genuinely surprised. "How can you possibly know that?"

"It stands to reason, doesn't it? Why else would our forefathers have built the dome and ELSA where they did? Of course they would have chosen the very best place for us."

I think about that whilst he grazes on more food. A bird flies overhead and I am captivated by the vivid colouring of its feathers. It soars high on an air current, skimming the top of the trees and vanishing out of sight.

Time seems to be slipping away from me and I still have no real appetite. Instead, I want to seize each moment and fill it with things I will remember all my life; cram it with every single thing I may never experience again. I pull myself upright. "Come on!" I take Grey's hand and pull him up too.

Without my shoes I am shorter than him, and I have to lift my head a little to look into his eyes. Hand on the waistband of my trousers, I undo the fastenings slowly. He watches me like I am that exotic bird which flew past only moments before.

My breath is caught in my throat as I step out of my trousers and top and cast them aside. I pull the pins from my hair and let it tumble around my shoulders. Now I am there in front of him, clad only in pants and a vest. I fold my hands over myself in modesty.

Wordlessly I turn away from him, and run to where the stream bottoms out into a small pond, before narrowing once more and running onwards. The water is cold, colder than I had expected and it steals the remaining breath from my lungs.

I make an involuntary strangled *whoop* of a sound, and it's so ungraceful and so devoid of sexiness that it makes me laugh, a deep string of sniggering.

But Grey isn't laughing. Shivering in the

water's cold caress, I watch him take off his top and trousers, fold them carefully and lay them next to where I had been lying, only moments before.

I have never seen him without his clothes before. Naked, his body is lean and muscular with a pure beauty that takes my breath away once more. My eyes roam over him and I know beyond any shadow of doubt that he can be the only man for me. The only love I will ever have in my life.

I feel my cheeks redden at my forwardness but I do not shy away from the picture he presents. He strides towards me and I am simultaneously eager for, and afraid of his embrace.

If he feels the coldness of the water, he gives no indication. But he stops short before he reaches me. I want to speak, want *him* to speak and yet I don't want the beauty of the moment shattered. I don't want either of us to say or do something that will mar the perfection of this instant.

And then suddenly and unexpectedly I am soaked, as he brings his hands up and throws a cascading fountain of water at me. Streams of water run down my hair and over my face as I throw back my head and laugh. Far from ruining the moment, he has taken the edge from it and kept it safe, kept *me* safe.

Delighted, I play him at his own game,

rushing towards him, making the water churn white and foamy around my hips, before bouncing my palms to the surface, causing a tidal wave to surge towards and over him.

"Okay I'm really going to get you now," he mock threatens, scooping up even more water and bounding towards me. I laugh and back away, moving out of his reach, but he throws the water anyway, splashing me harmlessly.

I hold my hands up. "Truce!" I call. I move closer so that we are within touching distance.

Droplets of water are held almost crystallised on his chest, caught in the thick hair which grows there. My attention is riveted and I let my gaze travel naturally downwards until his body is obscured by the deeper water. I am aware that my sodden vest clings to me and that every curve of my body above the water level is visible to him.

"It's not that I don't want to - you know," I struggle to express what I mean. He's standing so close and we are so alone. And he is naked. "I love you and I want to marry you but-"

He cuts across my words. "Any other day with us in this situation," he gestures around him at the perfect beauty of this place, "it would be different. But today, because of what this day means to you, it would just be wrong."

I can't tell him, because my throat is tight with emotion, but I love him even more for understanding this. I lean my head towards him, keeping our bodies modestly apart.

His lips meet mine and I open my mouth to receive the sweet probing of his tongue. Shivers that have nothing at all to do with the coldness of the water ascend and descend my spine, sending shockwaves of longing and hunger to the very core of me. That private area between my thighs is tingling and I want to mash my body to his and demand that he makes us one immediately.

But he's right. The consummation of our love would forever be sullied by events which happened on this day exactly a year ago. And with that thought, I am immediately ashamed. I step back, pulling away from him, wrenching my lips from his with an effort.

My throat is tight and I struggle to get words past it. "Winner gets to eat the best strawberries!" I throw back at him, as I turn and head for the bank, aware of the strange and unusual shakiness of my voice, the heavy thudding of my heart.

I clamber out, trying to step quickly over the sharp stones so that I don't cut myself. Slick with water and moss, the stones are slippery and I have to work hard to keep my balance. And then I am out and pulling my clothes over my wet underwear, working the material so that it falls uncomfortably back into place.

"That's it, you lose!" I call lightly, deliberately tossing one of the largest and most succulent looking strawberries into my mouth and chewing it with relish. Thankfully the tension between us is gone, now that I'm out of the water. We can be like we always are together and everything will be okay. I reach forward and choose another strawberry.

Grey is picking his way across the stones as I already did. But as I bite into the sweet fruit he stops dead, his momentum lost. I follow his gaze and see that his foot has become trapped beneath a shifting rock.

Not particularly concerned as the rock isn't big enough to crush his foot or cause damage, I watch him bend to move it... and then suddenly everything happens so fast, in stilted slow-motion.

And I witness every little detail of how my world is completely shattered.

CHAPTER 4

Grey bends down to his trapped foot. One of the larger stones has slipped from its original place and has landed on his foot, grazing it a little, so that a thin line of blood leaks out from a narrow cut. The blood oozes from his skin and then is diluted and washed away by the lapping of the water.

It's a small cut and he's clearly not in any pain. He shuffles the other foot, the one which isn't trapped, trying to plant it firmly on the wet stones whilst he bends to work on freeing the trapped one. But the stones are slippery, covered in moss, and he's suddenly having trouble balancing.

I see him windmill his arms, flailing at the empty air, pushing his body forwards and then back, trying to find his centre of gravity and all I can do is smile at the funny, jerky motions he is making.

I stand there with a stupid grin on my face as his free foot slips forward then lurches back, trying to find purchase that isn't there. And in my defence he's laughing too, berating himself for his awkwardness and stupidity. And he's cursing the rocks and... and then he is falling, dropping hard, and I don't even have the time or sense to stop laughing at his antics.

He goes down. Hard and fast. I see his face hit the rocks which jut out just above the water and those which lie below unseen, producing a sickening thud that can be heard even over the movement of the water. He is suddenly very quiet. Very still.

In seemingly inverse proportion to how quiet he is, my heart is thudding, pounding in my chest. At first I think that what I am listening to is some giant bird of prey that is even now sweeping down upon us, until I realise it is my heart and not the beating of wings, and that the laboured breathing I hear is my own.

"Grey!" I scream, calling his name over and over, as I dash to his side. But not once does he respond.

His face is immersed in the water and it's only when I reach him, dragging him onto his back that I see how damaged it is. Blood pours from a large gash on his forehead and already there are bruises beginning to form under his eyes and across the bridge of his nose.

It was a struggle to turn him over but now I face an even bigger task. Somehow I have to get him out of the water. The rocks which cut his face are the same ones which now lie under his neck and back. Unconscious and without something to cushion him, every inch that I drag him will hurt and cut him more than he already is.

There's nothing to use other than our clothes. I pull my top off again and use it and his own discarded one to cover the rocks directly ahead of him. It's not ideal but there's nothing else I can do.

Cushioning his head against my stomach as best I can, I put my arms around his torso and I haul. He's heavy and I can feel each and every one of my sinews straining but he's moving.

Inch by painful inch, I pull him from the water and onto the grass. My breathing is erratic and I want to stop and check that he's still alive but I daren't do so. If he is already dead, I know I won't be able to bear leaving him here, and if he's alive I have to get him help. Either way, I have to move him.

I keep hauling and pulling, even when it seems that my arms are about to snap out of their sockets, or my heart burst with fear and adrenaline, I keep going.

Finally he is out of the water. I lay him gently on the ground, wanting to cry, but I daren't let myself, for if I cry there will be no one to help either of us. I blink back tears and instead feel for a pulse at his throat.

There! Weak and thready but nonetheless

there, it's as if someone has given me a second chance at life and I am overcome with relief. "Grey? Grey can you hear me?" I speak right into his face, mouth almost touching his, but there is no response. "I have to get you back to the dome," I tell him, unsure whether or not somewhere in the back of his brain he can understand, even if he can't currently respond.

He's still naked and whilst I am unconcerned for his modesty or mine, I'm aware that getting him back will basically mean dragging him over a long distance. Not only is he taller than me by half a head but he is heavier and more muscled. But getting him back isn't a choice, it's a necessity. And if it kills me, I will not fail him.

Somehow, I manage to get his trousers on him and using his top and mine as roughly fashioned shoes around his feet, I figure I have done as much to protect his body as I can, under the circumstances. If only we'd carried our shoes rather than leaving them outside the dome! I curse my own stupidity.

I ignore the food but wedge a container of orange juice into the waistband of my trousers. For a moment I consider the wisdom of leaving him here and going for help – if I run to the dome and back, I could be gone for maybe only a couple of hours - but I have no idea what wild animals might be lurking and what danger I might put him in by leaving him alone.

Barefoot, I will ignore whatever pains I suffer, but there's no doubt it will make progress slower. Refusing to think any deeper than the immediate need to get Grey to the dome, I wrap my arms around him once more and begin to shuffle backwards.

It's all my fault - the fact that we're outside, the idea of going in the water, of choosing to ignore the dangers of the slippery rocks, the unfamiliar situation. Perhaps he might not even have slipped if he hadn't been just a little irate with me earlier over all my pointless, *needless* questions. Maybe too he'd have been paying more attention to the rocks, if only I hadn't presented myself to him, half naked and full of emotion and angst. Individually and collectively, all of it lays the blame squarely on my shoulders.

I have no idea how long it takes me to cover even a short distance, but it feels as if I have been dragging him beside me for years. My whole body aches, my arms feel fit to fall off and there's a pounding in my forehead that won't go away.

I look for landmarks that I stupidly had paid no real heed to in the daytime, and find none in the growing darkness. All I can count on is that we'd travelled in a fairly straight line and that if I do the same in reverse, I can't be far off course. But the light has faded entirely and I can't even be sure that I am not zigzagging across the landscape.

After a while there are noises in the dark, strange rustlings and feral calls that I don't even try to identify, for fear of what my imagination will conjure up. But I can't close my ears to them.

It doesn't take me long to realise that there are different qualities to the sounds, that some are blunt and guttural, whilst others seem sharper and more clearly defined. And closer. Much closer.

Because I don't know what else to do, I make my own noises that I hope sound as scary thrust into the night, as theirs do to me; sharp calls of defiance and anger, rising in pitch and volume like a tidal wave. I let my misery out on each note, each exhalation, but I keep my fear to myself.

Although I know nothing much of the world outside of the dome, I feel instinctively that there's more than one type of creature on our trail. I can only hope that they are as wary of me as I am of them, either because of my strange cries or despite them. If their desperation or curiosity prevails, I have no doubt who will be the victor between us.

Occasionally, a call sounds even closer than before, as if the breath it is issued upon dampens the hairs on the back of my neck, making them rise on pinpricks of terror, and I almost convince myself that if I turn around, it will be into fierce and unknowably savage eyes I gaze. But I don't let it stop me from moving.

Instead I intensify my own primal calls into the darkness; something between a wail and a bellow, hoping to renew the fears of whatever unseen beasts patrol around us. If nothing else, at least it's a way to vent my guilt and grief, to prove to the world that I'm not giving up on him, whatever the challenge.

I bump, pull, drag Greyson over every blade of grass, every loose stick and pebble on the ground - and I do it never once checking if he is still alive. I believe he's alive, because he has to be. It's that simple really. I'm alive, so he has to be too. He is my world and I can't go on without him. It's not an option.

Once or twice he moans and then is silent again. Each time it happens, I'm grateful for the small indication that he's still breathing. I choose not to dwell on whether the following inevitable silence is a bad sign, focusing only on the good, the positive.

The moon is high in the sky and I realise I'm talking to it, gabbling on incoherently and pledging my soul to it, if only it will spare Grey's life. Promising it anything, everything, including my life for his.

In the deepest reaches of my mind I wonder at myself. I'd always considered myself rational and yet here I am begging promises from the moon, as if it really could grant them. And yet I don't dare stop.

"Please, please, *please* let him live. Let him be fine and well and let us get married like we planned. I promise I'll be good my whole life. I'll be a good wife, a good mother, I'll never again complain about anything, if you just let him live. Or take me instead, my life in return for his."

Promises. Again. The idea haunts me.

Not even realising it at first, I step into brightness. It's only once Grey's face becomes slightly illuminated, and the crazy idea that the moon really has heard me, has granted my wish and saved him, fills my head and heart with relief, that reality reasserts itself.

This isn't a shining beacon of light direct from that sky-hung disk, but a subtle leaking of light from a far-away source, one far more earthy than the moon.

Not daring to put Grey down, I struggle to twist my head around. There, in the distance is the dome. Atop the steel walls, a slice of light can be seen and it's this which casts a diminishing pool of radiance all the way to where I now stand. My eyes measure the distance to safety. It's a long way, but much, much closer than the expanse I've already travelled.

I try to pull harder, faster, now that the end is in sight, but my muscles rebel, weak and quivering, as if the nearness of salvation has allowed my body to give up, even if my mind won't. I don't dare let my muscles win.

Fighting against paralysing exhaustion, I force my numb hands tighter around Grey's body, push my breaking back to straighten further, to walk taller and heave more.

The pain is unbearable and yet I bear it. I grit my teeth and think how more unbearable my pain will be if I let him die. I *will not* fail him! Once more, I begin my mantra to the moon.

Something hits me cold and hard on the back of my heel, drawing forth a hiss of pain from tight lips and I jerk my head around to see what it is, almost expecting it to be the strong muzzle of some ferocious beast with red blazing eyes and teeth as sharp as knives.

But I'm astounded to see instead that I have banged my foot on the cold metal lip of the doorway. I have reached the dome, dragged myself and Grey to safety!

But the doors remain closed.

I balance on one foot, unwilling to lay Grey down on the cool grass, as if having come so far, I fear that either he or the universe will take it as a sign that I am giving up on him at the last moment.

I kick at the door with a bruised and bloodied foot as hard as I can. But the steel resists all impact. My face is wet and belatedly I realise I am crying, shedding silent tears that course down my cheeks and over my neck.

I am done.

Defeated.

To have come so far and then fail, is the worst agony I can imagine, and almost makes me sink to my knees in despair. And then common sense kicks in.

The doors are closed because I have not scanned my wrist, not for any supernatural reason! But I can't do that and hold Grey at the same time, so very gently, I lay him down. But just before I straighten up, something catches the corner of my eye.

Our shoes lie where we discarded them. To one side of the doorway, my shoes and Grey's larger ones reside like an omen of things which were to come but were unknown to us at the time. My feet are raw and bleeding, but I instinctively know that I will never wear these shoes again. They are now from a different time, from a time when I didn't know how close I would come to losing everything.

I hold my wrist to the scanner and mutter under my breath at the time it takes for the big doors to slide open on their hydraulics.

"Welcome home Fortitude Smith and Greyson Ford," ELSA displays. *"You were expected back some time ago. However I hope your outing was pleasurable."*

Although only a machine, I feel as if ELSA is mocking me, as if she's aware of every single thing that's happened outside and that she's deliberately done nothing to help. But if Grey were able to, he'd tell me I'm being ridiculous. And I probably am. But the feeling remains nonetheless. I drag Grey through the doorway.

Inside, the corridor is deserted. Maybe most people are in bed or at least in their apartments, but I had thought that there would be a few people still up and about. Someone who could help.

"Help!" I shout, but all that comes out is a feeble squeak, not loud enough to pass to a person close by, let alone to other areas within the dome. I try again, summoning what little reserves of strength I have left. I call out again and turn my attention back to Grey.

Did he hear me shout? Have I finally managed to rouse him? His body is moving, even though I am no longer pulling on him. But when I look at him, his movements seem strange, uncontrolled and contorted. There is a fine line of white drool leaking from one corner of his mouth and the whites of his eyes are showing, the pupils buried almost completely under heavy lids.

As I watch helplessly, his body spasms, jerking like a fish out of water, his head flailing from side to side, some of that foamy spittle ejected over him. Whatever's happening, it's something bad. *Worse* than before! This new urgency informs my voice. "Help! HELP us! Please!"

This time my cry is louder, stronger, and I think it might be enough. It *has* to be enough, for it's taken all of my remaining strength. Someone seems to have turned the lights down, which is weird, because the corridor is always brightly lit, regardless of day or night.

And the floor is wrong. It's tilting towards me, listing at a funny angle... I shut my eyes slowly and sink to the ground, oblivious to the sounds of running feet, of help finally arriving.

CHAPTER 5

I wake up feeling like I have been trampled by something heavy and unforgiving. Every part of me aches and I can't quite remember or imagine why this should be so.

I'm in a bed but it's not my own. Instead, this one seems to be made with sheets that are stiff and crisp and a little too white for my eyes. I squint against the brightness, trying to figure out what's happened... and then everything comes back to me in a rush. Greyson, the water, the rocks... and then chillingly, his bruised, bloodied face fills my inner vision.

He's not here with me in this medical room and I am terrified of the significance. "Grey!" I shout, sliding my feet from the bed and pressing them to the floor. They are heavily bandaged and must be quite damaged, for the pain when I put my weight onto them is terrific and makes me immediately gasp.

Stumbling, I make it as far as the door, before the walls seem to shiver before my eyes, receding and advancing as if I am Alice and this is her

Wonderland. I grasp the door handle but don't immediately wrench it open.

What if Grey is dead? What if it took me too long to get him back? What if I *failed* him? I'm caught in a world of pain. There is no relief to be found in waiting here not knowing, but nor might there be in pursuing the answer, if it's not the one my heart needs.

I want to call his name again but it sticks in the back of my throat, burning there and suffusing my lungs with an acrid scent. The door is heavy but I manage to open it wide enough to squeeze through. When it bangs into my left foot as it begins to close, I am nearly hysterical with pain.

Fat, heavy tears slide down my cheeks with a languor as if they know they have all the time in the world to linger; as if they intend to be a permanent feature upon my face. I'm in no position to argue.

The medical area has many rooms leading off it. Without knocking, I enter each one. Every room is unoccupied. There is only one room left to check. I push open the door.

He is there! Head elevated slightly by thick pillows, his face has lost none of the bruising that I remember so vividly, but he's been cleaned up and looks slightly less brutalised.

Hooked up to a variety of machines, I am almost scared to touch him, lest I accidentally disturb any of the points which anchor them to his skin. His fingers are cool and relaxed and I curl my own around them protectively. His eyelids flutter open at the contact.

"Hey there, Superwoman," he says with difficulty. Perhaps his throat is dry, because his words are slightly muffled and strange sounding. "They told me you got me back here on your own."

I try to shrug dismissively, but my neck, back and shoulders scream in protest. "It was nothing." I attempt to laugh it off but my voice is flat, made insipid by the strength of emotions which I am trying so hard to stave off.

"Are those tears for me, or are you annoyed that I spoiled your picnic?" This time I hear the anxiety in his voice.

I try to smile reassuringly. "They're for me actually. I thought I had lost you." It's too close to the truth for it to be funny for either of us.

"Can't lose me quite that easily." It's a denial of the plain truth which we both choose to ignore.

"Do you remember what happened?" I ask.

He shakes his head and winces with the effort. "I remember my foot was trapped and I pulled it and then…" he shifts his gaze to the bare walls as if they help him visualise the memory. "I slipped."

I nod. I could tell him more; the sickening sound his face made when it hit the rock; the terror I felt. But none of those things will help him. "I was so scared, Grey!"

The door opens and a medic enters. "Miss Smith, you should be in bed, resting." She holds the door open, clearly expecting me to hobble back through it the way I came in.

"But I needed to find Greyson and-" I protest, unmoving.

The room is quite small so it doesn't take many steps for her to reach my side. "And now you have seen him, you can get back to your room. I'm assuming you can find your own way back?" Her eyebrows are raised, there will be no defying her, not right now anyway. And she's right. He needs to rest to get better, and so probably do I.

Two pairs of eyes follow my progress to the door but when I reach it and turn around, it's Grey I focus on. "I love you," I say simply.

"I love you too," he says in return.

For a split second it looks as if he is about to say more but then something strange and totally unexpected happens. His eyes which had been focused on me are still looking in my general direction, but instead of *at* me, his gaze seems now to go *through* me, as if he regards not me or even the space I occupy, but something worlds beyond.

There is too much tension in his every facial muscle, too much tautness in the lines of his forehead and the creases at the corners of his eyes and mouth, where his face had been paused in a smile. The rigidity extends now to his neck and back and as if controlled by demonic forces, his body is pulled into a flat line, so that his weight appears to be resting on the back of his skull and his heels, whilst the rest of his body is suspended above the mattress.

As he had done before I blacked out, he begins to spasm once more, jerking almost out of the bed and then back towards the mattress, white froth spraying from his mouth, teeth clenched as if in pain. His hands, tightly fisted, beat a tattoo on the top sheet and it is this one bizarre act which scares me the most.

I'm so riveted by what I am seeing that I don't even realise I have been pushed through the door until it closes in my face. As the internal locks seal the room from my view, I bang on it, screaming out his name, begging to be let in once more. But the door remains closed. My heart feels like it's stuttered to a stop.

From inside, I hear sounds of movement, of frantic action. Metal screeches upon metal and there is an electronic whine which is as loud as it is ominous. A claxon sounds nearby and as other medics arrive seemingly from out of nowhere, one of them takes my arm and firmly leads me away.

"The only way for you to help him is to give us space to do our job." The speaker is a tall man, handsome as all Alphas are, but somehow softer, as if his years as a medic have physically altered him.

"No, let me go! Let me back in there!" I try to pull away but he's much stronger than me, and I'm ashamed at how weak and pathetic I feel. And useless. "What's happening to him?"

"The best thing you can do right now is get yourself better," he says, hustling me down the corridor and back into my room. I try to resist, try to wrench myself away, but I'm not strong enough.

The room hasn't changed in any way since I left it and yet it looks as alien as another planet. Machines which have been switched off stand silently against the walls, their screens dark and brooding, as if threatening that if I don't behave, I too will be hooked up to them.

For a moment I wonder if the medic can read minds because he says almost exactly what I am thinking. "Do you want to be attached to those machines? Because that's what will happen Miss Smith, if you push your body any further. You're exhausted."

His voice softens. "Trust me, you have done all you can for your fiancé. It's our turn now. Let us do our jobs." He gently manoeuvres me into bed and pulls up the sheet, tucking it firmly around me, holding me in.

For a moment I am caught in folds of time. I

am eight years old and those hands which smooth the bed linen around me are those of my father. My eyes follow his hands. They are a darker shade of skin than I remember, a dark burnished olive, lined with a soft fluff of black downy hair, where I'm sure before there was none. But the fingers are the same - long, slim and tapered at the ends. They are the sort of hands you expect to see curled artistically around a flute; creative, expressive hands which should flutter into the air, weightless as a small bird and twice as graceful.

A syringe injector flashes before my eyes and then is gone. "Daddy?" I hear myself say, even though I know my father died a year ago. The name both saddens and excites me, the verbalisation of it suggesting that there is a possibility, however minuscule, that it was all just a bad dream, that my father really is here and that I truly am only a child. But I'm saddened too, for if my father is alive, if I am just a child, then the love that I have known with Grey is the dream, the unfulfilled fantasy...

Does one have to die so the other can live? Is that how life works? I ask myself sleepily. If it is, then it's so unfair. Is it some sort of giant cosmic scale where I am only allowed one shot at happiness, one chance of being loved? Are the people who should be surrounding me with love, destined to be lined up in a row, each given only an allotted time and hour to be in my life?

I see my mother, recognisable only from the photos of the young woman my dad had stuck to every wall, every mirror in our home. She is standing on the edge of a cliff face, a sheer drop just beyond her feet. Her hair, long and free, billows in the warm breeze. She looks back at me over her shoulder as she takes one step forward - and tumbles from the cliff. Silently she plummets downwards, her eyes never once leaving mine until she descends beyond my sight. Her mouth remains closed in a half smile, her scream unvoiced.

Even as I recoil in horror, I realise there is a presence to the other side of me. I turn my head to find that my father stands at another point at the cliff edge, feet shuffled forward, just as my mother's had been. This time I know what is going to happen as he turns his head over his shoulder to check I am watching. I try to run towards him. Try to grab at him, arms outstretched and feet planted firmly on solid ground, try to anchor him to this earth, but it is I who am rooted to the spot, harnessed in place and unmoving.

He takes his one fatal step and like my mother before him, he tumbles from my existence. I am distraught, hysterical with grief that I can no longer express. I want to rend my clothing to shreds, rip at my own flesh, destroy myself so that no one else is destroyed for the love of me, and yet all the while I know there is another figure who patiently awaits my attention.

I turn my head towards him, not because I want to, but because I am compelled to do so, forced by some intrinsic need to face that which I do not wish to. And he is there, exactly as I know he will be. Standing on the same spot that my mother stood on, only moments before.

"Grey, please," I beseech him, knowing that either he *will* not or *cannot* listen to my pleas. His gaze, too knowing, too hurt - too hurtful - holds mine and I feel something leave my soul through the portal of my eyes and enter his, through those same orbs. His lips remain closed but I hear his voice in my head anyway.

"I love you," he breathes into my heart and I am lost, utterly and completely and without any hope of ever returning. He takes his one step forward as by now I know he must, and with his fall, I feel my heart wither and die.

I want to reach that cliff face, to fly soundlessly from it, as all my loved ones did before me, but even though my feet are no longer stuck to the ground, every step I take towards it, leads me inexplicably farther away, as if I step not towards it, but a mirror image by which it is magically displayed.

Inexplicably, the landscape changes and

another figure is revealed. This one is smaller, more fragile than the others and not unaccompanied. Yet she makes no effort to communicate with those around her, to participate in their conversation.

It is the very fact of her self-imposed isolation, so obviously emotional rather than physical, which makes her so utterly alone. She sits at a table surrounded by others, yet apart from them all, just as she had appeared to be in real life, the one time I had met her. She lifts her eyes to mine.

Where were you? I hear her think at me. *You promised to come see me after my 'sessment! But you never came!*

Oh Willow, I think back at the image, *I should have come, should have kept my promise. I honestly meant to. But Greyson came up with the idea of a picnic and I just...* I just what? *Forgot*, I almost let myself think until I can accept the real answer, that my own needs had mattered more than hers. *I just needed to get outside for a little while. I'm so sorry...*

Her little face crumples in disappointment and then seems to fold in upon itself, melting and changing and reconfiguring until I don't know what it will become. And then it is me. *She* is me.

I regard my mirror image critically. Because of me, Grey is seriously injured. Because of me, Willow will feel abandoned and confused.

Because of me, my mother died in childbirth. My self-loathing tries to find a reason for the death of my father that can trace the blame back to me, but that one evades it. Still a tally of three destroyed lives is enough for any one person to accumulate by their stupid actions.

I look for the medic who helped me into bed. Perhaps he will know the answer to the question, but he is gone. I am alone in the room once more. There are strange noises in the corridor outside but they don't concern me. I float into a drugged oblivion.

When I awake again I'm no longer sure if it's the same day, the following one, or if several days have passed. My body feels stiff and sore, but it's more the soreness of lying too long in one position than the ache of overused muscles now.

I swing my legs out of bed to find that although I'm still in a medical gown, the dressings which had previously covered my feet are gone. The skin looks red in places but otherwise it would be hard to tell what I've been through. Whatever the medics and their machines have done to me has worked.

Pulling open the door causes only a slight discomfort in my arms and shoulders. I step out into the deserted corridor and make my way to Grey's room.

His bed is empty! I feel my heartbeat surge into panic mode but before I can fly from the room, crashing into every other one, looking for him or anyone who can tell me where he is, a medic appears behind me.

She's a different one to the others I have met previously. Arms full of fresh bedding she smiles calmly at me. "He's been taken to have some tests done," she says before I can even ask.

"What tests? Where?" I need to be by his side, to see him and touch him and reassure myself that he will be okay.

"He's been having fits, Miss Smith," she informs me as if I hadn't seen them with my own eyes. "We need to establish the cause."

"And then you can fix them?" I will her to agree.

"Well let's hope so."

It's not the answer I want, so I push her for more information. "Where is he? I want to be with him."

She shakes her head. "The tests are quite invasive I'm afraid." My horrified expression probably says everything I am thinking, for she continues, "Oh they don't hurt, don't worry, but they have to be conducted in a very quiet and sterile environment. No one will come in or out of the room until all tests are complete."

"How long will that take?" I ask impatiently. If I have to wait to find out the results I know I will work myself into a frenzy.

"A few hours at the very minimum."

"A few hours!" I can't sit in my room, worried for all that time. I have to do something, keep moving, occupy my mind. "Can I leave?"

"The medical section? Of course. You were physically exhausted and had some minor lacerations and bruising to your feet but otherwise you are fit and well. So if you feel able to, I'll fetch your clothes and you can leave."

"But I'll be back in a few hours to see Greyson," I assure her. "And if he's back before then you *will* send someone to fetch me won't you?" I bore my eyes into hers, demanding that she do so.

"Yes, of course. We encourage our patients to have visitors. It helps in the recuperation process. So if you'll head back to your room, I'll change this bedding and then bring you some clothes."

"Thank you," I say, and am already in the corridor heading back to my room as the words leave my mouth.

CHAPTER 6

It's midway through the afternoon, a day and a half since I dragged Grey back here. I feel a little like Sleeping Beauty, and wonder what I've missed during this time.

There's no point in looking for Willow; she will be at her schooling, and I can't think of a single other person I want to see right now. To have to face Grey's family with the guilt and knowledge that we only went outside because of how I was feeling, will be too much for me to bear. But I don't think I can face being alone either. With no other company, the voice in my head which repeats my stupidity over and over, will drive me insane. I need a distraction.

I go to my work section. Joy is surprised and relieved to see me. "I heard about how you got back! But no one really knows what happened to you both *outside*!" Her gaze lingers on my face but tactfully she doesn't ask directly, even though I can see she's bursting to know. The way she's said 'outside' makes it sound like another world, too strange and different to be safe within. Maybe she's right.

I cover my face with my hands, hoping to wipe away at least a little of the guilt. But when I drop them to my sides a moment later, I don't feel any different. "It was all so stupid, Joy. And totally my fault." I perch on the edge of my chair, knees buckling and muscles too weak to support me. I'm shaking.

"He slipped, fell on some rocks and banged his head. It was so quick. I couldn't stop it from happening." Tears form at the corners of my eyes and I brush them away. "There was nothing I could do. One minute he was fine, the next…"

I'm surprised at how calm my voice is, how detached I appear; even though my body quivers with every word, I hear myself speaking as if from afar, as if it's someone else and not me talking. It's only when Joy wraps her arms around me, that I let go of the tight hold I have on my emotions. The dam breaks and tears fall.

Joy hands me a tissue. And another when the first one is used up. "I was so scared!" And I want to believe that now we're back, the danger is over. I want to believe that one day, when we're married and settled, we will look back on this and see it as nothing more than a foolish adventure; that we will laugh at the risks we took and be grateful that everything turned out okay. But for now, with no Grey at my side, I'm unable to laugh about anything.

"Where's Grey now?" she asks.

Perhaps medics keep more information to themselves than I'd thought. I'm scared to think what they haven't told me! My voice trembles so much I'm almost incomprehensible. "They're doing tests on him. He's been having fits… they need to find out why. Oh Joy, this is all my fault!"

She looks astonished and pulls back from me. "Why would you say that? It was an accident! You said yourself that he slipped, that there was nothing you could do." She pulls out another tissue and wipes her own eyes.

I'm surprised. I've never seen Joy upset about anything before. She's always seemed a little cold to me, unemotional and unbothered about other peoples' feelings and motivations.

Maybe I'm staring at her, for she volunteers. "Sorry. I just thought how I'd feel if it was Brent." She dabs the tissue at her eyes once more. "How I'd feel if it had been my fault that we'd ventured *outside*."

So there it is. An admission that regardless of her words, she also thinks it's my fault. I don't pull her up on it. She's right after all.

Unaware of my turmoil, she continues. "They'll find out what's wrong and they'll fix him." She smiles brightly, full of belief in her own assertion. I wish I could believe it so easily. Saliva curdles in my mouth.

I stand and wipe my eyes and nose. "I have

to go."

"Of course. You have to see Grey's mum. And the rest of his family," Joy nods.

It hadn't been them I'd been thinking of. It hadn't been anyone in fact – only a desire to be away from here, away from Joy's easy assertion that everything will be fine. It's too easy for her to say. And too hard to not believe in.

Although I have known her for years, I realise that I've never *really* known her, not the part of her that could be called her soul, if such a thing exists. And if it does, I'm not even sure she has one.

Unaware of the direction of my thoughts, she says, "They'll want to see you and hear what happened."

I look at her, horror-struck. I can't tell Grey's family what happened. I can't tell them how he put his life at risk because of me... And yet, she's right. I have a duty to them. The fact that I have no family of my own, means that Grey's should have been of paramount importance to me. That they're not, says more about me than it does about them, I fear. Maybe Joy and I are more alike than I care to consider.

She walks me to the door. "Everything will be fine, you'll see."

I want to believe her, but for now there is a dread in my heart which refuses to be stilled.

***

There's no need to search for Grey's parents. They won't be at work. Not today. I knock on the door to their apartment.

His mother answers, ushering me into the small living space where his father and sister are already seated on the pale green couch. "We've been waiting for news all day," Grey's mother says, her face furrowed with worry. I nod in response because I'm not sure what to say.

"Sit down," she says kindly. "You look exhausted." She sits next to her husband and daughter on the couch, meaning that I either have to sit down next to them, or on the seat opposite. Neither option is good. Either I will be too physically close, or they will be able to directly scrutinise my face. I remain standing, indecisive. Finally I sit down opposite them.

"Are *you* okay, Tudie?" Grey's mother asks, making me even more ashamed that I am so physically recovered, whilst Grey is still so unwell.

I nod. "I'm so sorry about Greyson." I can't say any more, the words just will not come.

She smiles sadly. "None of this is your fault, Fortitude. And when Greyson is better that'll be the first thing he insists on telling everyone." Her assurance only serves to make me feel even worse. Because I know the truth.

"They're doing tests on him," I say, even though she already knows. "I'm not sure they know what's wrong with him."

"They'll fix whatever it is." She is so certain, so convinced of the truth of her words that I want to shake her. Wasn't that probably what my father had thought about my mother? That she could be fixed? Put back to proper health? That everything would be okay?

But this woman in front of me has led *her* life, and only *I* have led mine. Only I have lost my mother before I even knew her and my father before I reached adulthood. Up until now, there has been no tragedy to mar this family's life, no calamity or heartbreak to temper their faith. I pray that Grey does not prove to be the exception to the rule. That, unlike me, they don't have to learn that not everything can be fixed.

They insist on making tea and drink it whilst we talk. I only lift my cup to my mouth, and put it back in its saucer almost immediately. To be drinking tea whilst I talk about Grey's accident seems too civilised, too detached from the misery I feel.

Haltingly, I tell them most of what happened, leaving out only the fact that Grey was naked, which is both too private and too embarrassing. Besides, it has no bearing on what happened. Or on my culpability. But I do tell them that although the outing was Grey's idea, it was founded on his desire to do something that he thought would make me feel better.

When I get to the part about how I dragged

him home, Grey's father rests a hand on my shoulder. It's exactly what my own father would have done and is enough to make me start weeping again. This time I let my tears flow and am comforted in the sharing of love for Grey, with his family.

"You mustn't blame yourself," Grey's father tells me softly. But I do and I know I always will.

When his mother rises to make more tea, I make my excuses to leave. I've shared everything with them, answered their questions as fully as I can, and explained as much as I know. "If you hear anything, you'll tell me, won't you?" I move towards the door.

"You're not going to sit with us, until we hear something?" his sister asks sharply. She's said very little since I arrived and although she's not said as much, I feel that of the three of them, she does lay some of the blame of what happened on me. If not all of it.

"It won't help Grey, and I don't think I can sit still any longer." I say, because it's the truth. But it's not the only reason. The bigger truth is that the sharing of their palpable misery and pain only magnifies my own. And it's unbearable.

But when I leave them I do so half-reluctantly, full of a strange superstition that in departing from their company I will break some kind of collective consciousness that will keep Grey from harm. That in leaving, I will open the situation up to the winds of fate. It's no more than superstitious mumbo-jumbo and yet I can't shake it as I go in search of Willow.

In the corridors, children spew forth from the schooling rooms but she doesn't appear to be among them. But she is young and as I vaguely remember, new starters are released a little earlier than normal.

Perhaps she is already in the communal dining area. Loath as I am to go there, with its many food aromas and bustling atmosphere, I change direction and head that way.

It occurs to me that I haven't been back to my own quarters yet, haven't changed clothes from the ones the medic has given me, or exchanged the foam slippers for real shoes. Once I have spoken to Willow I will go home, shower and change, before going back to sit at Grey's bedside until someone comes to forcibly drag me away.

The dining room is exactly as I'd known it would be. Loud and too, too bright for how I feel. Even though I haven't eaten for a while, or perhaps exactly because of it, the smell of food is intolerable and makes me feel queasy. The only way I can think to combat it is with the comforting aroma of fresh coffee. Whether I can drink the coffee or not, is irrelevant.

I approach one of the little doors at the drinks station and proffer my wrist to the scanner. I press the button to request coffee. But no coffee appears.

Good afternoon, Fortitude Smith, the readout displays. *I'm glad you are out of medical section. Coffee is an insufficient beverage for you under the circumstances. ELSA suggests a fruit tea.*

"I would like a coffee, ELSA," I pronounce clearly into the speaking panel and simultaneously press the button again, so that my wishes are received loud and clear.

Coffee is an incorrect choice for your body today, Fortitude Smith. The miniature door slides open to reveal what I presume to be blackcurrant tea, judging by the sickly sweet aroma it gives off.

"I said, I want *coffee*." I hear the threat in my voice and am aware that heads are turning in my direction. I put my finger on the button and hold it there.

Once you have removed the fruit tea and consumed it, ELSA will be able to rescan your body for fluid requirements.

There is no arguing with the machine. I take the warm drink, down it in two swallows and say, "ELSA, I would like a coffee please." I put the empty cup back.

The door slides closed as if the computer is organising a fresh drink for me but the readout surprises me.

Fluid levels are adequate for optimal body performance. No further fluid is currently required. Have a good day, Fortitude Smith.

For a moment I stand gaping at the display. The little door remains resolutely closed.

"I want a coffee, you bitch," I say, through gritted teeth. Without conscious thought, without contemplating the wisdom of what I am about to do, I bring my clenched fist up hard to the readout and smash it so viscously, that shards of plastic fall around my feet. Tiny wires protrude from the gaping hole.

The action results in little noise and no one is even looking in my direction but I am ashamed nonetheless. ELSA is only a machine, I remind myself. Incapable of true understanding. I bend down and pick up the broken fragments of the display and deposit them in the trash.

And yet I wonder what might happen if I go to another drink dispenser. Will ELSA accuse me of trying to break her? Of trying to scramble her memory banks? Or will she finally give me what I want? But all of these reactions are too human for the computer. I am reading far too much into the situation.

I shuffle over to the next dispenser in the wall. "I want a coffee." I neither add please, nor thank you. I press the button.

No further fluid is required to enhance current body performance, Fortitude Smith.

"Do I need to smash you again?" I am shocked by my own words, stunned at their brutishness and remorselessness. It's almost as if they emanate from some other origin other than myself.

System incomprehension. Please repeat request.

I'm as disgusted with the machine as I am with myself for picking a fight with it. "I know my body doesn't need a coffee, but I would really like one." I try to sound placatory this time.

ELSA has scanned your body requirements and finds that coffee would be inflammatory to your physical condition, Fortitude Smith.

I am getting nowhere fast and time is moving on. I decide to move with it and forget the coffee. I was probably not going to drink it anyway. "ELSA hasn't got a clue about what I need right now," I mutter, turning away, no longer looking at the display.

There is a bleep which I ignore, then another, louder than the first. When I ignore that too, the bleeps intensify, becoming louder and with shorter intervals between them, until I finally turn back around to the display.

ELSA knows everything about you. The word 'everything' is not in capitals, it is not underlined or highlighted, or in any way different from the rest of the words… and yet it turns my blood cold. There is an implied threat in that one word. A world of meaning.

The display stops beeping. I guess its purpose has been accomplished.

What I do next, I can't explain even to myself, but I place my hand over the readout, covering the words so completely that I can't see them.

Then I scan the room. Over in the far corner I see a guy who works in the same department as Grey talking to a group of men I don't know. I don't actually know him either, but I recognise him from the times I've met Grey at his section. After only a slight hesitation I approach him.

"Sorry to interrupt, but..." I begin.

"Hey you're Greyson's fiancée aren't you?" he asks immediately. "I heard something happened. Is he okay?" He could be asking me if Grey had a cold, his expression is so unconcerned. Yet he's not uncaring, or just being polite. The truth is far worse. Like everyone here, he doesn't realise that life doesn't always go to plan.

Like everyone except for me, that is. "I don't know yet," I manage to stutter out. This isn't the answer he expects but I can't elaborate, not when there's so much that remains unknown. I step aside a little, hoping that he'll follow. What I want to ask, I don't want publicised. Maybe he senses I need a little privacy for he follows and waits for me to speak.

"Look something just happened. With ELSA. Is it possible that she knew I hadn't read the readout on the display of the drinks dispenser?" Even as I say it, I imagine how stupid and insensitive he must think I am.

"I don't know what it was that you think she wanted you to read. The readout is programmed to confirm delivery of the drink."

And that was what I had thought, until only a few moments ago proved otherwise. I don't let him in on the secret. "But can ELSA tell if it's been read?"

He doesn't even need to think about it. "Yes, I guess so. Set into every interactive station is a voice recognition system and a set of retina reactors." When he sees that I'm not entirely sure what he means, he uses a finger to draw a small circle in the air in front of one of his eyes.

"Why? The retina reactors, I mean?" I ask.

He shrugs. "ELSA uses them to scan for all sorts of things."

It's a logical explanation and yet it's one of the creepiest things I have ever heard. I had never thought about how much ELSA knew about me, now for some reason I can't stop thinking about it.

"Why? I mean that's what the scanners in our wrists are for."

He looks at me blankly for all of five seconds, as if even he can't come up with a logical reason. "I guess there are some things she can't scan through our wrists, in order to maintain her primary function of care," he says finally.

Except when did providing for us, change

to dictating to us? Even if it is for our own good.

"What happens to all that information? Does it get stored somewhere?" I ask.

He purses his mouth. "Don't honestly know. I wouldn't have thought so. Besides, what would be the point?"

I have absolutely no idea what the point would be, but I don't want to admit that. Nor am I comfortable with the fact that he doesn't know the answers to my questions. I wonder who does. If anyone.

I smile vaguely and fend him off with a different truth. "I'm sick with anxiety over Grey. It just took my mind off the wait to see him." It's not a lie, but bending the truth makes me feel even guiltier than before.

"Give him my best wishes when you see him. And tell him everyone in his section hopes he'll be back soon, even though his jokes are lousy!"

I smile weakly and turn away. In my empty stomach the blackcurrant seems to roil sickeningly; I ignore it as I move back towards the middle of the dining hall.

Young families have started to arrive for an early meal. I spot Willow's family amongst them, recognising the brother she doesn't like and who doesn't like her, according to her own account. I hasten over to them.

"Hi. I'm Fortitude Smith." This would be so

much easier if Willow was present but I guess she's either in one of the washrooms or at one of the many food dispensers. I've no idea what to say next, especially as they look at me with blank faces, so I glance around the room, hoping to spot her. But she's nowhere in sight.

"I sat here a couple of days ago." I realise the next bit of my explanation is sure to sound weird to them, so I put it as simply as I can. "Willow was excited about being assessed for school. I promised I would meet her that evening but something happened and I couldn't."

I sense they are waiting for me to tell them what had happened that had been so momentous that it had prevented me from keeping my promise to their daughter. Unable to meet their eyes, I give them the simplest version of my story that I can. "I was a bit down that day. Willow was a little nervous about school and I think I helped take her mind off it. But my fiancé was worried about me and so he arranged permission for us to have a picnic. Outside."

Willow's parents exchange glances. I see them think something. Probably, *so this is the girl who almost got her fiancé killed!* I swallow my pride under their silent scrutiny and continue. "I should have got a message to Willow to explain, but everything happened so fast." It's a poor excuse, but no less than the truth.

"You probably already know there was an

accident..." Saying it faster doesn't make me sound any less foolish for having brought the whole sorry scenario upon myself. And on Grey. "I've been in the medical sector until now."

I look around but still can't see Willow. I wonder what's taking her so long. Perhaps she's unhappy with the food that ELSA has chosen for her and is trying to trick the computer into giving her something else? I think if anyone other than me has the audacity to challenge the programming, strangely it will be this little girl.

"I just got out, so I came to find her." I realise that since telling them my name, I haven't looked at Willow's parents once. I raise my eyes to them now.

But where I expect their gaze to be inquisitive and maybe even a little sympathetic, instead I find it to be as soft and compassionate as flint. Surely after everything that I have said, all my explanations and evident sincerity, they cannot still be angry enough with me that they will not allow me to speak to Willow?

I look at their closed faces and wait for them to say something, anything, but they remain silent. But their silence, compounded by the strange look on Willow's brother's face, begins to make me even more anxious and uneasy.

Has she become ill with some childhood malaise and been taken to the medical sector?

Was she perhaps in a room just down the corridor from me? Expecting me to visit? Or is she fine, but so upset by my absence, that she has steadfastly refused to come to the table until she sees me leave?

But none of these explanations fit neatly into the niche in my heart. I truth is something else, I fear. Without further preamble I shift my eyes to Willow's mother. Still standing whilst she remains seated, I have a height advantage over her I intend to use. I lower my head but keep my eyes riveted on hers. "Where's Willow?" I ask abruptly.

She looks at me, irises as cold as steel. "Willow is gone. We no longer have a daughter."

CHAPTER 7

The flatness of her words and her eyes are at odds with both the context and syntax of her statement. My brain struggles to understand.

"Gone? Gone where?" And then her other words hit home. "You no longer have a daughter?"

I have almost repeated her words back to her exactly, and yet I feel as if I have spoken in a foreign tongue, so uncomfortably do they roll from my mouth. Their meaning is too strange, too frighteningly surreal to be true.

As she continues to gaze at me with that flat stare, that uncompromising challenge, my heart spasms in fear. I grip the edge of the table for support, sure that my legs alone won't hold me upright. The day is skewed - everything terribly, bewilderingly wrong. I would think that I were still in some horrific nightmare, if it wasn't for the constant anguish I've been in since awakening. It's the pain which makes me know this is real. No dream could ever hurt this much. Nor any nightmare.

"The child sat the assessment and

unfortunately was downgraded to Delta class," she replies without a hint of feeling; of shock. Of love.

The other voices in the room are too loud, too harsh, too full of raucous consonants and sibilant resonances. They reverberate through me with syllables constructed of daggers and vowels of panic.

How is what I'm being told possible? And even if it is, even if by the slightest chance that it's true, how does it explain Willow's absence? There's an answer there that my brain refuses to divulge. "I don't understand."

"Willow is not Alpha." She gestures around her. "She's not the same as all of us. She had to go."

I feel a huge chunk of comprehension slot into my brain. It neither sits comfortably nor easily in its slot, but lurches there, sickeningly.

"Are you telling me that you allowed her to be taken from you?" Now it's my turn to gesture around. "From her home and everything she's ever known, *just because ELSA has decided she isn't Alpha*?" My voice comes out in a rising crescendo and I don't try to moderate it.

Letting go of the table with one hand only, clutching at it ever more tightly with the other, I raise the empty hand to my mouth. Fingers splayed across there, I'm only dimly aware that my face feels strange, stretched by shock and grief into strange plains and contours that I don't recognise. Who am I now? Without Grey at my side and Willow as my sister? How can all this be happening? Grey, and now Willow?

Willow's mother doesn't miss a beat. "Of course we let her go. It's our civic duty to keep the classes pure. After all, what would happen if we continued to let Willow live here? One day she would marry, and then any children she produced would be intellectually compromised-"

I can't stand to listen to any more. I feel as if the inside of my head is on fire. I try to straighten up, staggering awkwardly to one side, jarring my hip painfully on the table. But I accept and harbour the pain, internalising it further and allowing it to sharpen my revulsion.

"You heartless fucking BITCH!" It's an insult that before today I had never voiced, never indeed felt a need to. Now I have used it twice in one day and find that it rises to my mouth with superlative ease.

And although the word is directed at the mother, I know that I mean it for all of them - for Willow's father and her brother, and everyone in our society who has allowed this to happen. If I could melt the very steel that surrounds us in ELSA's walls, I would do so, such is the heat of my temper.

Willow's mother looks back at me with neither rancour nor sympathy. "I'm very ashamed to have failed in my duty to produce two healthy Alphas." She reaches across the table for the support of her husband's hand. "Luckily I have a few more childbearing years left, where we can produce another child…"

I can't listen to any more of this. I'm not aware of picking up the plate of food in front of her, even less aware of lifting the eggs above her head and upturning them, but I see the resultant mess I make.

Perhaps because of my raised voice moments before, perhaps because word has spread of my exploits outside, or perhaps just because of my actions right now, all conversation in the dining room halts. Every face turns expectantly towards me.

A memory jangles in my head. Of how they had stood and stared just like this, when Grey and I stepped outside the dome. As if no one here has a desire for freedom of will. As if they're frozen.

But that egg gives it away. It slides slowly down her face, sticking here and there and then letting go of that patch of skin or hair, only to stick at another point, as if reluctant to continue on its journey to the floor. Reluctant to let go. Like them.

"Where is she? Where's Willow?"

She looks at me emotionlessly. "I already told you, she's gone."

"WHERE?" I shout, but she ignores me, they all do.

There is nothing more to say or do here, nothing that will change Willow's fate. And suddenly the horror that I feel seems to expand, as if it's a virus, staking claim to the whole of my being, suffusing me with a unique terror and urgency. There is no rationale to my fevered thoughts, no logic or reasoning, but I am suddenly terrified for Grey too.

Some chain of events has tethered itself to me; actions that I have initiated have somehow become linked and connected in a way that I can't even begin to understand. But without understanding, I recognise the primal fear that resides within the thought. This, *all of this*, is somehow my doing and only I can undo it.

I turn on my heel and run. Through the wide doors that led me into this room and out into the wide corridor again, I follow my instinct, letting my legs travel the route that my conscious brain cannot even assign. I pound hallways, finding intersections where one meets another, each one leading me closer to Grey. Closer to Willow too. I can only pray so.

My feet ache, but I relish the pain, taking it and storing it. It's my punishment, and strangely my reward. It's mine to feel and to keep and nourish, using it to prove that I, at least, am not an unfeeling bitch. That my love is not so easily discarded.

There are people everywhere, and even

though I know they are not intentionally getting in my way, I have no patience. I don't bother to mutter even vague apologies as I barge and elbow past them. Their opinion of me no longer matters. Only the fate of two people matters now.

The medical sector is quiet. Empty even. I dash to Grey's room but he's still not back from the tests.

There's no point in staying here, so I go in search of Willow. If she's not with her parents, then this is the next likely place I will find her. Although the fact that she had her assessment before I even left the dome, would seem to argue that she won't be here. After all, I didn't come across her when I searched these rooms before, looking for Grey. The reality is that I have no idea where else to look.

The other rooms are as empty and devoid of life as Grey's currently is. So I make my way back to his room in the hope that he has been returned there in the few minutes I have been absent. He's still not there and even though logically I know it's the same temperature as the rest of the dome, it feels cold in its emptiness. I sit on the newly made bed and try to wait. Surely he can't be much longer?

I am desperate to see him and even though I am worried about how he is, I know that I will tell him about Willow. There's no way I will be able to hide this pain from him, selfish as that is.

And it's that exact selfishness of mine that caused him to be in this mess, isn't it? Yet, I will share my feelings of how wrong and unfair this treatment of Willow is. Because that's what love is, isn't it? Talking and sharing feelings?

And I know too that he will understand how I feel. Less emotionally involved than me, maybe he will be able to figure out how I can find out where Willow is and how to help her.

I look around the room. Waiting and mulling things over in the quiet stillness has allowed my previously frantic heartbeat to slow, and whilst I am still concerned, I'm comforted by the fact that soon my problem will be shared. And that the sharing will bring forth the answer. Somehow.

The walls are drab here, much as they had been in mine. My eyes drift to the space where the patient's name is displayed above the bed. Strange – because the electronic display is dark. I'm sure that when I'd entered the room before, Greyson's name had been there, but now it has been removed, erased – as if it had never been there at all. As if *he's* never been here at all.

A slow, cold dread makes ice of my hands and it's with numb, trembling fingers that I press the buttons at the side of the display, ensuring that it's on. A small red light glows. The unit is working.

I know with a horrible aching certainty

that this is bad. That it's beyond bad. Catapulting myself from the bed I run headlong into the corridor, almost colliding with a medic coming the other way.

"Where is he? Where's Greyson?" My own words sting me, so closely do they resemble the question I've just asked of Willow's family. I am panicked and I expect the medic to try to calm me down. She doesn't.

"There were complications," she says distractedly, dismissively. She moves as if to walk past me, but I grab her arm, harnessing her in place. Her face is so close that I can feel her breath against my skin, reminding me of that moment outside, when the unknown animal calls seemed so close… but only for a second, before she turns away.

"What do you mean, complications?" I manage to spit the entire sentence out, even though the words threaten to choke me. Bile coats the inside of my mouth and I can't seem to entirely swallow it back down. I am more afraid than I have ever been.

"The tests show that his fall has caused permanent damage." She looks at me blankly, as if those few words are supposed to relay everything to me.

"His fall's caused permanent damage?" I'm repeating her words, just as I did with Willow's mother, but I can't find any of my own.

My heart should be hurting, but instead it seems to have the density and weight of a stone. I wonder if it has slipped its internal mooring and now resides at the lowest extremities of my abdominal cavity.

Perhaps the medic thinks I'm an idiot, for she explains. "The fall he had... it made him different to how he was before."

"Then he's not dead?" Relief floods me and from the frantic drumming of my heart, I realise it's still in its correct position after all.

"No, he's not dead." Her face changes as if she's thought of something unpleasant. "But he might as well be!"

My heartbeat syncopates with my breathing so that words tumble from me thick and fast. "What do you mean? Where is he? How can you say something like that?" And then when she doesn't respond immediately to any of my quick-fire questions – finally - the question I should have asked all along, "What's wrong with him?"

"The spasms you witnessed are a symptom of a condition called epilepsy."

"I've never heard of that before. What is it?" I ask urgently.

If she is trying to look kindly upon me, she's failing dismally. Instead she looks haughty, superior. "No, you wouldn't have heard of it before. ELSA has ensured that all Alphas born are perfect in every way."

"So fix him," I demand. "If ELSA can prevent it then surely she can fix it!" But perhaps I am being premature? Perhaps this is already underway, and in fact explains why Grey is not here? My heart thuds with anticipation. A quiet delirium fills me. Perhaps he's already fixed and looking for me!

Her face refutes my hopes. "I'm afraid that's impossible."

"But didn't you just tell me that ELSA makes sure Alphas are perfect? So ELSA can just fix him." It seems like perfect logic to me.

Now she really does look at me like I'm dumb. "ELSA can't 'fix' as you so technically put it, something of this magnitude."

We are still standing alone in the corridor but it feels smaller than before, as if the walls have shifted imperceptibly. The air feels different too. I'm aware that it's the same clean, pure filtered air that I breathe but here it seems tainted, tinged with something I can't quite identify. Whatever it is, it seems to cause my breath to stick in my windpipe, refusing to find its way down to my lungs and back up again.

"Besides, what the tests discovered, was that not only has this condition been triggered in him by his fall, but that unfortunately it is of a type where there is a raised likelihood of any offspring inheriting the condition."

"You're saying it can be passed to his children?" I wonder if I am simplifying the situation too much, for the solution seems to be perfectly obvious. "Then we just won't have any children!"

She smiles. Perfect white teeth lined up in two neat rows - and yet her smile reminds me only of a shark about to devour its prey.

An uneasy shiver travels down my spine, each vertebra seeming to loosen itself from its neighbour, before re-fusing together, but without the strength it had before.

"You are Alpha class!" Her tone has become strident as if it is I who has offended *her* in some way, as if it is me giving her unpalatable news. Nothing about this scenario makes sense in my head and I struggle to unravel it. "It's your civic duty to have children and to populate the dome with the very best that the human race can aspire to."

She tilts her head to one side. "Do you think it's a choice you have, dear?" she laughs and the sound grates in my eardrums. "Do you really think you can choose to have just one child, or none at all? My dear where have you lived all your life, that you can be so ignorant? You have a *civic duty* to provide."

I am shocked by her words but more than that, I am scared to the very core of my being, by the hard look of her eyes; the twist of her mouth, which continues to speak acid words through smiling lips.

Is what she states true? I'm aware that I am being side-tracked, that this whole conversation has still not revealed to me where Grey is. But like the feeling that had overtaken me earlier, I am somehow sure that none of this is random, that in some way, fate has conspired to link all of these things, these events and conversations, in a way that is not as disjointed as it first seems. If I can only just grasp...

Impatient as I am, I realise that there is a destiny at play here and that whatever entity controls it at its whim, I am just a pawn and as such must await my cue. I pray that I will recognise it when it comes.

"You're saying Grey and I can't choose not to have children, so that this thing he has, won't be passed on?"

She looks at me with a tenderness I haven't seen in her until now, and speaks to me like I am Willow's age.

"My dear. You are an Alpha. Alphas bear other Alphas. That's what keeps our world turning as peacefully and smoothly as it does. What would happen if one couple were allowed to go childless? Our whole system would be undermined. Maybe other couples would decide not to have children, and then our population would destabilise."

But I don't care about any of that. I just want Grey. I am cold. So terribly, terribly cold. "Where is Grey?" I need to feel his arms around me, touch his lovely face... everything else can be sorted once we are together again, I'm sure.

She manages somehow to pull away from me. "Miss Smith, I'm afraid I have given you all the time I can spare. Now please excuse me, I have patients to attend." Even though I know all the other rooms are empty.

I want to run after her, to grab her and arrest her progress up the corridor but I don't. An intuition that seems to start in the marrow of my bones tells me it's the wrong thing to do, the wrong course of action to take. If I'm sedated 'for my own good' I will be helping no one.

Trying as hard as I can to keep my voice level and calm, I repeat my question. "Where is Grey?"

Either the words or the tone of my voice stops her dead in her tracks. Very slowly, deliberately, she turns around to face me again. I take in the slackness of her features, the lack of empathy around her eyes that even from this distance I can clearly make out. I wonder what other subtleties are lost, viewing from this far away, what pities or horrors I am being spared.

"The epilepsy will not kill him but it will make his life sometimes difficult. That alone would be enough to seal his fate. But there was the added problem of his future children."

Every word is like a dagger to me. Every syllable, every inflection and shade of intonation impales itself in my vital organs. Without hearing what is yet unsaid, I already know. The parallels are too deep, the connection at once too strong and unfathomable.

She confirms my greatest fear. "Greyson has been reassigned and relocated. He is no longer Alpha."

CHAPTER 8

I backup against the brutality of her words and slump against a wall. But it seems that even that structure is unable to hold me and I slide towards the floor. Even as my knees buckle and my heart almost stops, my fists clench and my legs tense, push me back upwards, ready me for the action I don't even know I'm preparing to take.

I fly past the medic, uncaring what she thinks of me or whether my passing causes her to falter in any way. Barging through doors and past people who are just obstructions in my way, I dash to Grey's family with the awful news.

I don't even bother knocking, just charge into their private quarters as if I belong there. Without Grey, I'll never belong here or anywhere. His parents and sister look up as I enter, their faces stained with tears, eyes red and swollen.

"Oh Tudie!" his mother holds her arms open to me and I let myself be enfolded into her embrace. "Have you heard?" she asks, although from my entrance and the look which is surely on my face, the answer must be obvious. I nod, for a moment unable to speak.

All three of them resume a quiet mewling. For a few moments I join them unashamedly. Their pain echoes and amplifies mine. With no family of my own, they are all I have in the world – them and Grey, and it is he who ties me so firmly to them.

I'm aware that the tears aren't abating and that comforting as this shared grief it, it is also time consuming. Whilst we sit here grieving, Grey is already being moved somewhere away from us. Every minute is another distance we are being separated.

"What are we going to do?" I raise a swollen face to his family, uncaring that my eyes are hot and red, that my lips burn with a feeling akin to pins and needles and that my underarms leak sweat like liquid woe.

All three of them look blankly back at me. "There's nothing we *can* do," Grey's mother sobs.

I pull away from them in shock. "Of course there is! There must be something!" Although what that something might be, I have yet to work out. They resume their crying, trying to pull me back into their arms. But as if they mean me harm and not comfort, I fight against them.

"No this is wrong! You can't just accept it!" An image from earlier in the day assaults me - Willow's parents, not just resigned to her fate but bizarrely accepting of it, as if their child meant nothing to them at all any more. I know that Grey's parents are hurting, but that doesn't stop me lashing out at them for their apathy.

"What are you going to do? Just have another child and replace him?" It's unfair of me to compare them to Willow's family but I'm not exactly thinking rationally any more.

There's a momentary silence, a short cessation of sobs and I'm aware that I have shocked them. I no longer care. Nothing matters but Grey and Willow, who have become strangely linked by fate. Whatever I can say or do to spur Grey's family into action, I'll do it, regardless of how they might hate me for it.

Answering my question as if it was genuinely conceived and not fashioned in grief and despair, his mother responds with only the simple truth. "We are too old to have another child, Tudie."

Perhaps this is not all she means. Perhaps she doesn't actually mean to imply that Grey could be so easily replaced in their hearts but in the heat and terror of the moment, that's how I take it. I recoil in horror from these people I had thought shared my true grief.

"Is that all this means to you?" I shout. "Are you just sorry that you have failed in your *civic duty*?" My temper explodes the words from me. My retinas burn into them. Once more I am deathly cold.

"What is *wrong* with all you people?" There's a bitter, rancid taste in my mouth that I'm forced to either swallow or spit at them. I swallow. And wish I hadn't.

I don't even glance as them as I leave their quarters, hearing their protestations that there's nothing that can be done and ignoring them all. Their feeble words are lost on me.

For a few minutes I wander the corridors aimlessly, lost in internal dispute. What can I do? How can I find Grey? How can I save Willow? Without any conscious decision, I find myself at the medical section once more. This time I walk in quietly. I'm convinced that I will achieve my goal quicker and more easily if I am calm and rational, although it pains me.

I find a medic. She's a different one to the one I spoke to before. Younger. Perhaps around my own age. I attempt a weak smile. "Greyson, my fiancé – what class has he been reassigned to?"

She looks at me with sympathy. "I'm sorry I don't know. You should just forget about him now though."

So fast she doesn't even have the time to lift her arms up to protect herself, I have her by the collar and have thrust her hard against the wall, pinning her there through strength and sheer desperation. "Where is he?" I demand.

"I...I don't know!" she stutters, eyes huge

and terrified.

I'm not even ashamed of my behaviour. It's merely a means to an end; this girl merely someone who stands in my way. "Then who does? Who does know where he is?"

She tries to shrug, even though this must be difficult for her to do, being held so tightly. "I don't know. ELSA-"

At the mention of the computer, I drop her. Of course! It should have been immediately obvious to me where I can find the answer. But I guess my brain has been so befuddled that it wasn't apparent who held all the answers. ELSA.

Without apology I rush from the place, letting the door slam shut behind me. With Grey's workstation only a short distance away, I cover the ground in what must be record speed.

His workstation is unmanned. Luckily the others working in this section avoid me when they spot me. I wonder if they think I have made the trip here, just to reminisce. I let them carry on thinking that. I position myself in the exact spot where he usually works, flicking dials and switches, to ensure that ELSA is in prime running condition.

It's weird to be here without him. Weird to be about to interrogate the computer for his whereabouts, as if in some sort of role reversal. I almost feel like a wronged wife... It's too freaky and unnatural, and yet there is more than a grain of truth about it too.

I hold my wrist to the scanner. Let her know who I am. *ELSA where has my fiancé Greyson been sent to?* I type.

Good afternoon, Fortitude Smith. There is a pause, an electronic whirring that might exist only in my fevered imagination. *My logs show that at present you are not engaged with anyone to be married.* If the words had been spoken and not displayed on a screen, I am sure that they would have emphasised the second sentence.

This time I choose to speak directly into the microphone. I enunciate every word. "ELSA, where is Greyson?" I know that the computer isn't supposed to be able to deal in anything other than logic and yet I feel that it's being deliberately evasive.

There is no Alpha with the name of Greyson.

I am clenching the side of the control station with white knuckles. Pain radiates up the length of my fingers where I am forcing flesh so cruelly into steel, but I use the pain to focus my mind.

"Search your memory banks, ELSA. Greyson Ford was my fiancé." It almost kills me to use the past tense but I suspect I must play ELSA at her own game if I am to win.

Greyson Ford, past status as Alpha is confirmed. If it could have spoken, the computer's tone would have been sulky, I am sure of it.

"Where is Greyson now?" I ask. "What class has he been reassigned to?"

There is a definite pause where I hold my breath but the next display surprises me.

Fortitude Smith, it is ELSA's belief that you attempted to harm the operating system earlier today. Please report to medical bay for psychological assessment and evaluation.

I am scared now. And I act accordingly. "ELSA, tell me right now where he is!" I screech at the screen. I'm aware that all work in the section has stopped. Is everyone waiting to see how I will react? Do they expect me to dissolve finally into a puddle of my own tears and then just accept that he is gone? Like everyone else seems able to do?

There is no response.

"Where is he ELSA? And where is Willow…" I realise suddenly I don't even know the child's last name.

There is no Alpha named Willow, Fortitude Smith.

And yet I know ELSA knows exactly who I am talking about.

"Where are they? ELSA, this is the last time I'll ask politely." But we both know it's an empty threat. I can't after all grab ELSA by the collar and get the information.

That information is not available to you, Fortitude Smith.

"Then I will find it out by myself," I say

challenging her once more. "ELSA, please open the main exit to the outside." It's more of a demand than a request.

The display doesn't even take a second to respond. *ACCESS DENIED*, it flashes up.

"ELSA, OPEN THE MAIN DOORS!" I'm aware I'm shouting at a machine, but somehow it seems completely logical.

One word flashes onto the display and stays there, highlighted as if it is a final decision on my life. *No.*

There is a lever at the side of the console. Designed to be pushed gently upwards or downwards, I have no idea what it's actually for. With both hands I yank it sideways, wrenching it until it twists and tears from its moorings.

It's not quite a weapon but I use it like one anyway, bearing down and beating upon the display until the screen is cracked and the one *No* is a flickering, continuously scrolling plea for mercy.

No No No No NoNoNo...

Am I irrevocably harming the computer system which operates the dome? I don't know, nor do I care. But others will. Before anyone can reach me, I am off again, fleeing this time down the corridor, in the direction of the huge front doors which lead to the outside world.

I'm panting by the time I get there, covered in sweat and stale odour, but I don't even pause to take stock. I swing the metal lever at the computer terminal there, smashing as much as I can before I'm stopped. Through the sounds of tinkling glass and cracking plastic, I can hear many heavy footsteps heading my way. Running. Time is not on my side.

Even though the screen is cracked and broken I can see my name there, the letters jagged and uneven as the internal lights have broken but recognisable nonetheless.

Fortitude Smith, STOP! it says.

"Never!" I hear myself say, turning away from the console and towards the big doors.

I had hoped that they would open, that perhaps in order to save itself, the computer would open the doors and release me. Either I haven't done as much damage as I had intended, or I've done more, too much, causing the mechanism to freeze in place.

With the steel bar placed between the doors, I push with all my might, trying to prise the doors open enough to slide through. But they are solid. I'll never do it.

And then, even though I haven't consciously summoned it, I see a picture of Grey's face before my eyes, his mouth laughing, his eyes dancing with merriment as we shared some joke or story together.

If I fail I will never see him again. His image fades away and is replaced by Willow's. Was it not enough that I had to fail one person? Did I have to fail two? I take a deep breath and turn back towards ELSA's display. I raise the bar above my head and I give it everything I've got.

When the bar crashes down, the display finally goes dark. Only then do I turn back to the doors, pushing harder at them, prising the bar into them, giving every last ounce of strength I have and then more that I didn't even know I possessed. The doors slide a fraction apart.

No more than the width of my hand, the gap is enough for me to insert the metal bar. I wiggle it into place, aware all the time that my pursuers have arrived behind me.

At any moment I expect them to wrestle me to the ground, to remove the weapon from my grip and perhaps even to bind my hands safely behind me. But none of those things happen. Instead they just halt there as if now that they have caught up with me, they have absolutely no idea what to do next.

I pay them no attention, working diligently on the bar, twisting and manipulating it so that rather than it being lodged width ways between the doors, it's becoming locked across its length, affording a wider space by which I might be able to slip though, although it will be a tight squeeze. I think about Joy implying I'm a little underweight. I hope she's right.

The foolhardiness of what I'm about to

attempt doesn't escape my notice. The metal bar is strong but not strong enough to hold back the weight and force of the doors indefinitely. Even now the bar appears to be quivering, trying heroically to resist the strain of the doors, and I can see the metal beginning to warp and buckle.

There is a dire but very real possibility that the bar will prove inadequate to the strain, even as I am attempting to pass through the doors. Perhaps there will be a series of resounding cracks as every bone in my body splinters into a thousand pieces. Perhaps there will be only one loud complexly fatal crack. Or perhaps there will be no splintering sounds at all.

Perhaps instead, there will be loud squishing noises as blood vessels and vital organs rupture under the pressure. My eyeballs will explode and my tongue will loll from my mouth as the final breath is squeezed from me. I don't care. Whether I die trying to save Grey and Willow, or die here without them, it amounts to the same thing.

Except that it doesn't. To die through the slow agonised missing of them is a betrayal both to them and to myself. I will not go quietly. And I will not let ELSA make me.

I force myself sideways into the gap. It's tight and frightening but I wriggle and push and squirm my way through until I am fully out the other side.

Almost shocked that I have made it, I stand on the outside of those huge doors and look down at myself. I am completely intact. No fingers have been severed, no limbs crushed or mangled, and yet I am out and free.

And then I look back at the people I have left behind. The metal bar is still holding, but only just. It quivers in place. But there are so many people there, that surely if they had a mind to, they could wrench the doors fully open and somehow secure them there. Yet none of them do. No one even attempts to leave.

Instead they stand more than a foot away from the opening, as if afraid of the outside world and all that it contains. They seem bewildered by my actions, baffled and confused, and stare at me in astonishment. They look at me as if I am not one of them, but something different, something separate. Unrecognisable. I try to see myself as they do.

I have no food, no provisions, nothing to help me on whatever journey lies ahead, other than the clothes on my back. And yet unlike them, I'm unafraid, unperturbed that I am in sole charge of my life. I no longer know if they are scared *for* me, or *of* me.

And then the inevitable happens. There is an earth-shattering racket of splitting, rending metal, and despite the bar placed across its opening, the metal doors begin to close once more. Sealing the Alphas back into their living tomb.

I watch the people disappear from sight, the ones at the edges of the gap first and then those towards the centre. Perhaps I should feel some emotion, something to indicate how momentous a time this is, but there is nothing. Perhaps there's no emotion left in me right now. Not for these people, anyway.

If they had chosen to come with me they wouldn't just have left. They would have *escaped*. But the doors slide shut and all I can think is: *Now I am really on my own.*

Until I can find them - my family, Willow and Grey - I am alone.

CHAPTER 9

I turn in a circle. I have absolutely no idea where to go, how to begin the search. The landscape looks fairly uniform in all directions, but somewhere, out there beyond the distance that my eyes can see, Willow and Grey need my help. But which way? Left? Right? Behind the Dome or running in a straight line in front of it? I have no way of knowing.

With only the Dome and the empty land to focus on, there are no other clues. I close my eyes and let intuition guide me.

When you came outside with Grey you walked straight ahead. You have already travelled that route a little. Your path now lies elsewhere.

I try to reason with the inner voice. *But the fact that I have already been in that direction, even a little way, makes it more likely surely that that is the route I should take. Besides there is fresh water there.*

I receive my answer not in my own voice, as I have come to expect, but in that of my father's. *Life works hard to keep its unpredictability, Tudie. You who lost your mother before even knowing her, should know that. Take the path not yet taken.*

His modulated tone, the gentle rise and fall, treads so gently on my heart that the pain is a melancholy note, rather than a brash jarring symphony. As if the softness of my hurt is an insult to the deep connection there had been between us, I am shamed. I keep my eyes tightly closed, in case when I open them, I will find him standing there, appraising me and finding me wanting.

His voice finds me captive inside my head. *There are many kinds of love, Tudie, and every one is as valid to the soul as it is to life itself. Without love there is no absence of love; there is merely nothing.* Whether the words come from myself or actually from him, there is no real difference, I know that they are the truth.

I play a memory of myself laughing with him at some silly story or another, the way his face creased as he beamed back at me, the obvious love which connected us, evident in our every shared moment. In my imagination, I plant a kiss on his cheek, and for a second, I would swear that my lips graze lightly across the short bristles there... but when I open my eyes, he is not there. Perhaps he never was.

I turn my back on the direction that Grey and I had gone in. And face the dome. Walking around its circumference to travel straight ahead will take longer than choosing to go to the right or the left, so for this reason, if for no other, I dismiss that idea. So which is it to be, right or left? Right or wrong?

I glance both ways but there is little to distinguish between them. Both directions lead off flatly for as far as the eye can see. In the end, I choose the left path for no other reason than conversely, it *feels* right.

Placing one foot in front of the other, I walk. Not once do I turn and look back at the dome. If Grey, Willow and I return here, I have no idea to what kind of life that will be. But that is a concern for the future, not for the present. There's already enough to worry about for now.

I want to hurry, to run as fast as I can until I find them, but logically, moving too fast, expending too much energy will leave me depleted and in danger. I have no food, no water, and nothing to defend myself with, should any wild animals decide to attack me.

Trying hard to keep my pace measured, I use the time to think. To push at least some logic into the situation, frightening as that is. I have no idea where Grey has been sent, or what class he has been reassigned to, but I do know that Willow was reclassed as Delta. With the timeframe so similar – Willow and Grey have been reclassified within mere days of each other – it's possible that they have been sent together to the same sector.

I hold on to this hope, even though I think

that it's not going to be so simple, that finding one of them will automatically lead me to the other. If anything, I'm inclined to believe the reverse, that in locating one of them, I will have moved further from finding the other.

It's as if they are on some sort of cosmic see-saw, where every move I make towards one or the other, will affect the delicate balance, so that as one side comes down, the other will go up. It's such a horrible image that I shiver. I cannot choose between them, not even if my own life depends on it. So I'm resigned to work with fate, work with what I do know. I focus my mind.

Delta are farmers. Would Grey have been sent there for that reason? His size and strength would clearly make him suitable for working the land. Except that now he has fits. So perhaps they will give him lighter work to do, I tell myself. But apparently I'm not a good liar, even to myself.

A fear nags at my brain and I try unsuccessfully to push it aside. Grey has no knowledge or experience of farming. How much use to them, will the people of Delta sector actually consider him to be? And if they think he will be nothing but an unwanted drain on resources, a burden for them to carry, already cast out from Alpha as unworthy, then what? How likely are they to take pity on his condition if it turns out that he cannot work? What might they do with him? *To* him?

Fear clutches at my heart and there is nothing with which to still it. Logic only takes me further into fear, not away from it.

The reality is that Grey is injured, defenceless and alone. With no family wherever he is, no ties, there is no one to stand up for him, no one to watch his back. And if his own family are unwilling to support and provide for him, why should these strangers be any different? I fear that the Deltas will not react with open arms to his arrival. Perhaps the exact opposite.

And Willow? How will the Deltas react to her? She's only a child, not yet capable of the type of work carried out in this sector. Will the people of Delta find a home for her? Give her shelter? Food? Love? When she is long years away from being of any use to them? Or will they cast her out too?

Yet Deltas are people, flesh and blood the same as Grey and Willow. Surely they will not turn them away, cast them out from their sector? But I'm plagued by the image of Grey's parents' faces; Willow's family's refusal to acknowledge her as part of them. If their own families could cast them so easily aside, why should the Deltas feel any obligation to provide for them?

I'm terrified in equal measure for these two people who mean the world to me, but I dare not wallow in despair, for if I do, I sense that although my feet will undoubtedly continue to seek them out, my heart will not detect the subtlety of the path I must follow. To save them I must first believe that I can.

There are several Delta areas. I know this because of the information I send out to them. Delta sectors vary enormously over different types of terrain; the different crops or animals they tend, and the general weather conditions they work under.

Does that mean that there are more Deltas than Alphas? It's something I have never even considered before, having always assumed there were other domes, other Alphas elsewhere.

Are Grey and Willow more likely to be accepted as part of a bigger society? Or less? Perhaps there are less Deltas than the size of their sectors would suggest? Are they spread wider across areas due to the needs of their work? And would this have an impact upon the likelihood of them accepting Grey and Willow? I have absolutely no idea.

Logic tells me that Willow and perhaps Grey too, will be at the first Delta sector I stumble upon. Why would ELSA take them further than she had to, in order to relocate them? The question therefore is whether I am heading in the right direction. Or whether each steps moves me further from those I seek.

My feet plod onwards, my path dictated by the pull of my heart. Whether this will eventually lead me to where I need to be, I have no idea. All I have is blind faith.

But because I need something to cling to it, I take each step decisively, with no hesitation and no looks cast over my shoulder; until I step over a largish rock right in the middle of the path. Instinct tells me to pause, turn around and pick it up.

My fingers close around it, judging its weight and feeling for jagged edges which might work to my advantage should I ever need to use it. It might not be the best weapon in the world, but it's more than I had a moment ago.

The idea of crushing it into something's skull is abhorrent; but then so is the thought of failing Willow and Grey. When the time comes, *if* the time comes, then I will use the rock, in whatever way I have to.

My feet are aching, my limbs heavy and sore and I have no idea how far I have walked, what distance I have covered, or how long ago I left the dome. But when I eventually turn around to look back the way I have come, the dome is just a tiny speck, far, far in the distance.

The horizon gives up no clues as to how far I must still travel to find what I seek, and the landscape around me is bleak with solitude. Worryingly, I realise that night is falling and with it the temperature is dropping. I become aware that I'm shivering. And it's only with this discovery that I know I have been trembling for some time; that I am working on adrenaline alone.

What will happen when there is no adrenaline left? When fear overtakes determination and there is no way forward? What then?

I know that I will have to stop soon and rest, if for no other reason than that if I carry on walking in the dark, I will have no way of knowing whether I am walking in a straight line or just making wide circles, expending the last of my energy in a fruitless loop. But the thought of sitting alone in the vastness of the night terrifies me.

Just as I have this thought, there's a sound which brings a fresh wave of terror to my heart. It's a snarl. Closely followed by a yelp and a deeper growl. It takes only seconds to know that one rock isn't going to be enough to protect me.

I freeze on the spot, heart lurching between fear for myself and fear for what this means for Grey and Willow. But when the sound comes again, I realise that it is no closer than before.

It's followed this time by a series of yelps and howls that sound more immersed in battle, than readying for battle to commence. Is it possible I have stumbled upon something that has nothing to do with me? Nothing to do with the scent of fresh human that I am no doubt casting out into the growing darkness around me? Is it possible that the growls are not intended for my ears?

Caution tells me to walk as quietly and quickly as I can in the opposite direction, but curiosity compels me to hasten forward. Towards the unseen creatures whose cries fill the night air.

Even though I know it isn't the wisest course of action, I attempt to justify it to myself. Maybe if I learn more about what these creatures are and how they fight, I will be better able to defend myself from future attack. Assuming I survive that long.

It's madness, I know, walking toward the increasingly savage growls. Somehow, I manage to stop myself from committing to another step. What good will I be to Grey and Willow if I fall here, throat torn out and bleeding slowly to death? If my last words bubble from my throat in a pool of cascading blood? What good will I be to either of them then?

But just as intuition has guided my feet until now, so it continues to guide them. Forward. But quietly, with a stealth I didn't suspect I had.

The darkness seems to part before me, and in the silvered moonlight the creatures I recognise from my schooling as coyotes, look less like they are fighting, and more like they are performing some elaborate dance; circling one another, creeping forward only to jump back, connecting and disconnecting to some unheard rhythm.

Mesmerised by the thrusts and parrying of the two creatures as they first lunge then leap back from one another, I barely notice the rest of the pack, huddled to one side, not moving in on the scene but watching intently. Waiting for the victor; the spoils of victory.

Thin and rangy, with matted and unkempt fur, they are unlovely creatures. And yet I see a beauty in them too, a symmetry of line and fineness of bone structure, that hints at an uncompromising truth: here is nature, something I have spent my entire life shielded from. Raw and merciless.

Do the pack watch the fight so closely they don't see me approach? Or do they consider me to be of so little threat to them, that they intend to dispose of me at their leisure? Ripping and tearing my flesh with the abandon of those who know no defeat?

Am I momentarily dismissed, considered merely the second act to the greater savagery of coyote against coyote currently on display? The thrill of the taking of a human to be all the greater for the delay in gratification?

I am terrified but I am also strangely fascinated. This is like nothing I have ever witnessed. So brutal and ruthless. Uncivilised. And yet... Isn't this only a more honest depiction of what already took place within the dome? Didn't the Alphas betrayal of Grey and Willow amount to the *same thing* as is being played out here before my eyes, in the shape of these wild animals?

The thought of Willow and Grey in this way, brings a fresh wave of pain and I avert my eyes from the bloody battle before me. Closing my ears to the ferocious cries, nauseated by the scent of blood in the air, I try to disconnect them from this scene, separate the two events. But I can't.

Nearby, fresh kill lies bleeding on the ground. Too still to have any life left in its body, its death is no doubt attributable to the coyotes in a very real way. I wonder how long it took to die. How much pain and fear it felt. Whether it knew its death was inevitable.

Sorrow for the animal cannot reinstate it to life, but I feel it anyway. I am reminded of my earlier feeling that everything is connected, that to save either Grey or Willow, I will have to put the other in ever-worsening jeopardy.

I am drawn to the dead animal by a need to touch its still flank, as if in the doing so, I will be better informed. I creep quietly forward. But there is no knowledge mystically imparted through the contact. No secrets of the universe are unveiled, no confidences bestowed upon me.

A deer of some sort, it looks large enough to provide food for the whole pack, and is certainly larger than any of its attackers, not that its size advantage was enough to save its life, I note nervously.

I wonder if it's a left-over excitement from the chase and recent kill, which has sparked the feud within the pack. Or whether it's something else, some inability of one of the coyotes to fit in with the others.

Because I've been drawn into this scene, not quite against my will, but certainly for some reason that I can't define, I know now that I have some part to play. I turn my attention back to the fight.

Mouth so wide, it almost appears that the lower jaw has become unhinged, the bigger of the two animals swipes a paw at the other one and advances. In apparent fear, its opponent cowers down before the attack and I wonder if it has decided to give in, when just at the last possible moment, it hurls itself through the air and lands almost on the larger coyote's back.

Teeth grappling into fur, there is a tussle and the two animals become wrapped together until they are no more than a fighting, howling ball of matted hair; fangs glinting in the moonlight, blood spraying in a wide arc.

Neither of the coyotes has my support against the other. I have no knowledge with which to judge them and find one or the other failing. I am merely a spectator here. But my gaze latches onto them, trying to follow their twists and turns, attacks and counter-attacks, trying to work out who is wining and why - what strategies they have used - so that I might be at least a little prepared when they come for me.

And then suddenly, the creatures separate, become untangled, and the smaller of the two is on its back, belly up and unguarded to attack. For a long moment, the victor stands over its enemy and just when I think it is all over, that the feud at least will not end in a loss of life, it lunges for the smaller coyote's throat.

Perhaps it is the difference in size and muscle power between the two. Perhaps it's the thought of Willow, defenceless and needing my help and of Grey whom I love with all my heart, but I am running towards the coyotes, unable to remember making the decision to do so. Running and screaming with all my might.

The sounds which rip from my throat are almost inhuman. They are unrecognisable as words, containing noises which are so primal, so primeval and ancient sounding, that I wonder how and from where I have conjured them up.

Life, I realise, is more raw and brutal than I had ever imagined. It is also unfair and unjust. These coyotes are not my concern. Grey and Willow are. And yet...

And yet here I am hurtling towards the big one with the stone in my hand, as if I am set on a path to avenge every injustice in the world. I see its eyes, up close and beautiful, and completely unaware of the danger I pose. I don't know if it even sees the heavy rock in my hand or understands how I intend to use it, for its eyes hold only mine, as I bring the stone crashing into the side of its skull.

There is a nauseating thud and I am reminded of Grey's fall, of the horrible pallor of his skin and the terrible, terrible weight of his unconscious body as I dragged him home.

Without even thinking what I am doing, I raise the stone again but I don't need to bring it back into contact with flesh and bone. The big coyote, taking perhaps the full measure of me, or perhaps just stunned by the unusualness of the assault, staggers back to its feet. But it does not attack me.

Turning tail, tucking it right in-between its legs, it scurries over to the rest of the pack and then miraculously they all disappear, vanishing into the dark, like bad fairies.

The smaller coyote has not run away with the others. This surprises me most of all. Despite the ferocious battle it has just lost with another of its pack, I had expected that it too would flee, preferring the known dangers of pack life to whatever it feared from me. But it holds its ground.

So do I. For a moment we gaze at each

other. Both wary, neither of us acknowledging our fear or how much we have underestimated the situation.

Can I just back away? Will it let me do this? Or will it, once I have shown my fear, leap up at my throat? The stone is still in my hand. Its weight calms me somewhat. I'm not *totally* defenceless. But I doubt that I can strike again with the force and accuracy I managed before. Instinct guided me then.

Now the idea of bringing the stone down once more onto a living creature's skull appals me. If the coyote was to attack me it would be different, but whilst it is just lying there seemingly at my mercy – do I have it in me to kill like that?

I take one tiny step backwards. The coyote, still on its back, makes no move to get to its feet. I have been watching its face in the dark until now, looking for signs of what was going through its mind. Assuming that I could interpret them, at least a little. Now as an enshrouding cloud moves from in front of the moon, no longer cloaking the world with such darkness, my eyes adjust to the available light and track the length of the animal's body.

A thin stream of something that looks like black mud leaks from a gash on one side of the coyote's underbelly. Forgetting entirely what it is and what I'm *not*, I take a step forward again. I slowly drop the hand with the stone in it to my side and tentatively reach forward with the other hand. Perhaps I am sealing my own fate but I choose to believe that the coyote knows I saved its life. And that it will spare mine in return.

It tries to back away from me, but it doesn't once growl or snarl. Instead it pulls its muscles together and giving a faint whine, manages to drag itself just out of my reach. Just far enough away that it can watch what I do next.

Unhurriedly, as if we two have all the time in the world, I drop to my haunches and ease forward until I am once more within touching distance. I slowly raise the rock until it's in front of the creature's face.

"You see this? This is what saved you. *I* am what saved you. But I'm putting it down now." I place the rock on the ground where the coyote can see it. "Whatever happens next is down to destiny, I guess," I tell it, watching it watch me speak, looking somehow as if it understands every word.

I reach forward towards the wound but do not touch it. Its breath is hot against my neck, its eyes flicker across my face and then to the soft flesh of my throat. In my mind I hear the bones and cartilage being crushed between the animal's strong jaws. I try to swallow my fear. "I'm just going to see how bad this is," I say, reaching forward towards the wound, fully expecting it to be the last thing I ever do.

Its fur is warm and softer than I would have imagined and although the coyote looks thin, there's a wiry strength that's evident in its thinness from even the most tentative of touches. Gently I part the fur on both sides of the gash.

The coyote's head is raised, watching every move. I'm acutely aware that my fingers are within biting distance, that my whole face is within a fraction of the animal's sharp teeth. I try to hold my breath, scared of bursting the bubble we seem to be caught in.

Its scent is musky, its breath warm with a strange but not unpleasant smell. I breathe it in with the crazy thought that in doing so, I will be considered part of it. Slowly and deeply I pull the coyote's muskiness into my lungs, filling them with the power of the animal, holding the breath for as long as I can, before quietly exhaling and blowing the animal's smell back to it. And then, with what sounds so much like a human sigh that I am startled, the animal lowers its head to the ground, as if letting me do what I will.

I'm not naïve enough to think that I have gained its trust. It's merely beaten from the unfair match, cowed, injured and in pain. Any moment now it will regain some of its strength and will to live, and then it will attack me. But still the attack does not come.

I rip a strip of my cotton top to use as a

bandage and wrap it around the wound, binding it as tightly as I can. To do this I have to get one arm underneath the creature, putting me at a serious disadvantage. I hold my breath whilst I work, afraid that the human smell of me will finally be too much temptation for the coyote to endure.

I don't know how much time has passed, but suddenly I feel as if many eyes are upon my back. The hairs on my arms are standing on end and I have that same horrible feeling of being watched, that I had when I was dragging Grey to safety. Am I destined to repeat this scene with variations for the rest of my life, I wonder.

It stands to reason the pack would regroup and come back. For a start their food is here. But I am hungry too. And for now, surely I am the victor? And with victory come victor's rights.

I pick the stone up and move over to the dead deer. What I am about to do makes me feel ill, but I steel myself to do it as quickly and calmly as I can. The animal is already dead and can't be hurt further. But its meat can save my life and in doing so, save Grey and Willow too. It's this thought that I focus on.

Using the sharp points of the rock, I rip and tear through the deer's flesh, carving out a section of flank. I cut enough for me and for the injured coyote but am careful to leave enough for the rest of the pack to feast upon. If I am quick and sensible, then perhaps they will be lured more by the scent and promise of meat than the thrill of another chase.

Because I have used the stone to previously attack a coyote, I'm aware that blood and chunks of gore are probably already stuck to it, but I can't afford to let this put me off my task. I work swiftly and diligently, aware that every minute that passes puts me in greater danger.

Separating the meat from the rest of the carcass is harder work than I would have imagined and I'm sweaty by the time I'm done but finally I have a large chunk which I wrap in the top I am wearing like an apron. I put the rock there too. Just in case.

I shuffle back to the injured coyote who hasn't moved. I've made even more of a target of myself now, being covered in and carrying fresh meat on my person but I don't waiver in my path.

"I can't carry you," I tell it, looking it in the eye. Maybe I'm wrong in what I'm about to say, but gut instinct has served me well so far. "You have to get up. You have to walk." I'm convinced that if the pack move in they will show no mercy to their former companion. I am convinced he will be killed. And that if I let that happen it will be another weight on my conscience, another failure of mine.

The coyote looks at me and although he has no way of understanding me, perhaps he sees something in my eyes which communicates my fear for him, for he tries to do as I say. But his wound obviously pains him and he has trouble in getting his legs under him enough to raise himself off the ground. As gently as I can, I shuffle one arm under him once more, using it to lever him up and to his feet. He is surprisingly heavy. Swaying slightly on his paws he stands but does not follow me. I decide to show him the meat held inside my top.

"This is for us. For you and me. But first we have to get to safety. Away from the other coyotes in your pack." Except I think we both know they are no longer his pack.

He takes one step forward. I keep facing him and take one step backward. He follows in my footsteps. But this is not a hunt, nor is he stalking me, instead I lead him forward with gentle words of encouragement. "There you are. Keep going. You can do this."

I deliberately don't look behind him, to the pack which watch us with every step we take but it's only a short time before I hear movement and see them come creeping forward. But they stop when they reach the deer and the fresh meat available there.

The pack are feasting and have forgotten about us. For now, anyway.

CHAPTER 10

I keep us moving, at least another hour or so, judging by the changing position of the moon in the sky, and the fact that the night seems to have gotten deeper and darker than even before. I know that night follows day, which follows night... but despite that logic I'm ready to believe that I have entered some sort of perpetual night, where I will spend the rest of my mercifully short life, desperate for the day and never finding it.

I purposely don't estimate the time by how utterly exhausted I feel – I am already running on empty and dwelling on it will do no good at all. Putting enough distance between us and the pack that we will be out of their range, outside of their territory, is a necessity, not a whim.

But the bigger worry doesn't escape me. Moving beyond the point of exhaustion and in this poor state, drained and starving, how will we be able to defend ourselves?

The obvious answer is that we won't. I shut from my head the equally terrifying thought that if we are moving out of one pack's area, then who or what might we be heading straight towards? Perhaps the known problem of the coyotes will turn out to be the lesser of two evils, less terrifying than the possibility of the unknown one, still ahead.

I push the thought away. I can't let myself by paralysed into inaction by my fears. For if I do, if I let fear override my heart, I will be the same as all those people inside the dome; the ones who stood near the threshold and the open doors with me, but never dared to take a step towards freedom. Never stepped outside. Never dared to venture into the unknown. I can't be like them because I'm not.

Finally I allow myself to sink to the ground. For the last half-hour or so, the coyote has travelled almost by my side, only a step or two behind, allowing me to turn around and face the direction we are heading in, rather than having to walk backwards, coaxing him with every step.

Whatever has passed between us, it has engendered a vague trust that neither of us is entirely uneasy about. I have enough confidence in him now that I think he too will stop once I do. And I guess he no longer sees me as a threat, which is absurd enough that under other circumstances I might laugh. Now, I merely accept it as true.

From my slumped position on the ground, I turn a little towards him. His gait is halting, limping, and he is clearly in pain and scared. My makeshift bandage has held the wound closed but it can do nothing to alleviate his pain. I wish I could help him more.

He stops as if waiting for instruction and on impulse I pat the ground beside me. "Come and sit here." He ignores my words and regards me warily, settling where he stands, not on his haunches, but lying flat a few steps away. Perhaps his closeness is dictated not by choice but by fear, hunger and exhaustion. Perhaps I am nothing more than another unwanted pack leader.

I have walked with the meat still held firmly in the fold of my top, feeling it gently hit my body with every step I take, until I no longer noticed it. Now I take it from the congealed cloth it's stuck to. The blood around the flesh has soaked into the fabric and it pulls away with a deeply unpleasant sucking sound, which makes me wince.

Even though I cut this slab of meat from a dead animal, I have to force myself to touch it now. At the time I was running on adrenaline - perhaps anything might have been possible. Now I'm just me again and some things seem beyond me. But I can't let them be.

I take hold of the meat firmly and using the rough edge of the stone again, I cut it into two portions, a big one for the coyote and a smaller one for me.

I have no way of cooking the meat even if I knew how to, and no knowledge of how to make a fire, to even attempt it, so I'm stuck with raw meat. I try to tell myself that this is only a small step from cooked meat, but the truth is far different.

I have seen the animal this came from. I have actually cut the flesh from the still-warm carcass myself, and with a rock that I had already used against the skull of a wild coyote. Yet, as well as making me feel sick, the ludicrous image makes me giggle a little. It's too far beyond the me I thought I was.

I'm quiet, but the unusual sounds are enough to disturb my coyote companion, who tries to crawl on his injured stomach a little further away from me. Seeing this quells the laughter in my throat. Slowly I get to my feet and approach him, his portion of the meat held out in front of me.

"I don't know why it's turned out to be important that I have you on my side. But somehow it is. I guess it's just destiny." The sound of that one word seems to echo on in my head. "Destiny. That's what you should be called."

I lay his meaty chunk between his front paws but I don't back away. Instead I sit down right next to him, as if we are old friends. He eyes the chunk in front of him, sniffs it, then looks back at me as if seeking permission. I have to be wrong about this because it doesn't make sense. He's a wild animal. Perhaps it's more that he's still scared of me and the unpredictability of what I might do. I hold my own chunk of meat up for him to see. "That's your bit, Destiny. I have mine here."

He eyes my chunk and then bends his head over his, holding it down between his front paws whilst sharp canine teeth tear at the flesh. I watch for only a moment. Raw meat clearly hasn't killed him. Why should it kill me? Apprehensively I raise my own piece to my mouth.

The aroma is rank, coppery and too wetly musky to be thought of merely as under-cooked meat. I try to ignore what my nose is telling me and sink my teeth into the raw flesh. Like rubber, it seems to rebound from my attempts to separate any small piece of it, and I resort to having to slice a sliver off with the rock.

I pop the smaller piece into my mouth, try to chew it at least a little, and then swallow it in what must be its entirely, as I feel every single millimetre it sinks down my throat. It's disgusting, but I force myself to eat another seven or eight chunks anyway. But when they sit so heavily in my stomach that I fear they might soon revisit my throat, I give up and pass the rest of the meat to Destiny, who takes it eagerly.

"Fortitude and Destiny," I say quietly. "It kind of has a ring to it." I don't ask his opinion. I'm not quite mad enough yet to think that he has one or even that he understands. But his presence is comforting enough.

I try it out together with the other names in my manufactured family. "Fortitude, Greyson, Willow and Destiny." They go together nicely, I think.

However disgusting the meat tasted and smelled, it has done the job of placating my growling stomach and I am sleepy. Destiny has finished eating but his eyes are still open, still wary. But I can't let that worry me. After all he is my destiny, right? I close my eyes and lay my head on the ground.

When I wake, the sun has banished the moon from the sky and the day is warm and fine. I am surprised to find that somehow during the night, the coyote and I have curled around one another, sharing body heat.

Raising myself onto one elbow I look at the flattened grass beneath me. I don't appear to have moved much at all in my sleep and so I suspect that it was Destiny who moved towards me and not the other way around.

The coyote is awake but seems calm and content to be by my side. Only hesitating a few seconds, I raise my hand and stroke the fur down one side of his flank. He does not shy away from me; his eyes hold mine and for a moment I see not him, but Willow – the look of complete honesty and trust is the same.

It causes me to swallow hard. *What am I doing? A girl alone out here? Attempting to rescue the people she loves and taking on even more responsibility along the way? How stupid I am!*

I argue with myself as I continue to stroke the coyote's coat. *But it's not like there was a choice, is it? This is just how it is. I couldn't have left this animal to die. Besides, if it really is my destiny, then it will play itself out, as fate intends.* It's not much of a consolation. But it's all I have.

"Time to get moving again," I say, pulling myself to my feet. For a long moment the coyote remains on the ground watching me sadly. Pinpricks of fear needle my heart. *Is he dying? Is his wound too deep, too grievous to heal? Is it infected? Did I walk him too far without food and in pain?*

I'm at a loss for what to do and I'm not surprised when tears slide down my cheeks. I lower my face to him. "I'm so sorry Destiny."

The coyote's tongue darts out from between his brilliant white teeth and licks the moisture from my face. I stumble backwards in surprise, almost falling down on my behind. As if he has perpetrated some great joke on me, he hauls himself to his feet, tongue lolling from his open mouth, as if laughing. But his stance is slightly wobbly and his head hangs a little lower than I think it ought to.

I was right the first time. He's struggling.

I look down at the state I'm in and realise that I'm kidding myself if I don't admit that I too am pushing myself beyond what I could normally endure.

"They need us," I hear myself tell Destiny. "When we find them, everything will be okay. I know it will!" But I don't know it, not for a definite fact. I just hope it will be. That has to be enough for now.

Standing side by side, we regard the terrain ahead. There's been a subtle shift from how it looked immediately outside the dome to how it looks here. The grass is longer and coarser than it was around the vast structure, with little bits of flowers or plant seed at the top, which blow majestically in the gentle breeze.

I run one finger and thumb up the length of a stalk, feeling its texture, realising that I have never experienced anything like it. Nothing here is old to me, all is fresh and beautiful. And even though I am compelled urgently forward, I recognise that there is much here to fill the heart with wonder and joy.

I look upwards at the sky. It's not the first time that I have seen it, although inside the dome, ELSA provides our lighting. Blank walls or carefully chosen artwork line our rooms and corridors; there is nothing to hint at the beauty which lies outside of that sterile place.

The sky is so vast, so infinite. I have seen it

only perhaps a handful of times in my life, and yet it's only now that I really wonder at it. It's not as it first appears, one uniform colour. It's made up of a variety of shades of blue, some darker and more profound than others, some lighter and wispier, as if swirled gently with cotton wool. There are clouds too, white cotton candy balls of softness that remind me of pillows.

The vastness of the sky above me should make me feel small - but it doesn't. It makes me feel incredibly alive, connected to the earth and the grass and the trees in ways I can't explain even to myself, as if I am as vital a part of everything as the air and the rain and the wind. I lower my head and look in the direction I'm travelling.

The land is more undulating than before and I can't tell what lies beyond what I guess must be at least a half day's walk from here. Perhaps only more of the same, perhaps something different. Time and distance will tell.

I begin to walk, hoping that the coyote's initial wobbliness is due to stiffness and will be walked off. Eyes on the far horizon I don't look down at my feet lest I catch sight of him struggling. He has to make this journey with me. He has become a part of my quest without me even realising it, and if I am forced to leave him behind, to fail him, I fear I will fail all of us.

But he keeps up with me. I feel his flank against my leg every few steps as if he walks deliberately close, guarding me and letting me guard him in return. After a while, I lower my arm on that side, letting it trail gently along his back as we stride forward. I think he finds it as comforting as I do, although why that should be, I have no idea.

I'm becoming increasingly hot and thirsty and I know that we won't survive to the end of the day if we don't find water soon. I pull my tongue from the roof of my mouth to break the silence and find that it is almost glued there.

"We'll find water soon," I say reassuringly, but even if the animal could understand my language, it would have had difficulty in interpreting the sounds into words, so thickly and slurred do they exit my mouth.

We carry on. But my mind is no longer on our route, instead I am reliving events of my past. I hold my arms out as my father picks me up from the ground and swings me around in his arms. He hands me a glass of water and I drink it thirstily, hand it back to him and beg for more. The water is cool and clear and soothes my arid throat.

"Drink it all, Fortitude, your body needs it," he says. And I try, I really do. But when I look down at my hands again, it's not a glass that I hold cupped there, but tufts of dry, spikey grass. I spit them out.

I'm crying, hot stinging tears that leak moisture from my eyes; moisture that I can ill afford to lose. I wipe my hands across my face and stumble onwards. It's only then that I realise Destiny is no longer by my side.

As if finally disgusted by my inability to look after us, the coyote has moved away from me, walking not straight ahead anymore, but on a diagonal from my path, distancing himself from me with every step. It's clear he's had enough. Whatever his real reasons for following me, nature has now kicked in and he is leaving me to find his own kind. I can't say I blame him.

I watch him go, from my knees. I don't remember sinking to the ground but I am there, hands palm down in the dirt, knees planted firmly on the dusty ground as if I am so bereft at losing him, I'm trying to become a coyote too. Maybe I am. Maybe death will come to me and I'll be reborn as one of his kind. Maybe *that* was the destiny between us, after all.

Barely able to keep my eyes open, I watch him disappear behind a clump of trees, favouring his injured side slightly with every step he takes. I wonder what the other coyotes will think when he reappears within the pack, smelling of human and with a strange thing wrapped around his middle. I hope they are pleased to see him. That they forgive him his mistakes and accept him back.

Even though he is no longer my concern by his own choosing, I hope his wound heals and that he lives a good, long life. If there's nothing else I can give him, I can give him my good wishes.

My eyes close. The lids are like the doors of the dome and I know that it will take a supreme effort to get them to open. I don't bother to try. There's no point. I am so hot, so thirsty, that I can hear my brain whirring inside my head. It's a strangely comforting sound and makes me feel -

Something closes around the collar of my top and tugs at the material there! Something that breathes heavily on the exposed skin of my throat, that smells alarmingly like wild animal! Instinctively, I pull sharply away.

It's a coyote! My eyes dart open to find that I am millimetres away from sharp white fangs which lunge towards my neck once more. I raise my hands in defence but am too late, the fangs are too close, too ready. Mouth holding tight to my collar, it drags me a short distance from where I lay.

So this is how it will end, I think. Coming all this way, only to die stupidly without even having the energy to defend myself. No wonder Destiny left me!

My palms are flat on the ground but there is something under one of them. Slowly my fingers curl around it. It's a stick. Neither long nor broad, it's not much of a weapon, but at least I could use it to jab at the coyote's eyes. Its blindness in exchange for my life.

I prepare for the punctures and inevitable pain, the sickening sounds of my flesh ripping from my bones, fingers tensed around the stick in readiness. But the coyote releases me and steps back, playing with me, cruelly giving me hope, before it comes in for the kill. And for the first time I see it properly. The coyote is Destiny.

My brain tries frantically to make sense of this unexpected betrayal. From my position on the ground I look up at the traitor. It's only then that I notice that he's wet, that his muzzle is darkened by water and that his underbelly drips onto the dry ground. His legs and tail are wet too. I sit staring at him, trying to figure out what the significance of this is.

He approaches me again, grabbing at my clothing with his teeth and tugging gently. He wasn't attacking me! He was urging me to move! I struggle to my feet. My knees are weak and threaten to give up on me at any second but I make it upright. Staggering, weaving a crooked path, I follow the coyote to a small stream.

Not wide, but deep enough to come to my knees, I wade into its centre. The cool water swirls and ebbs around me and my heart tries to fool my brain into believing it's a few days ago. That this water is where Grey and I stand, and that if I just close and reopen my eyes, I will find him there, handsome and healthy and absolutely fine. That all of this will never have happened, never have existed.

I close my eyes but when I open them again, the scene is exactly as it was before. Only Destiny stands watching me, all four legs in the water, the surface of the stream reaching above his stomach. His eyes are bright and I can see that his wound is immersed in the water. Whether this is accidental or deliberate I have no way of knowing but I know that him getting me here is neither chance nor accident.

"You saved me!" It comes out on a sigh as if I'm not grateful. I try again. "You saved my life, thank you." I bow my head at him. He emits no noise in recognition but lifts his head a little in return, like an acknowledgement of sorts. Like he knows he's paid his dues.

"I guess we're even now," I say. "I saved you and now you've saved me. So if you were just sticking around to pay your debt, then you can go now." I hope he won't though. I am giving him his due 'out' but I don't want him to take me up on it. I pray he won't.

He just stands looking at me, mouth open in a kind of half-smile. I scoop handfuls of water up and into my mouth and when I have finally sated my thirst, use my cupped hands to wash the dirt from my face and neck. Finally I am refreshed.

Destiny hasn't moved once and I know what I have to do, what he's waiting for. I reach forward and gently remove the bandage from around him. Because of being soaked in the water, it comes away easily enough but what I find underneath scares me. The wound is a livid red, much redder than I think it ought to be. It's hot to the touch too and there's a yellow pus which seems to ooze out from somewhere in the middle of it. Without any medical training, I know that it's infected and that soon, he will die, unless I can get help for him.

I wash the bandage out in the stream. It has dried pus on it but comes away clean when I rub the material together. When it's as fresh as I can get it, I wash it again, then use it to gently wipe the pus away from the open wound.

What I'm doing to him must hurt like mad, but Destiny bears it stoically, never once yelping or baring his teeth at me. Gently I pull at the yellow discharge, sickened as it comes away sometimes in globs and at others in a thin glutinous stream. I take my time, both so that I'm as gentle as I can be, and also because the running water is helping, cooling the wound and washing away the debris.

Only once does Destiny pull away from me slightly. I let him go and when I think the pain has subsided a little I place my hand gently on the flat of his back. "Lie down," I say.

The water is too deep for him to actually lie down, but he suffers himself to be more immersed than before. I keep him like that for as long as I think he can bear it, and when I encourage him back up, I'm relieved to see that some of the redness has gone from the wound and whilst it's still raw and open, it looks both cleaner and healthier than before.

I wish that I had something to carry some water in but there's nothing. I curse myself yet again for being so unprepared. The coyote follows me out of the stream and stands still whilst I re-bandage him.

"Once we find some people we will have medicine that will help you," I tell him, not daring to think how long that might be or how far away. We have gotten this far. Together we will make the rest of the journey.

With renewed vigour on my part and sheer determination on his, we march back to where we had left off from our trail. The sun is in a noticeably different position in the sky, and I wonder how long we were in the stream. I can't let myself worry about it. We are going as fast as we can and will continue to do so. Anything else is down to fate.

But another thought comes gnawing into my brain. Now that we have found water we have tended one need, but this will soon be overtaken by hunger. Without food, Destiny will have little energy to stave off infection.

My heart sinks with the thought that one

worry has been merely superseded by another; that this entire journey might just be a series of trials. Fear, dread and anxiety quicken my gait and I am no longer looking at the far horizon to keep my path straight and true. I am beyond that now. I am beyond trusting in myself to get to where I need to be. I am too small, too insignificant under this vast sky.

Now I can put my trust only in whatever force controls the wind and the rain, the seas and the spinning of the earth; Nature or some other unseen force, it doesn't matter which. All that matters is that I believe, and that it, whatever *it* is, listens.

Destiny at my side, eyes down, I press forward.

CHAPTER 11

For another day we walk. The sun is too hot, too unrelenting in the sky and seeks to make no more than a puddle of sweat and tears of me. I'm aware that I'm hallucinating at times and at others, I wish that I was. The relentless empty landscape, devoid of shelter, or people who might help us is breaking me and I *almost want it* to be the end. There is nothing in my world except heat and hunger. And Destiny.

I don't dare forget him, for I think that he's what keeps me going. More than my fears for Willow and Grey's futures in Delta, I'm worried about Destiny, for I'm fairly certain that if he dies, I will not last long beyond him. What that means for Willow and Grey, I dare not contemplate.

At some point during that day, we come across a dead animal. It's a rabbit. Small with soft, dense fur, it's the first of its kind I have ever seen, other than in pictures. It seems little more than a portent of doom that this first one I see is dead, but when Destiny picks it up and brings it to me, I realise I am mistaken. Once this was a rabbit, now it's merely food.

Destiny lays it at my feet and I pick it up and examine it. I can't tell if it was old or young when it died, and certainly not what it died of. But there's one thing there's no mistaking – it has been dead some time, at least a few days. The stench from the meat is unbearable and when I look closely I see little things wriggling there too. I drop it back at Destiny's paws. "Be my guest if you want to eat that," I tell him, "but count me out!"

He takes me at my word and I settle on the hard ground whilst he gnaws at the carcass. My stomach rumbles, but it's not enough to make me want to partake of the only food available.

After he's eaten we rise again and resume our walking. But by nightfall we still have found no signs of life anywhere, human or otherwise. I begin to wonder if this whole damn planet is as empty as the route we have so far followed.

With the slipping of the sun from the sky, it begins to get colder so I huddle into Destiny for warmth. Sleep claims me quickly but it's neither restful nor relaxing, filled with wild nightmares and even more terrifying memories.

And waking doesn't put an end to the horror, it merely illuminates it with bright light. We are in the middle of nowhere. The only choice we have is to carry on, or die where we lie. I get up.

We walk for hours and hours. I don't dare

track the progress of the sun in the sky for fear that it will make me give up. I keep my eyes firmly fixed on the horizon and my feet pointing forwards. After a while I notice that Destiny is no longer walking by my side. I pause and wait for him to catch up but he seems reluctant, walking slower than before and acting strangely nervous. Apprehensive, even.

"Stay with me," I say, running my hand down across his flank, hoping to calm and reassure him, my eyes scanning everything around us. Whatever has spooked him is not immediately obvious to me but I trust his judgment.

He is hotter than I think he should be; perhaps an indication that the infection in his wound is spreading. And perhaps it's this which is making him edgy. We are both exhausted and hungry – the hollows in his flanks are even more pronounced than when I first encountered him and I'm aware that my clothes are hanging off me. We've managed to find sources of drinking water along the route we have travelled, but no food for me and not enough for him. Perhaps he too is now suffering from hallucinations… like the one that I am currently having.

Just ahead are buildings that look remarkably like those of olden times, before the world was ordered into sectors and regulated by ELSA. They're like nothing I've ever encountered before. I'm slightly surprised by the amount of detail my addled brain embellishes them with; the occasional plume of smoke that wafts from one or the other, spiralling on and on into the air until it finally disappears. And the smells! And sounds! A multi-sensory hallucination!

I take a step towards the mirage, and another, expecting it to disappear in front of my eyes. But it doesn't! I blink, close my eyes for a count of ten but when I reopen them everything remains the same. Except that it's real.

Just ahead, small, round, square, and sometimes irregular shapes made of wood and stone, are topped with some sort of plain tile. All the buildings are small, hardly enough room for more than one or two people at a time surely, and they are sprawled randomly across a meadow. But they are one of the most beautiful sights I could have wished for.

More astonishingly, there are people everywhere! Women and children, men and... I try to gulp in surprise but merely splutter with a dry, cracking sound. There are people so old here, they look like they might have been around in the world before ELSA was even constructed.

I stare at their lined, craggy faces, at lids drooped low over cloudy eyes that struggle to focus on me, hands which shake with the effort of being still. I have never seen such apparent age, such obvious decrepitude. And I can't pull my gaze away.

Strangely, for all the attention I pay to these ancient humans, I receive little in return. Their gazes roam over me and are gone, as if they see nothing in me worthy of note. Not so everyone else, the men and women of normal longevity; the children. They look at me wide-eyed in horror.

No, not at *me* directly, but at the extensive and cruddy gore which stains my top. Their scrutiny travels the length of that stain and finally comes to rest on something behind me. Befuddled by lack of food and proper rest, I wonder vaguely what has captured their attention. It's almost my downfall.

Moving so fast, I barely see the man who lunges past me, brightly glinting steel held tightly in his hand. For a moment there is so much noise, so much colour around me, that I struggle to make sense of the situation, and by the time I do, by the time I realise the threat, I fear I am already too late.

Weakened by starvation and infection, Destiny doesn't have the muscle power to run away from the man who holds the large shining blade above his head. Kept by my side by my words, he is at once too close to the crowd and too far from escape to be able to save himself.

He has slunk low, dropped to the ground in acceptance of his fate, his eyes lifted not towards his attacker, but to me, his former rescuer. That I have saved him from one fate only to present him to another, sickens me. He doesn't deserve to die, and certainly not like this.

With a dark portent, the blade gleams in the sunlight, and begins to descend. I see it fall, see in my mind's eye the coyote's head severed from his body, rolling away from me in the slight tilt of the meadow. And I know for sure that if that happens, if I *let* that happen, then I too will be doomed.

There isn't time to scream at the man to stop. To make him stop and listen. There's no time either to pull Destiny to safety; the blade is already on the descent. I do the only thing I can. Mustering every last ounce of strength I have, I charge the man from behind, throwing myself at him in such a way that he is thrown to one side. He doesn't see me coming and he certainly doesn't expect to be tackled, for he lands away from Destiny, the blade falling harmlessly from his hand and onto the grass.

I tumble down with him, rolling over and under him with the momentum of my attack, shrieking like the wild animal I have become, words inaccessible to me in the heat of my terror. And before he can try to get up I am sitting on top of him, preventing him from rising.

I grapple for the weapon, fingers closing around the hilt of the blade, mind desperately trying to put words together that will be coherent, more than the babble I have produced so far.

"No! He's tame! He saved my life!" I shout breathlessly, pushing each word from the depths of my lungs, loud enough that everyone will hear. The man struggles to free himself from underneath me, pushing hard at me and in return, I'm shocked to find myself resting the point of the blade at his throat. But if the choice is his or Destiny's life which must be lost this day, I know which one it will be. I won't hesitate.

I harden my voice so that they realise it's not an idle threat. "The coyote is with me. He needs help and so do I. But if you hurt him, I swear I'll cut this man's throat!" I take a moment to look around at them, to assess them. "Is that a price you are willing to pay?"

I hear my own voice, my own words as if they belong to a stranger. Is this what I have come to? *It's what you have to do*, I tell myself. *And as long as you say it like you mean it, you will never actually have to carry the threat out.* I hope I am right about that.

I see the doubt in their faces but I also see fear. I dig the point of the blade in a little harder. My eyes feel hot and gritty and I'm aware that I probably look at least half-mad to them. Maybe that's just as well. Maybe then they will take me at my word. The blade continues to rest on the man's throat. It hasn't drawn blood yet but I'm aware that a fraction deeper and it will. I hold the blade incredibly steady.

Beneath me, he's no longer struggling, instead he's looking at me with a disconcerting intensity. If he continues to regard me like this, I know it will be hard to do what I have sworn I will, what I *must*, to avenge Destiny, if anyone decides to test my word and hurts the coyote. But so help me, I *will* do it!

"Whatever you do to Destiny, *my* coyote. I will do to him!" I nod my head towards the prostrate man beneath me, muscles in my neck straining, fingertips quivering in fear. But my voice is level as possible.

"Destiny, come here," I call softly, my heart fluttering in my mouth with every word. I don't know if it's safer for him to be closer to me, or farther from the man currently trapped underneath the blade he was so eager to use. The chances of things going right are incredibly slim, but I must hold onto my courage. I use my free hand to pat my thigh, encouraging the animal towards me.

By the slow, reluctant way the coyote drags himself over to me, it's clear that in his present condition he's not a threat to anyone. He's close to dying. Perhaps unsaveable even if these people were willing to help. My heart lurches painfully at the thought of losing him.

I take a moment to rub my fingertips up the

length of his muzzle in a way that I have learned he likes. Perhaps he is still afraid, but he places all of his trust in me and closes his eyes. Gently I lower his nose until my hand and his mouth are almost touching my captive's cheek. I remove my hand from the coyote and delicately trail it across the man's face. Destiny's nose gently follows me.

I'm aware of the gasps and mutterings that have accompanied my every move. I'm aware too of how they suddenly cease, as if the people behind me are holding their breath in fear and nervous anticipation. I hope that this isn't the lull before the storm. Destiny's tongue darts out from between sharp teeth and it is my turn to hold my breath. If for only a millisecond this is misinterpreted, I know that we are all doomed – me, Destiny, Willow and Grey. This can't fail! *I* can't fail!

Long and pink, the coyote's tongue flicks over the man's face and whether it's the relief that once again Destiny has done the most perfect thing he could have, or whether it's just a bizarre reaction to the tension, I am laughing.

No one joins in. I have lost. They are not won over. They will kill Destiny and then they will kill me, or perhaps just turn me away, which amounts to the same thing. I am beyond despair.

"You can see that you can trust him," I beg. "He's tame!" But my words are less battle-cry and more resignation. I'm all out of ideas, exhausted and starved. If they won't help us then I have to accept that no one will. "What more do you people want?" I cry in desperation, voice breaking, heart breaking even more so.

Without waiting for an answer, without even thinking about the wisdom of my actions, I climb off my captive and hand him back his blade, positioning myself in front of Destiny, making clear my intention. "If you want to kill us, then there are enough of you that you will easily be able to overpower us." I shrug my shoulders dejectedly.

"I'm only a girl who needs help and he's only a defenceless, sick animal. It's your choice." I cast my gaze around the crowd before looking directly at the man in front of me, as he raises himself to his feet. Only a little taller than me, I hold his gaze as steadily as I can.

"And it will be on your consciences, not mine." In the periphery of my vision, I see them look at one another apprehensively. I allow my shoulders to droop lower. I am defenceless and I let them see it. "But you better be prepared to kill me first, because this poor animal saved my life! And I owe him that."

The man in front of me shows no desire to use the weapon either on me or on Destiny. He holds it loosely, down by his side. "You are Alpha!" he says as if in awe of me. It's so strange to think that looking like I do, I can still be recognised as the sector I belong to. My hair is matted and dirty and my clothes ragged and bloody. I nod. "What are you doing here?" he asks.

Whilst they are thinking about me, they are not worrying about Destiny, and that can only be good. I tell them the truth. It's all I have. "I have a friend, a little girl called Willow. She was Alpha too. Until she was re-classed. And there's a man, Greyson. We were to be married but he had an accident and was also re-classed. I've come to find them."

He seems to think about this a moment. I watch his hand with the blade. It doesn't move. Just continues to hold the knife as if he's undecided what course of action to take. I wonder how soon he will make up his mind. Or whether this can be just a rouse to keep my attention on him whilst someone else kills Destiny. But no one moves.

We are all standing still. And for the first time, I think I understand how the other Alphas felt when that door opened. They were afraid to stay and equally afraid to go. But understanding them isn't helping the situation now. I focus on the man in front of me, the way his eyes seem to bore into mine as if he's memorising every detail of the conversation, every detail about me. "And when you find them? What will you do then?" he asks.

I shrug as if there are a variety of outcomes

for me to choose from. "I don't know yet. That's not the important bit right now."

Very subtly, there seems to be a shift in him, perhaps a loosening of muscles as he stands there, maybe a more openness to his face. I can't quite pinpoint it, but I sense it. "I haven't heard of the man you mention, but yes, Willow, that name rings a bell." He looks towards the crowd. "Beulah, didn't you say there was a new girl in the next village?"

A little girl no older than Willow steps forward, shuffling from behind the legs of the older, taller villagers. Plain of face and demeanour she has an earnest look to her that makes me instantly trust her. She smiles shyly at me but keeps her distance for a moment. "The coyote won't bite me?" she asks, before taking a step closer.

I move slightly to the side, revealing Destiny again, who is now lying on the ground, head between his paws and looking pained and desperate. I'm shocked to notice that his breathing seems to be shallower and more rapid than before. "No. I promise," I say, thinking that even if he wanted to, Destiny is too weak to do anything to anyone.

She steps forward and surprises me by reaching into her pocket and withdrawing a little bit of sugary snack. "Would he like this?"

I honestly don't know, all I know is that

we're running out of time. "Try him and we'll find out." I say. I want to hurry them all up. I need information and Destiny needs help, but the situation here is so precarious, so delicate, that I dare not push any of them beyond the limits to which they are prepared to go.

I watch her bend and offer the treat to Destiny. He takes it daintily from her, licking her palm and wrapping his big tongue around her little fingers to catch the remainder of the sugary crumbs. The child laughs delightedly and raises a wholesome face to mine. "Willow is in the next village," she confirms.

"You met her?" I ask.

She nods. "Yesterday. We played." She smiles at the memory before her face falls. "But she's really sad." She thinks hard for a moment. "She said she misses her sister. Trudie I think she's called."

At the mention of how Willow misses me, my heart flips inside my chest. "That's me. But it's Tudie," I correct, "Fortitude actually. And we're not really sisters. It's just that we became friends and I didn't have a sister…" I hope the explanation is enough for her, for them all.

"Do you want me to take you to her?" she asks.

I nod but then the reality of the situation assaults me. Destiny will not make another journey in his current condition. "First, I need medicine to treat Destiny, to make him well again." I direct my words to the man whose life I threatened. I hope he won't hold that against me now.

"It's a coyote," he says sceptically. "We don't help them."

His gaze is hard. I challenge it. "Have you ever known one that was friendly? That had saved a human's life?"

He shakes his head. "No, never!" I get the distinct impression that despite what he's seen with his own eyes, he doesn't believe me.

"But *he* is. This little girl..." I search for her name, "Beulah, has petted him. He saved my life and I've saved his. That's not something a coyote would normally do, is it?" I'm speaking to the man and the girl but the whole village is listening. I think about how out of the entire dome, all the Alphas, I am the only one to be seeking Willow and Grey.

"We are not just defined by how we look. Sometimes we are defined by how we feel and how we act." But they are unswayed by my words. If they will not help Destiny, then I have no choice but to somehow get him to the place where Willow is. If someplace took her in, there's a chance they will help Destiny there too, I reason. "How far away is this village, the one where Willow is?"

But it's the man, not the little girl who

answers. "It's a day's travelling. From the look of you and your..." he struggles, "animal, I think it's a journey you can't make without proper rest and food. Stay here tonight and we will start out at first light tomorrow. You have my word."

But appealing as the idea of rest is, I'm not sure Destiny has that long. Yet neither of us are in any fit shape for travelling. But before I can admit that, he takes a step towards the coyote, the blade still in his hands. "No," I say. "Your word is not enough." I block his path just in case.

"Relax," he says. "I'm just going to take a look at the coyote and see if I can help." He doesn't smile but he does hand the weapon back to me. "Just don't point it at my throat again," he says ruefully, "I'm not used to being threatened by a girl." I feel my face colour crimson at the memory of how I treated him. But although I don't like the fact that he considers me just 'a girl' I move aside.

He bends down and touches the rough bandage around the coyote's wound. The strip of cloth came to the end of its useable life some time ago, and now hangs ragged and soiled from the coyote's emaciated frame. "Can I see what's under here, fella?" he asks, but doesn't lay a hand upon Destiny. Instead he looks expectantly up at me as if seeking my permission. I grant it by nodding, the knife held loosely in my hand.

"Can you help him?" I ask anxiously.

"I'm going to try. Perhaps you can tell me

what happened for a start."

I watch him gently peel back Destiny's bandage. "He was in a fight with another coyote. I helped him." He takes his attention away from the wound for only a moment, looking back at me in a way that makes me think he's re-evaluating me.

"Seems to me, you might be more dangerous than the coyote!" He pauses, smiles a little. "I'm Devlin. And it's just as well you didn't stick that blade in my throat, 'cos I'm the one who tends to the sick livestock around here and probably the only one who can help you. Apart for Beulah, that is!"

He's perhaps a few years older than Grey and I, and quite a bit shorter than the average Alpha male, so if he were still standing we'd be almost level. But crouched down like this at my feet, he seems less hostile and aggressive and there's an unmistakable warmth to his voice, now that neither of us are threatening the other's life. I smile back at him but mine is tempered with uncertainty. "Can you really help him?"

He neither shrugs nor continues to smile, just looks at me with a totally unreadable expression. "Folks need to get back to their work now. Cows won't milk themselves and butter won't churn itself either." Without looking directly at the crowd, he has raised his voice to be heard by all. I follow his lead and don't look at the dispersing mob. Soon there are only the four of us left. Me, Destiny, the girl Beulah, and Devlin.

"Come on. You can fill us in when we get him inside." Devlin heads off towards one of the funny little buildings, whilst I wonder who he means by 'us'. But Destiny is too weak to walk more than one or two steps and collapses at my feet.

Sobbing, I scoop him up into my arms and carry him the short distance to the entrance of the hut. I'm scared by how light he is, how small and thin he seems - how quickly things are moving beyond my control. Again. Devlin beckons me quickly inside. "I don't have much more than antibiotics and ointments and the like, but it should be enough to fix him back up."

Inside the hut, the furniture is sparse and basic but it's clean and it's tidy. I place Destiny on a long metal table that reminds me of the ones in the medical bay back in the dome. The coyote's eyes are open but his gaze is distant. I'm afraid that it's the hereafter his eyes seek.

Devlin rummages in a drawer and produces two tubes, bottles and an old-fashioned syringe. Painkillers." he tells me. "And creams to fight infection and encourage healing."

I look at the wickedly long needle on the end of the syringe. "Haven't you got anything else you can give him? No one has used needles for decades back at the dome!"

Unfortunately he seems to take my remark

as an insult. "Well we don't have the finer things here that you Alphas have. We are just common old Deltas, not worthy of your finer things!"

"I...I didn't mean it like that!" I protest. "I just don't want him to hurt."

Devlin looks at me as if he understands but his next words make me wonder if he really does. "Sometimes you have to have a *little* pain to make sure you don't have a whole barrel full of the stuff."

"What's that supposed to mean?" I ask.

"Exactly what I said."

I decide not to press him further. I need his help, not his wrath. I watch him draw some sort of fluid into the syringe. "I tried to keep the wound clean but I think it got infected anyway."

He bends down, strokes Destiny with one hand, looking into the coyote's eyes and murmuring softly to him. With the other hand, the one containing the syringe, he moves fast, bringing the arm around and sticking it into the coyote's rump so quickly, the animal doesn't have time to react. Destiny's eyes roll back in their sockets and his head lolls to one side. I am horror stricken. "You've killed him!" I launch myself at the traitor, fists flying. He catches me easily.

"Whoa there, Miss Alpha," he says, pinning my arms to my side. "I gave you my word remember? Maybe that doesn't mean much to an Alpha but it means a lot to a Delta. And it means more than even that, when that word is mine."

I focus on the important bits. "He's not dead?"

"Of course not! The painkiller just put him into a deep sleep so that I can do whatever needs to be done to fix him up."

"I'm sorry," I say. "I thought -"

But he doesn't let me finish. "You thought that only Alphas stuck to their words." He's wrong, but I don't tell him so, it's unimportant. All that matters is that he tries to help Destiny, not what he thinks of me.

Devlin cuts the bandage away with scissors to reveal the wound as he talks. The gash is worse than it was the last time I saw it; thick and congealed with pus, it has an over-ripe, putrid stench to it that turns my stomach.

"How long has it been like this?"

I try to think back. "The last time I saw it was yesterday and it wasn't as bad as it is now." I'm aware I haven't answered his question.

"What caused it? You said there was a fight?"

"Yes, between him and another, stronger coyote. I saved his life and then later he repaid me by saving mine." I sense this isn't the time to go into details.

"That accounts for the strong bond between you then. Shame you couldn't have managed to save him before he got so torn up."

I bite my tongue. This man is unbelievable. First he tries to kill Destiny, then he berates me for not being quick enough to plunge myself into a fight between two coyotes!

But if he senses my annoyance, he doesn't let on. "Beulah, fetch me the cotton pads and the sharpest scalpel we have."

The little girl scurries off out of sight, presumably to carry out his orders. Despite my concern for Destiny, and my annoyance at Devlin, I am surprised enough to ask a question. "Isn't she a little young to know what you need?"

He snorts derisively. "Don't know much about life for you Alphas, but round here, outside of the dome, if you want to eat, you have to work. Those're the rules!"

"But there must be other things she could be doing? And then there's her schooling."

Just at that moment, Beulah arrives back with the things he has asked for. "I brought the sewing kit, just in case. I figured we'd need it," she says, placing it nearby. I stare at her. It doesn't go unnoticed.

Devlin looks up just long enough for me to see the self-satisfied look on his face. "Beulah, tell Tudie what your job is," Devlin instructs her, turning his attention back to Destiny.

"I'm apprentice animal carer," she tells me proudly.

"You see, Fortitude, we might not be Alphas

around here, but we know what's important!" He takes the scalpel and begins to cut.

I bite my tongue again and watch in silence.

CHAPTER 12

He cuts away some of the flesh from around the wound. "These bits of skin are too infected. Easier to take them away than try to heal them," he explains.

Beulah helps him, holding back the sides of the wound with long metal scissor-like things, which don't actually cut. In one or two spots the child actually takes over from him, wielding the scalpel into smaller, tighter sections of the wound than he can easily fit his hands into. I am amazed at both her dexterity and her confidence.

Unable to help in any way, I position myself at Destiny's head and stroke the soft fur there. Devlin says it's unlikely that the coyote can feel anything, however the rhythmic actions serve to reassure me if not the animal. "He will be okay, won't he?"

There's a tense silence which goes on a lot longer than I want it to. They look at each other. Neither of them look at me. There's too much contained within that look for my liking. Too much they're leaving unsaid. "If you'd found us any later, he would have died of the infection," Devlin says finally, looking up at me. I suspect he's trying to temper his answer with the vague smile he fixes on his face, but he's more or less avoided the actual question.

"So he'll be okay now?" I press. "We found you in time?"

Again he takes his time answering. "If we can cut out every bit of deep infection and he responds well to the antibiotics and creams, then yes, hopefully he'll be fine."

I don't like the fact that the answer is so qualified, that its likelihood depends on lots of different factors. I bite my lip though – words won't help Destiny, only actions will, and any talk is surely getting in the way of Devlin's concentration. I watch him and Beulah in silence once more.

They cut and wipe, stem the blood that rises to meet them and cut again. And again. Below my fingertips I feel the warm breath Destiny expels, the steady even flow of his pulse. I see the rise and fall of his chest. But none of these things are enough to provide reassurance that he will live.

"If you want to help," Devlin says in a tone that makes me think he's fairly sure I'm incapable of his request, "you can count the beats of his pulse and let us know if it changes."

He flicks his eyes towards me. "Do

you think you can do that?" I'm stung by the suggestion that it might be beyond my capabilities. But I don't let it show. Devlin and I got off to a bad start and although I instinctively bristle at his every word, Destiny's fate is currently in his hands.

"Yes," I say, holding my anger in. I place one hand over the area where destiny's pulse seems strongest, and use the other to continue to stroke him. *These are Deltas.* I'm not immediately sure in what way this thought is significant, but it spins around my head. I give it space and time to unravel itself.

Yet they know what they are doing. And they're saving Destiny's life! Deltas! I watch them delicately snip away at some parts of the wound and avoid damage to other bits. None of this was what I would have expected from their kind.

Their kind? My conscience mocks me. What exactly do I mean by that? That Alphas and Deltas are so far apart they are almost a difference race? I scan my memory for what I have always been led to believe and hear Joy's voice in my head. *Deltas are several notches down the scale in attractiveness compared to Alphas.* In my mind I compare Grey and Devlin. I expect it to be easy, but find it's actually an impossible task. Grey is tall, handsome and muscular, everything an attractive person should be.

Devlin is much shorter and stocky without

being particularly muscled, by what I can tell. His lips are perhaps a shade too thin to meet Alpha standards and his nose is hooked. Yet there is an unmistakable appeal to his face. His features are bold and somehow... manly. In comparison to him, Grey seems almost beautiful rather than handsome, as if his attractiveness is too feminine to be thought of as manly. But that's ridiculous!

But more than his physical attributes, it's Devlin's obvious intelligence which surprises me. I think of the job I do at the Dome, interpreting ELSA's weather information, sending it to the terminals in the outpost sectors; all those places where people who are not Alphas live and work. If anything, my work requires *lesser* intelligence than does his. All I'm doing really is using information gathered from a machine, whereas he is interpreting and skilfully acting upon real situations. Making decisions that are life or death. Much as I don't like the man, I can't help but be impressed by his abilities.

"That's it now. I'm going to stitch the wound back up and give him some antibiotics to help him fight the infection." Devlin loops tight, even stitches across the edges of the wound, drawing the skin together and securing it in place, using the sewing kit that Beulah had fetched. "He'll start to wake up soon. He'll be confused and sore but I think he'll heal absolutely fine."

I'm on the brink of thanking him, when he adds unnecessarily, "Even if his surgeon was only a Delta." He's so hung up on that fact, that I feel my eyes tightening, the tears that blur my vision drying a little in reaction to his unnecessary sharpness. If he wants to keep the animosity going between us, then that's fine by me. I am grateful for his help but I won't prostrate myself over it.

"Thank you for what you did," I say, "I'm very grateful." And I am. I just wish it had been anyone other than him who had helped me.

The smile he turns on me is too radiant. "No thanks needed actually. It's the best feeling in the world to be able to help a sick or injured animal. That's the real reward."

I think he's telling the truth, but the way he states it seems designed to make me realise how little value I am to him in return. That it was never me he was helping, only Destiny.

Letting his vague insults pass, I swallow hard and wipe my face with my dirty hands. Now that the crisis is almost over, I realise what a mess I am, how filthy and grime encrusted. "How long before he wakes up?" I ask.

"Not long," Devlin says. He eyes me up and down with what looks like distain. "We can keep an eye on him whilst you get cleaned up," he suggests.

I grimace. "I've nothing to change into."

I'm not ashamed of this although I suspect it surprises him. He looks at Beulah. Again there seems to be something unspoken which passes between them, something I am not privy to.

Beulah considers me. "You are about the same size as my mother. You could borrow something from her."

"She wouldn't mind?" I ask uncertainly.

"You're not in *Alphaland* now!" Devlin scoffs, as if it's the funniest thing he's ever heard. "We share, here in Delta. We have no choice!"

It's the second strange thing he's said about my home and I want to challenge him on it, but now isn't the time.

He senses my indecision. "If you go get cleaned up you'll feel better and be better able to look after him," Devlin nods towards Destiny, "when he wakes. But it's your choice."

He's right. Again. I just wish I could find the right words to challenge his authority. But it seems that fatigue and worry have robbed me of my former sharp wit. With a quick glance at Destiny to make sure he's still asleep, I follow Beulah out of the hut. I'm relieved to be leaving Devlin behind.

"We live on the other side of the village," she says, walking briskly past a variety of huts of different shapes and sizes.

"What animals do you and Devlin usually tend?" I ask, trying to keep up with her, whilst also glancing curiously into all the huts with open doors. What is revealed to me, each and every time, is a sparsely furnished home. The people I pass look curiously at me in return, but if they are inclined to chat, I don't notice, I'm too busy rushing after Beulah.

"We have cows. We make butter and cheese from the milk."

"So you tend the cows?"

She laughs. "Not just the cows. Do you think we could exist just on what little we are left with, after Assignment?"

It's a phrase I have never heard before. "What's Assignment?"

"It's what the Alphas allow us to keep for ourselves." She looks at me like I am dumb.

It isn't an adequate explanation but I file the word in my brain for now and come back to my original question, sensing it wasn't fully answered. "What other animals do you tend to then?"

"Sheep, hens, pigs, some wild dogs and anything that we find injured – wild birds and the like – oh and the people of course." She states it like it's nothing.

"Aren't they all very different?" Even I realise how dumb the question sounds. "I mean people and animals…"

"Oh yes, very, very different. Inside them and how their bodies work and even what medicines work on them and everything. There's a lot to learn. I mean you wouldn't expect a cow to lay an egg would you? Or for a hen to give you milk." She's almost skipping at my side. "A cow has four parts to its stomach…"

I struggle to match her pace. "You really love helping animals, don't you?"

She gives a final extra-long skip and halts outside a hut. "It's what I do. And this is where I live." She pulls on the wooden door, swinging it open and gesturing me to enter.

Inside, it's brighter than I expect. Warm light issues from objects placed around the room that glow softly, creating bright areas and shadowed ones. Unlike the uniform lighting of the dome, this light makes me feel instantly more relaxed, more at peace with the world.

"I wondered when you'd be bringing her back, Beulah." A woman comes out of the shadows to greet me. "I'm Genesis, Beulah's mother."

Long auburn hair left to fall softly around her shoulders, there's a softness to this woman that I instantly take to. A little shorter than me, she's also fuller around the bust and hips but I think we are around the same size.

"You'll be needing to get cleaned up, I expect. I have put some clothes out for you in case you had none of your own. The reports were that you arrived here with only the clothes on your back and an injured coyote for company." She speaks as if she knows the reports are correct but that she doesn't hold my lack of provisions against me.

"How did you know Beulah would bring me here?" I ask.

Genesis leans forward and ruffles her daughter's hair. "It's what she does. She brings back all the strays she finds."

Is that what I am? A stray? It's perhaps closer to the truth than I would have liked to believe. Certainly until I can locate Grey and Willow, I am without family. Just like I've always been. Maybe a stray is *exactly* what I am.

Genesis looks at me with concern. "I didn't mean any offence. It's just that –"

I cut her off. "You were right. I am a stray. Until I can find the people I'm looking for." But there's no time to get into all that now. Destiny will be awake soon and I need to be there.

She seems to sense my hurry. "There's time for explanations later. For now, do what you need to do. I find that's the best way to approach problems." She strokes a hand down the length of her daughter's hair, reminding me of how I stroked Destiny, only minutes before.

"Come on," she says and I follow her through to a small bathroom. It's nowhere near as luxurious as I am used to, but it has all the basics of toilet, shower and sink. On a chair, lies a clean set of clothes. "They are not as new or as fancy as I'm sure you're used to wearing, but it's all I have to offer," Genesis says warmly.

I smile in return, although rather bashfully. "I'm just so grateful for all your help. You and Beulah... and Devlin." I'm almost pained to admit that I'm in his debt.

Her smile falters a little. "We have little to offer, but what we have, is yours for the taking. I wish it were so in all sectors."

I sense an undercurrent in her voice. "You mean it isn't?"

I ask the question innocently. I have no knowledge of life other than in the dome, but had assumed that without ELSA, it would be at least fairer, less strictly controlled and regulated.

The look she settles on me is searching. Is she trying to decide whether I am genuine or whether I have some hidden agenda? Whether I'm out to trip her up in some way? Even as I watch, her face softens. "You are different to how I would have imagined."

Her statement unnerves me and I want to ask in what way am I different. But I am so aware of time ticking away, aware that at any moment Destiny might wake and find me gone, that I dare not question her. Nor do I admit that she is different to my expectations too. That all these Deltas are.

"I have to hurry back," I say but I don't

move. Will there be time later for explanations? On both sides? I hope so.

She shoos me into the bathroom. "Go. Clean yourself up and do what you must and there will be time for talk later, at dinner." I nod and close the door.

The water from the shower is little more than a trickle and not particularly hot, but I manage to get clean. Dressed in someone else's clothes I feel strange, like I have stepped out of my own skin and into another life. But there's no time to dwell on my feelings, I have to get back to Destiny. I roll my soiled clothing into a bundle and tuck it under my arm.

Beulah is waiting for me outside the door. "Put your dirty things in here. Mum'll wash them." She holds out a wicker basket in front of her.

"It's okay, I'll clean them myself," I say. Even though I have never cleaned clothes in my life before, there's no reason I can't, surely. If Deltas can... I stop the thought almost immediately.

"Mum said she'll do them while you're busy with Destiny."

I don't move, forcing Beulah to stand hands on hips and consider me. "She's not going to steal your things if that's what you're thinking."

I'm immediately ashamed she would think that's what I'm worried about. "No of course I wasn't thinking that! I just, well... it just doesn't seem right, that's all."

"Mum says many things aren't right in this world but while it keeps on spinning –"

Genesis appears, takes the basket from her daughter and finishes her sentence. "While it keeps on spinning, we just have to keep trying to make it better for each other. Let me help you make it better." When I don't answer she holds the basket forward again. "I think maybe someone with a name like Fortitude, might just be able to change the world, don't you, Beulah?"

I realise that the child has taken the time I spent showering to fill her mother in about me in detail. As much as she knows, anyway. "Do I have to change the world?" I ask. This wasn't what I'd counted on when I left the dome. Only on finding Grey and Willow.

"We all do what we have to do," Genesis says cryptically. "And for me, right now, that's the laundry." She looks pointedly at my bundle. I feel bad about the imposition but perhaps when Destiny's better I can be of some help in return. I drop my things into the basket and follow Beulah out the door.

We virtually run back to Devlin and Destiny, although it's the coyote I am eager to see, not the man. Coming into the hut, I find Devlin sitting on the floor, Destiny's head cradled in his lap. He shuffles to the side when he sees me, letting me take over comforting the animal who is just starting to come round from the anaesthetic. "Keep your hands away from his mouth," Devlin instructs me.

I am almost incensed at his suggestion. "He won't bite me!"

Devlin sighs, as if I really am the stupidest girl he's ever met. "He's not fully conscious yet. He doesn't know what he's doing. He could bite your hand off and not even realise it."

As if to demonstrate the point, I see the coyote's legs begin to paw the empty air as if he's dreaming of running across a wide meadow. Devlin is right, but I can't give him the satisfaction of knowing that I realise my mistake. I keep my mouth shut.

Sitting so close that I feel his body heat, I'm strangely excited about our proximity. I want to move away and yet at the same time I find myself leaning closer, letting my arm brush against his, in the gentle swell of Destiny's breathing.

I wonder about my unanticipated reaction to him. *You love Grey*, I tell myself. *And yet this man has sparked something in you, something you didn't even know existed...* Is it the fact that he's different to what I thought a Delta should be? I don't know.

Or is it the challenge he poses? The fact that he clearly thinks I'm stupid, is that what's really bothering me? It's ridiculous and yet it doesn't make it any less true. I need him to realise that I'm not dumb, not just some girl who has been mollycoddled all her life.

But his opinion shouldn't actually matter to me. All that should matter is that Destiny will be okay and I will find Grey and Willow. That we will all be together.

I stroke Destiny's head and think about Grey. Of all the Alphas our age, he is without doubt the most attractive. He's funny, kind, considerate, and I can't think of a single way in which he isn't perfect. In fact we are perfect together. I consider an image of us in my head. We are perfect *for* each other.

Although my face is turned towards the coyote, my thoughts have lain elsewhere, these last few minutes. I turn to Devlin intending to ask him if Destiny can be fed tonight, and find him looking at me so intensely that I blush. "What?" I demand, rather more brusquely than I intend.

"You're not at all what I expected," he says.

Since this so closely mirrors what Beulah's mother had said, I'm more than intrigued but also a little put out by his tactlessness. "What would you expect? How could you expect *anything*? You don't even know me! Or anything about where I come from."

He smiles and raises an eyebrow at the ferocity of my words. "Although I can see why you and a wild coyote would hit it off," he says.

I bristle. "What did you mean by that remark?" I shake my head at him, lest he misunderstands. "Not the bit about me and Destiny, but about how I'm not what you expected."

He stands up and moves away a little, busying himself with checking Destiny's wound and clearing up. "You don't seem like an Alpha," he says finally. I'm about to question this statement when he expands upon it. "I mean you are *astonishingly* beautiful and you're clearly intelligent but you don't have that…" he gestures into the air, hands waving as if trying to catch the right word, "hard-edged attitude to you. Well not when I see you with Destiny. Or Beulah." He leaves out how he considers me to be towards him, I notice.

Astonishingly beautiful. Of all the things he has said, those are the words I focus on. I have to work hard to keep my breathing even and I struggle to concentrate, to say something relevant. I try to think about what he might have meant by, 'hard-edged attitude', but 'astonishingly beautiful', rolls round and round in my head.

I'm about to refute his words on behalf of all Alphas, deny I know what he is talking about, when I remember Willow's family; how her mother just sat at the table and calmly informed me that she no longer had a daughter… Wasn't that exactly what he meant?

"What do you know about Alphas?" I don't

mean to sound as terse and loaded as I do, but I can't help myself; he seems to bring out the worst in me. Or maybe it's just that everything here is so unfamiliar, so different.

"A lot more than you know about Deltas it would seem," he says, unfazed by my outburst.

"Maybe you only think you know about..." I suddenly don't know whether to end the sentence with the word *Alphas* or *us*. Wasn't I the one who had ripped open the doors of the dome? Hadn't I stood alone outside whilst everyone else, all the other Alphas, some of them friends, colleagues, even Grey's own family had remained inside? Watching me but not helping, not joining my cause.

Can I really be the same as the rest of the Alphas? Do I even want to be classed as the same? I'm no longer sure. Luckily Destiny chooses that moment to open his eyes, sparing me the need to finish the thought or to answer it.

Bleary and unfocused, the coyote is instantly afraid and confused. I lower my face towards him and speak softly. "It's okay, Destiny, I'm here. We've been looking after you. You're going to be fine now." Then searching for more reassurance and finding none, I speak as I would have done to him if we were alone. "We're in Delta Sector and we'll be okay."

The coyote looks back at me. His gaze seems a little more focused and his breathing which had become harsh and ragged when he first began to wake up, now slows and levels. I run my fingers over the top of his head, smoothing down the fur there.

"So is he an Alpha coyote then? Is he used to feasting on prime meat, eaten from a silver plate?" I can hear the suppressed mirth in Devlin's voice but I ignore it. I won't lower myself by responding to it.

I look around for Beulah and find her missing. "Where's Beulah?" I ask.

He doesn't bother to hide his condescension as he answers me. "We all have more than one job here. We *work* for our living in Delta. For the food we put in our mouths." He doesn't bother to hide the animosity in his words.

"Beulah helps me here, but she also has a flock of sheep to help look after."

Despite how he has helped Destiny, I'm angered by his attitude towards me. What gives him the right to judge *me*? "And what's *your* other job then? Intimidating anyone who wanders into your village and threatening them with a big knife?" My voice drips acid. I don't even try to modify it.

He stops tidying away and focuses on me, giving me his full attention. "Only if they wander in with what looks like a wild coyote at their side, that might just kill every animal we have." He pauses. "And even then... only if they are Alphas."

I know that I can't stay in this man's company any longer than I have to. He's rude, and infuriating, and just too righteous for my liking. "Well I'm sorry that me being an Alpha is such a big disappointment to you. At least *you* are everything I expected from a Delta and more," I lie, hearing my voice rise to a crescendo in temper. "You are ignorant and ill-informed…" It's so far beyond the truth that I am sure he will see through the lie but I work at sounding convincing.

He snorts derisively. "Well Miss Alpha, when you have a gash in your stomach the length of my arm, you just feel free to go right ahead and fix it yourself," he says pointedly, looking at Destiny.

I recognise the stupidity of our argument. And the danger of it. I can't afford to make an enemy of him. Too much is at stake. "Look, I'm sorry. You hit a nerve, I guess." I soften my tone and my words. "I'm tired, I'm worried about Destiny and I still have to find the people I came out to find."

His face alters, as if he too is sorry for our spat. "Yes, the Alpha you are going to marry and the little girl." He says Alpha like it's an unsavoury word. I try to ignore it.

Destiny is struggling to his feet and under cover of helping him, I turn my face away from Devlin's gaze. What I will say will only further his low opinion of Alphas, if that's possible. I think it may already be at rock-bottom.

"We were, I mean we *are*, engaged." I wish I could explain this more easily but I clearly can't. "There was an accident and when they ran tests on him, they found that he had developed an illness because of it, something that could be passed to our children."

I expect him to cut in, to ask what the illness was, or perhaps how the accident had come about, but he doesn't, so I'm forced to carry on. "He got re-classed as something else and sent out to another sector. No one but me even cares."

My words must have shocked him for I hear him draw his breath in the stillness of the room. "You must love him very much."

I nod. Only then, do I wonder why his voice sounds so tight.

CHAPTER 13

Destiny is a little wobbly on his legs but noticeably cooler than before, a good sign that the operation and medicine are working, Devlin tells me curtly, avoiding looking at my face as he speaks.

I wonder what I've said to upset him. From being talkative before, even if it was mostly insulting, he is now quiet, restrained and unwilling to enter into even the smallest of discussions with me.

I don't let on this bothers me. Why should it, after all? Why should I care what Devlin thinks, or why; whether he's bored of me, or considers me an unwanted intrusion upon his village?

But I can't stop myself from sneaking looks at him whenever I think I won't be caught. He is an enigma, different from anything I've been led to expect.

Destiny's eyes are clearer, and his tongue, when he lolls it out of his mouth, is pink and wet. I kiss him on the top of his head, relieved that he already seems improved.

"Genesis will feed him and provide a soft bed for you both," Devlin says in that still too-tight voice. "He should be able to walk there now. Just go slowly while he finds his feet again."

For reasons I can't quite determine, now that I have been summarily dismissed, I avoid looking at him, concentrating fiercely on Destiny instead. "I don't know if I can remember which hut belongs to Genesis." I say honestly, annoyed at my own stupidity. I wait for him to say something, anything.

"Then it's probably just as well that I'm going there too." He sounds reluctant, as if walking with me is the worst chore he can think of. I don't want to agree or disagree. In fact I'm no longer sure what I *do* want. All the anxiety and fear has caught up with me and I stand unmoving and undecided what to do or say.

"We should talk." He strides ahead of me to the door.

"What about?" I ask cautiously, following him, keeping Destiny at my side. He's leaning a little, favouring his good side still but he looks less groggy, less pained by the minute, and I'm relieved. Slowly the three of us make our way out into the open.

"Your arrival has brought us an opportunity to learn more about each other's lives," he says evenly.

I manage to resist the temptation to

enquire what little thing it is about Alphas that he doesn't already know, since he's clearly an expert on the matter. "What do you want to know?"

He surprises me again with his answer. "First of all, what you know about life as a Delta."

I say the first and most obvious thing that comes to mind. "That you don't live in a dome."

He nods as if I have said something profound. I carry on. "That Delta is the fourth class, coming after Alpha, Beta and Gamma. And that Deltas are farming people."

He interrupts me. "Why do you think Delta is the fourth class? Why are the classes in any order at all? And order of what, exactly?"

I hesitate. "It's what we're taught. In the dome. That Alpha is the first, the intellects," I'm more than a little embarrassed and consciously decide to leave out the bit about them also being the most attractive, sure that he'll take it as a slur. "Beta are the creatives, the artisans. Then there's Gamma, the industrialists who make all the things we use, and then Delta…"

He interrupts again, forcing me to stop. "So the intelligence levels drop with every sector, that's what you're saying, right?"

"I don't know anymore," I say truthfully.

I'm relieved to recognise Genesis, standing just inside the doorway to her house. I keep my voice level. "It was certainly what I believed before I met you, what I've been taught in schooling. Now I just don't know."

He lets me go through the doorway first, Destiny still close to my side. "Why aren't you so sure now?" He is relentless.

With me standing just inside the hut and him still outside, I take the chance to really look at him whilst my own face is shrouded in shadow. Brown eyes so dark it's hard to differentiate between the pupils and the irises, I feel they are so bottomless I could be forever lost in them. If he were at all attractive to me. Which he isn't.

His hair is dark and cut raggedly, as if he became impatient with it and hacked at it with the huge blade he had at first threatened Destiny with. He should look shabby, unkempt. Yet I have to admit that he doesn't. Instead, he looks as if appearances matter less to him than anything else. I wonder what does really matter.

"You see, Fortitude, that's the thing. I mean if you can be wrong about such a big thing, then what's the likelihood that you're wrong about lots of other, smaller things?"

I'm saved from having to answer by Genesis, who comes to the doorway to welcome me back. "Give the girl some time to relax," she rebukes Devlin. "Hasn't she been through enough right now?" She wraps an arm around me and leads me further inside her home. There's a delicious aroma of cooking food but I can't identify what it's from.

"I've made a bed for your animal." She helps me settle Destiny on a pile of soft blankets on the floor, and places a bowl of warm scrambled egg in front of the coyote. "I'll give him something more fitting for a coyote a little later," she says, "once he has come round more and his stomach is less empty."

I pat Destiny briefly, using the time to try to compose myself. Unsure of what the food is at first, he sniffs it before delicately sampling a morsel. Then when he has found the taste pleasing, he sets about polishing the rest of it off, before closing his eyes and drifting back to sleep. It seems he's accepted the people here more easily than I have.

"We'll let him sleep for a while, before giving him more food," Devlin says. He needs rest as much as nourishment to aid the healing process."

"Yes, and he's not the only one," Genesis notes, ladling something hot into four wooden bowls. She passes one of them to me and indicates I should sit at the table.

I sit down and wait for the others to join me. Beulah sits beside me and opposite her mother. Devlin takes up the empty space opposite me. I keep my eyes focused on the bowl, away from his searing glances which seem to require me to bare my soul for his inspection. And let him find it wanting.

"What is this?" I ask, resisting the temptation to stir it with my spoon, hoping she doesn't think me rude for asking.

Genesis laughs. "It's chilli. An old recipe handed down through the generations."

I sample the spicy concoction. Meaty and hot, it's like nothing I've ever had before. It's delicious and I'm only aware that I am gulping the food down when I look up and find them all staring at me, their bowls still more than half full.

"I guess you like it then," Devlin says and I feel as if he is deliberately making fun of me. "Another strike against Alphaland."

"Ignore him," Genesis says kindly. "There's plenty more in the pot, if you are still hungry later," although she doesn't qualify what she means by later. The idea of eating what I want, whenever I want, is new to me.

"In the dome, we are given whatever food ELSA decides our bodies need," I reveal, "but here you eat what you want. When you want."

"Not quite what we want," Devlin says. "Only what we are left with after each Assignment."

I spoon another load of chilli into my mouth and swallow. "Beulah mentioned Assignment earlier. What is it?" I ask.

A look passes between the two adults. "You don't know?" Genesis says, sounding as if she can't quite believe that.

I shake my head. "I've never heard of it."

She looks at me for so long before she speaks, I begin to wonder if she's decided not to tell me.

"Every month there's a *request* from ELSA. Most of the food we produce is taken, leaving very little for us here," she says.

I frown. "We are taught that ELSA organises the production of each sector, and makes sure that everyone has food, everyone has clothes..." I don't know enough of what all the other sectors do to make my point stronger. "But she wouldn't leave you with so little that..."

"I assure you that's exactly what happens," Devlin throws in, before Genesis adds, "And we aren't the only village with cows."

I look at her, failing to understand.

"This Delta sector is huge," Devlin says. "But there are other Deltas spread all over the country. Some of them produce milk, butter and cheese like we do. Others produce only meats. And then there are all those which produce wheat and barley and all sorts of other crops."

"Yes, and everything gets shared out fairly by ELSA," I say, "so that every sector has a range of things it needs. So it's all fair and equal." I wonder why I am so eager to defend ELSA. Haven't I already stood up against her control? But this is different, I tell myself, this isn't personal, it's for the good of all.

But Devlin barely lets me finish before he bangs his fist on the table so hard I actually jump in my seat. My empty bowl rattles on its base, falling over onto its side and rolling around the table in a wide arc.

"I can't believe that as an *Alpha*, and according to you anyway, at the top of the intellectual tree, you don't completely understand what I'm saying." He manages to make it sound like an insult. "So I can only think that you don't care."

As usual, he has put me on my guard. "I don't know what I have ever done to you -"

He cuts me off. "Really? You really have no idea that every month the people who produce the food, are the very ones who are left with the least of it for their own use? That the people who make the butter that the Alphas spread so thickly on their morning toast, are half starved?" His face has taken on a red hue and his eyes are hard, glittering.

I stare just as hard, back at him. "Well it seems that I'm not the only one who knows nothing! I already told you that we don't get to choose what we eat."

I search for further ammunition to throw back at him. "We don't even get to choose how much butter we use. It's all calculated for us." Instead of making me sound righteous, this information has just made me sound incredibly immature and ridiculous.

He has the audacity to laugh. "My heart bleeds for you."

Unaccountably, I am stung by his attitude. "I suppose you are going to tell me next, that in the sector which produces clothing, all the people have to walk around naked, because ELSA takes every item of clothing they make!" I realise too late I've gone too far.

Genesis's lips set into a thin line. She places a hand over Devlin's, silencing him from whatever he might have said. "We are fortunate in this village, Fortitude. We keep hens for eggs and we have sheep and some cattle for meat, so we can subsidise our meagre diet. Others are not so fortunate."

This time I think I catch the meaning of the look Devlin flashes at her. She faces him directly, turning her attention away from me momentarily. "There's no point in trying to hide anything from her. She's seen too much already. You yourself told her that Beulah cares for the sheep!" She turns to me and despite the implied threat of her words, her voice is soft, calm. "ELSA doesn't know that we have chickens and other animals here. If it did..."

"Then you wouldn't be able to keep them?" I infer. She nods. None of this makes sense to me. I wait for her to continue.

"ELSA delivers grain and other supplies to

us. But it's only just enough to keep us going. We don't starve, but we don't do great either. We have what we are allowed to keep of our own produce and our ration from the other farming sectors. So to bulk it out, we have our own extra supplies. It's not much but it's something at least."

"But if ELSA knew you already had food, then you wouldn't be given the amount you are assigned?" I ask, hoping I've got it right, finally. But also conversely hoping I'm wrong.

This time it's Devlin who answers. "More than that. We would have those animals taken from us. The only reason that we don't, is that ELSA doesn't know about them."

"But that doesn't make any sense! Why would they be taken from you?"

Devlin rises from the table as if his words burn with such a passion in him, he can't remain seated and still express them. "The best guess is that ELSA needs us to be dependent on all the other sectors, just like they are upon us. Except for Alpha Class of course." This time he doesn't bother to hide his animosity.

"What does that mean?" I show that I too can be forthright and aggressive.

He doesn't back down. He looks at me as if he sees right through me, as if I am nothing more than a pile of bones and gristle to him.

"What do you do in Alpha to help even one of the other sectors? What do you make or produce that helps anyone in any way to live their lives, Fortitude?" He's being deliberately aggressive, deliberately antagonistic. I try not to rise to his bait.

"My friends call me Tudie. And I interpret weather patterns. I send information out to the sectors telling them when to bring their livestock indoors because of inclement weather, when to harvest their crops-"

He cuts me off harshly. "And in the hundreds of years that people like me have been out tending animals and crops, do you think, *Fortitude*, that we have learned nothing?" His eyes mock me but I cannot look away. "Did it never even enter your head that we don't need someone who lives their entire life inside a *dome*, without ever setting foot on a blade of grass, a handful of soil, telling us what the weather's like and what we should do about it?"

I blink, letting his words sink in. My voice when it emerges in the aftermath of his anger is low and quiet. But not broken. Just truthful. "No, I never once thought about it. I thought my job was important."

The silence which follows is profound. Inexplicably I feel very much like how I did when my father had died. I am adrift, alone on a sea of loneliness. Even if the people here in the room with me, Devlin, Genesis and little Beulah know how I feel, they cannot possibly understand it.

Nor can they change it.

"You left the dome to find your fiancé. Maybe you should just concentrate on that." Some of the fire has left Devlin's voice but it's been replaced by something that's frighteningly close to contempt, as if I'm incapable of deeper, less selfish thoughts.

I look at Beulah who has followed this entire conversation without comment and at Destiny who lies asleep on his bed, wound exposed and so, so vulnerable. Already I have more now to think about than just myself.

"Yes I did," I don't try to deny his words but I do add to them, "and to find Willow. But so much has happened since." My voice falters and I hesitate to say more. How will I know if I say the wrong thing?

Surprisingly, it is Beulah who comes to my aid. "They still need you. Willow needs you. And Destiny needs you too."

I blink back tears. "My fiancé had an accident..." I'm aware that Genesis doesn't know the full story. I try to find the strength to explain. "He-"

She halts me with a hand on my arm. "The village is full of talk about you. Some of it true, some of it speculation. What you said, what you did. Why you are here. But I will take you as I find you, Tudie. Nothing more and nothing less." She says the last words pointedly, as if they are meant not for me alone. I suspect they are also meant for Devlin's benefit.

"I had to break my way out of the dome," I blink back tears at the memory. "There's something very wrong with the people there. No one *really* cares about anyone else." *Perhaps I'm being too harsh though.* I was in shock, maybe I would have perceived things differently if... but I wouldn't have done. I know it's true.

"But, that's not it exactly," I continue. "My fiancé's family were devastated when it was decided he was no longer Alpha – but they still didn't do anything about it. They just accepted it. Like they accept what they have for breakfast, how much to eat, what to do, where to go. How to *think*!" I spit the last sentence out.

"But not you, Tudie." Genesis's tone is meant to be comforting I think, but it serves instead to mark me out once more as different.

A shiver snakes its way down my back and I wonder just how different I might actually turn out to be.

CHAPTER 14

I stand at the sink, washing dishes. Genesis demonstrates what I should do with the first bowl, her fingers, nimble and quick. I am slower in my movements, running my hands over the bowls, revelling at the feel of the wooden grain under my fingertips, the smooth metal of the cutlery and cooking pots. It is these smallest, simplest of things which anchors these people to their homes, their land, I realise. And the absence of it, which distances me from mine.

"It's almost like we are two separate races, us in the dome and you out here," I say. It's almost an absurd suggestion but no one scoffs.

"Well we know which one is the *superior* one," Devlin says but makes no qualifying remark to suggest whether he means his own beliefs or anyone else's. Mine in particular.

Genesis dries the dishes as I pass them to her, stacking them neatly to one side. "Do you know the history of the dome?"

"You mean who built it?" I ask.

"More the *why* they built it," she says.

I shake my head then nod, confused. "Well I know what I've been told. They built it because..." I almost use the phrase I was taught in school, *the dome gave Alphas a better way of living.*

She waits for a second, then when I don't conclude the thought she steps in. "They built it because they needed it for ELSA."

"I don't understand."

"People didn't always live like this." She takes the last bowl from me, dries it and sets it with the others. "Living in sectors according to how intelligent and attractive they are deemed to be, by a *machine*."

She notices how my eyebrows shoot up in surprise. "What surprised you there, Tudie? That I figured out we'd be considered less attractive, as well as less intelligent? Or that I called ELSA a machine?"

"Both, I guess," I say honestly.

She drags a chair over to the fire, where Devlin has already positioned himself, next to Destiny, keeping a close eye on the coyote who is awake again and eating slowly.

"Hundreds of years ago, people lived together in towns and great cities but there was so much inequality, so much hatred, that one day the government, the men and women who made the laws, decided that it would be better if people were separated into sectors."

She hasn't invited me to sit down but I

dry my hands on the discarded towel and drag a chair over to them anyway. As I approach, Destiny struggles as if to try to get up. I halt his movements with a hand placed gently on his back. "Stay down Destiny. You're still weak." I stroke his head while turning my attention back to the humans in the room.

"But the people were willing to go into sectors." I say. This is what I was taught anyway. Is she suggesting something different?

Devlin nods. "To some extent there were no major differences. Not to begin with anyway. The farmers stayed on their farms, the people who worked making things stayed within the industrialised sectors but it ended the idea of people travelling from one area to do their job and another to live in."

I can see how that would be a sensible change. Still, I don't get their point. As if completely understanding my lack of deeper comprehension Devlin speaks again. "What it also did, straight away, was to remove all the really intelligent people from every town, city and rural area and bring them all to one place."

"The dome," I anticipate.

Devlin shakes his head. "Not the dome. Not then. There was no dome at that time."

"Okay, then to wherever Alphas lived before the dome," I say. I'm impatient to get to the point. "But where's the problem? You said that all the people were in agreement."

"Every sector lost its doctors, its surgeons, its people who created things, the ones who had *ideas* about change and progress."

"And?"

He is inexplicably angry with me. "You don't get it, do you?" he places the heels of both palms on his temples as if I am causing him physical pain. "The segregation was initially intended to create a better world. It was thought that by separating into their natural levels, humankind would work more efficiently, more happily. That people could live more happily alongside others who were just like them, the same as themselves. But that caused a real problem of its own."

"Why?" I genuinely don't understand.

"Because without all the exceptionally clever people, without their interaction and their discoveries and their drive, every sector was on its own."

"But it's not like that!" I protest. "Everyone in every sector pulls together to create the whole." In my head, I hear my class repeat the words together. *We are Alpha. We are the best of humanity. But everyone in every sector...*

"Isn't it?" he challenges me. His hands have dropped from his face and his eyes, so dark, blaze with temper.

"Everything is shared out across the

sectors," I say.

He ignores me as if I haven't spoken. "And then the Alphas created ELSA and everything changed. Again." I keep quiet, sensing that if I interrupt now, I will miss something vital. I listen intently.

"They constructed her inside a dome, so that the computer was a part of the entire structure, the entire purpose for the place." He looks at me dispassionately, at odds with how he spoke just seconds earlier. "You are beautiful. But how do you think you got that way? How do you think it is that every Alpha is so good looking?"

Under the circumstances what should be a compliment seems to be a slur more than anything else. I am defensive. "We are born that way."

He nods. "Exactly. But that's not nature, Tudie." I notice the use of my preferred name but don't comment on it. "ELSA controls it. Like it controls everything else. Like it wanted to control us by extending out to the sectors. If she had been able to do that, nothing could have stopped her having ultimate power. She'd have made every Delta child exactly how she wanted it to be. Just like she does with the Alphas."

I shake my head. "No, that's not possible," I say, horrified at the idea.

Devlin looks at me again as if I am stupid, as if he really can't believe exactly how stupid

I am. "Are there ever any children born with defects in the dome? Any Alpha babies born with a cleft palate, six fingers on their hands instead of five? Any with heart defects or whose bodies are weak, unable to thrive? Are there any who are not perfect?" He doesn't even wait for me to shake my head. He already knows the answer. Like he knows everything else.

"Somehow pregnancies are scanned, monitored, and if needs be, modulated in some way to ensure that Alphas are aesthetically pleasing. And that they're *just clever enough* to do ELSA's bidding."

I don't want to agree. It's too horrible to think that I might have been artificially created, that my whole life I've been manipulated. Even before birth... "No, you're wrong, I'm sure of it." But even as I protest, I wonder which of us is right.

Devlin laughs but there's no humour in it. "Last year we had a foal born from our best horses. The mother is a beautiful creature, dark brown with a steady gait and a willing nature. The stallion who fathered the foal is the very best of his kind, with a thick sheen to his chestnut coat. But their foal – well that was the sorriest thing I have ever seen. Muddy brown in colour it's neither graceful nor pleasing to look at. More than that, it stumbles over every tuft of grass, suffers from a variety of illnesses every time the wind changes direction, and is severely lacking in personality. Neither ornament nor use, it's the clumsiest, most awkward animal I have ever encountered."

Genesis cuts in. "What Devlin's trying to say, in his usual confrontational manner, is that nature doesn't work like how life does in the dome. Nature doesn't just take two perfect things and make a third even more perfect thing from them. Only ELSA does that. Nature likes to mix things up a little, add some spice!"

I shrug. "Okay, I see your point, but even if ELSA does something to make Alphas more attractive," I oppress the shudder that threatens to overwhelm me at the thought, "it doesn't mean that she means you harm, does it?"

Genesis doesn't smile. Her face is so straight and serious that I know this is not the first time she's thought about this. "If ELSA does something to Alphas before they are even born, why should it wish to do anything less to us?"

Despite the warmth of the fire, I'm cold. I think about all the check-ups and scans and procedures that pregnant women are subjected to in the dome. Never once before did I consider them in a sinister light; now I can't do anything else. I wonder what my own mother went through without her knowledge, wonder how I was modified from how I should have looked, how I should have been. Is my hair my own natural colour, or lighter than it was destined to be? Are my eyes larger, a different shade to what they might have been? I'll never know.

I take a good look at the people around me. Different to Alphas, they are smaller and stockier but there is a wholesome appeal to their faces, a warmth that Alphas don't have.

"Why, though?" I ask. "Why would it be important to ELSA that Alphas were attractive?"

Devlin shrugs. "The only reason that I can think of, is that ELSA wants it that way. Maybe it makes the Alphas concentrate on something other than what's going on around them, both in the dome and outside."

He's quiet for a moment. "Tell me something. Who is in charge at the Dome?" he asks.

"In *charge*?"

"Who makes the decisions? The rules you live by?"

There is no hesitation before I answer. In fact I'm surprised he's asked this. I thought he already knew. "ELSA." I bite my lip. "ELSA controls everything. From what we eat, to granting permission to leave the dome, for a few hours. Or not."

None of us speak for a few minutes. Destiny has finished his food and is snoozing again. Beulah has taken up a spot on the floor next to the coyote, listening to our conversation without interrupting. Her eyes are wide and I wonder just how much of this she's taking in. It must seem like another world to her. I know it feels that way to me.

Genesis sighs. "That's what we thought." She doesn't clarify who the 'we' are and I'm not inclined to ask. "Look, it's getting late and tomorrow is soon enough to finish this conversation." She looks pointedly at Devlin.

"There's no time like the present," he says but stands reluctantly anyway.

"And there's no present like some time," she counters, sticking to her decision.

He returns the chair he's been sitting on to its original position at the table. "You'll call on me if you need help?" he asks Genesis. She nods, although it's not clear what kind of help she might need. I wonder if he means with me.

"We'll see you tomorrow," she tells him, smoothing Beulah's hair with her hands.

Devlin nods but doesn't smile. "Night Beulah. Night Genesis." He takes a breath and I think he won't bother acknowledging me. And then, "Goodnight, Miss Fortitude."

"Goodnight, Mr Devlin." I echo his formality back to him, allowing my voice to be slightly off, to let him know that I can hear his scorn. And that I am more than capable of giving the same in return. But instead of annoying him, I see the corners of his mouth lift in amusement.

He walks away without once glancing back.

Genesis shuts the door behind him. "Right then, Beulah, bed for you, young lady."

Beulah doesn't move. Her arm stays wrapped around Destiny, little fingers entwined in the coyote's fur. "Can't I sleep here tonight?" she asks, managing to make her voice sound pitiful and pleading all at the same time.

"No. Bed for you. Otherwise there will be nowhere for Tudie to sleep!" Genesis states firmly.

Destiny opens one eye as Beulah is hauled to her feet. But the child will not go so easily. Shaking loose from her mother's hands, she slides to the floor, small face pressed up close to the coyote. "Good night Destiny," she says, planting a quick kiss on the animal's nose before getting back to her feet.

I watch the exchange with eyes which seem suddenly to see beyond the superficial. It's me who has brought the coyote to this place, me who saved his life and had my own saved by him in return, and yet whilst this is the strangest thing that has ever happened to me, these people have taken the coyote just as much to their hearts as I have, but without either cause or reason. Just because.

Genesis is gone only a few moments. I hear her talking to her daughter, settling her into bed. I can't discern their actual words but I hear the lilt and inflection in the voices, the to and fro of the short conversation. More than that, I hear the love they have for each other, which shines clearly through, and I think for the second time this evening of my own mother. The woman who crafted me inside of her. The one I never knew.

"Where is her father?" I ask when Genesis returns. I don't mean the question to be blunt, but it comes out that way.

She hands me a blanket she has brought for me. Perhaps she is surprised by my abrupt question but she doesn't show it. Her face is sad.

"He died. There was a problem with the cows a couple of years ago. Some of them were injured and when he tried to help, they panicked and the herd turned on him."

I am shocked at the brutality of his death. "The cows killed him?"

She nods and takes a moment to move the remaining chairs to their places at the table. She is concentrating too much on her task, as if the memories are still too fresh, too raw to be lightly discussed.

"He was trampled by them, caught underneath their hooves. Devlin tried to save him but his injuries were too bad. Internal bleeding from multiple sources. Devlin did what he could but it wasn't enough."

An unexpected image comes to my mind, that of little Beulah helping Devlin try to save her dad. "Beulah wasn't…?"

Genesis nods. "She'd just started to show an interest in what Devlin does. She was too little to help back then, but she used to sit in the hut he uses and watch whilst he worked. It was clear that when she was older she would naturally become his apprentice." She wipes a hand over her face, as if trying to rub away the horror of the memory.

"She was there that day, just as she always was, when they brought her father in. None of us knew what was going on until it was too late and he was there, dying on the table in front of his daughter."

In three quick steps I am at her side, wrapping my arms around her as she had done for me earlier. I have no words with which to help her. I'm not from her world and anything I will say is likely to be wrong, but I can give comfort to her.

In silence we cling together, two women who have lost so much and who cannot bear to lose any more. Finally she pulls away. "He likes you." She wipes her tears away with the back of her hand and smiles shakily at me.

I don't know what she means. "Who? Who likes me?"

"Devlin."

I examine her face for jealousy but there's none. Nor is there humour. She's being totally serious.

"Aren't you and he together now? I mean

since your husband died and you're alone... not that I'm suggesting you were together when he was alive, you and Devlin, I mean." I frown in the attempt to get my words to come out correctly. Somehow they are coming out all wrong and I sound stupid and insensitive.

"Devlin was my husband's cousin. We are close. But not like that. And there could never be anyone else for me when my husband died."

"But Devlin had feelings for you?" I'm shocked to hear the words come out of my mouth but even more shocked at how intensely I listen for her answer. *What does it matter to you?* I ask myself. *You have Greyson. And you will find him and marry him, just like you planned. And everything will be okay.*

Will I? I throw the question back at myself, unsure whether it's my ability to find him that I am questioning, or something else.

"No, not at all," she says, oblivious to how intently I watch her face for signs that she is lying to me, lying to herself. "It's never been like that between us. Never will be. But with you he's different."

I force a laugh. "You mean he's not this charming with all the girls?"

She takes my sarcasm and turns it around on me. "Yes that's exactly what I mean. "With everyone else he is polite, even-tempered." She shrugs. "Distant, I would say in truth. Like he can't really be bothered to make the effort to talk to them." She smoothes a hand down the front of her dress as if she feels awkward talking to me like this. "You are the only girl I have ever seen him react to. In fact, if I didn't know better, I'd say you are the woman he has been waiting for."

With that, she bids me goodnight and leaves me to the warm room and my uncomfortable thoughts.

CHAPTER 15

I'm woken by the sounds of people moving around. Between the warmth of the dying fire on one side of me, and the coyote on the other, I have been a little overwarm and have only dipped in and out of a dream-filled slumber during the long night.

Thoughts of Grey and Willow have flitted in and out of these night-time visions. Each time that I seemed on the verge of discovering them, of finding and staying with them, they flew away from me, transformed into something else, some inanimate object, and were lost to me once more. Or I would reach for Grey, grasp his hand and pull him towards me, only to find that it was not Grey to whom I clung so fiercely, but instead Devlin. And yet I would not let go. As if in the absence of Grey, I was resigned to Devlin. Consequently I am more tired than I ought to be. And more confused.

"How do you feel?" Genesis is already cooking something. I have no idea how long she's been there. I look around to see who else might be here, watching me whilst I slept. "Don't worry, he's not here yet," she says.

"Who? Who's not here yet?" I feign indifference. But the dream memory of Devlin is not so easily pushed aside. It haunts my waking thoughts.

She raises her eyebrows. "Devlin. That is who you were looking for, isn't it?"

Was I looking for him? The image of his face comes too quickly and sharply to my mind. How he looked when he said that I was beautiful. And then, the exact opposite – when he mocked me and my beliefs, the sneer on his face, the dismissal in his eyes... I stretch and get up, folding the blanket neatly. "Destiny seems much better today." I say, avoiding the issue.

The coyote is already awake and sitting up, watching Genesis's every movement with keen interest. His nose twitches as he sniffs the aroma of cooking food. "Yes, he does." Genesis looks from the coyote to me once more. "Devlin will be pleased." Yet her expression doesn't match her words. I wonder what else she's thinking.

I grimace. "Yes. Now he can be rid of me."

She stops what she's doing and turns to face me. "I wouldn't be so sure of that," she says.

I'm undecided about her exact meaning. Whether it's that he won't be glad to be rid of me, or that he intends to stay with me in some way. Even though there's a part of me that hopes she's right, either of these possibilities are inappropriate, so I don't question them. What could I possibly do with the answers she might give? And yet I have to admit I'm intrigued by Devlin.

I watch Genesis spoon some of the food into a bowl for Destiny, then the rest onto three plates. I presume Devlin will not be joining us for breakfast.

"Good morning, Tudie." Beulah looks as tired as I feel. Standing in the bedroom doorway in rumpled pyjamas, she makes me instantly think of Willow. And of how time seems to be slipping through my fingers. How long is it since Willow was taken from the dome? How long since Grey was stolen from me? Only days, and yet it seems like a lifetime. So much has changed.

"Good morning, Beulah. Thanks to you, Destiny is much better."

The grin she displays is wide and only a little abashed. "It was mostly Devlin," she says.

"But without your help he would have been lost," I say. And as the words leave my mouth I think about the girl's skilled contribution to the operation.

I'm not the only one who appears to recognise this. Destiny gets off his haunches and moves towards her, settling at her feet and allowing her to pat and kiss his furry head. Genesis sets the cooled bowl of food at the coyote's paws. "Let him have his food in peace

Beulah, and come and have yours."

Bacon and eggs with thick slices of toast are exactly what I need. I eat slowly, savouring the taste. Nothing ever tasted this good in the dome. Perhaps it's the fresh air, the freshness of the food – or perhaps it's just the freedom I feel; the ability to only eat as much or as little as I desire. I wonder what other desires are better here…

Unbidden, an image of Devlin's mouth creeps into my mind and I almost choke on a piece of egg. Genesis slaps me abruptly on the back and Beulah regards me with interest as I cough and splutter.

"I don't know about in the dome, but here we say that you were having bad thoughts, when that happens," Genesis laughs, as I manage to draw in a whooping breath. From the crimson that burns my cheeks, I wonder if she realises just how close to the mark she actually is.

"When you have finished eating and choking, you can take a shower. You might want to let the water run a little cooler, take some of that heat out of your face," she says, barely controlling her mirth.

I am even more embarrassed. To cover myself I ask, "What about my clothes?"

"I have put fresh clothes out for you in the bathroom. Your own clothes were ruined so there was no point in washing them."

Whilst I'm even further in her debt, I'm

glad I won't be wearing my own clothes. They were from the dome, the old me and I suspect that 'me' is gone forever.

I nod. "Yes I tore a strip off my top to use as a bandage on Destiny and the rest was covered in blood and gore." I almost tell her that I had used it to carry fresh meat from the animal the coyotes had killed, but change my mind. I am concerned that she will pass the story on to Devlin and quite frankly the less that man knows about me, the better.

"Thank you for all you've done for me." My plate is empty but I feel churlish just walking away from the table and leaving them to do the clearing up. I lift my plate and Destiny's bowl and carry them to the washing bowl.

"Go get in the shower. I know you're eager to be off," Genesis says. "You have bigger issues to attend to. Whilst you are getting dressed, Beulah will take Destiny to do his toilet." I am shooed away to the bathroom once more.

I strip out of my clothes but before I step under the water I look for something to wash my hair with. I should have done this yesterday, but I was so desperate to get back to Destiny that I didn't dare take the time. But although I am in a hurry to set out on the search for Willow and Grey, five more minutes won't make that much difference.

Bottles aplenty line a thick wooden shelf

but none of them are labelled and sniffing at their contents doesn't help much either. I wrap a large towel around me and go in search of Genesis. "Is there anything I can use to -"

Devlin is there, standing next to Genesis and regarding me with wide eyes, that slowly crease at the corners as his mouth forms into a grin. Once more, I have confirmed his suspicions that I am nothing more than a stupid girl. I clutch the towel a little tighter around me, conscious of how naked I am underneath it, and try to compose myself.

My heart races. I feel Devlin's gaze like it's a physical heat. And when I let my eyes be drawn to his, there's a fire there I can't deny. I wonder how he feels about the fact that he's physically drawn to someone he dislikes so much, someone he considers stupid and beneath him? I hope it disgusts him as much as he disgusts me, with his all-knowing attitude!

Genesis seems to be the only one of us who is enjoying the situation. She looks between me and Devlin as if we are a picture show, her eyes dancing with amusement. I have to prod her into answering me.

"Shampoo? Is there any? My hair- I need to wash it." I'm dismayed at how disjointed my words come out. Devlin is probably laughing hysterically inside his head at me. I wonder how he manages to stop himself from mocking me to my face!

Genesis tries to straighten her expression. Perhaps she sees how uncomfortable I am. "Use the pink bottle by the faucet for your body. I'm assuming that's what you used yesterday. And if you want to wash your hair, use the thick green stuff on the shelf. It has Aloe Vera in it."

I nod, even though I haven't got a clue what that is. "Okay, thanks!" I turn as elegantly as I can, whilst also trying to maintain my dignity, keeping the towel from parting where it joins around me. But there's nothing elegant about the waddle I'm reduced to, clutching the towel at its top and bottom. I close the bathroom door behind me and unwrap myself, placing the towel with the clean clothes and stepping under the shower.

I close my eyes under the water but even that can't stop the image of Devlin's face lingering in my thoughts. *Go away*, I think at it, *I'm in love with Grey and all you do is annoy me!* But as I towel myself dry and dress, it is still his face I see every time I close my eyes.

When I come out of the bathroom he is sitting at the table with a drink and a large bag in front of him. Seeing me, he reaches in and withdraws something from the top. It's a rope connected to another smaller rope fashioned into a loop.

"I brought you something to put around Destiny so you can hold onto him," he says. He demonstrates the device by slipping the loop over the coyote's neck. I expect Destiny to struggle or pull away, but he accepts the rope as if he now trusts Devlin implicitly.

"He doesn't need to be controlled by me," I say, looking straight into Devlin's eyes. Challenging him.

"Well if you don't want a repeat of what almost happened yesterday, every time you turn up in a new place with a coyote at your heels, I think you'd better use this. For your sake but mostly for his." He holds the lead rope out to me.

I don't want to take it, especially since it's Devlin's idea, but then common sense kicks in. Destiny's life is at stake. And I mustn't forget that because of my foolish pride. "Okay. You have a point," I concede reluctantly. "But he doesn't need it until we are close to a new village."

Devlin shrugs like it means nothing to him either way. "Your choice." He removes the rope and loop and places them back in the bag. "I've packed some things we will need for the journey."

I interrupt him. "*We* will need?"

He ignores me. "Food, blankets, anything that I thought we might make use of."

There's that *we* again. I dive straight in. "So you mean you're coming with me?"

He jerks his head back a little as if I have lashed out at him. "How else do you think you are going to find your way around? You only found your way to us with blind luck." Once more he has a point, although I'll never admit it.

Genesis watches our exchange with a faint smile on her lips but contributes nothing to either side. I wonder whether she has divulged her conversation with me last night. I hope not. Devlin is horrible. Yes, I admit that he has a strange attractiveness about him and also that he saved Destiny's life, but as a person he leaves a lot to be desired!

"So in the entire village, there's no one else who could be spared to accompany me to the next one?" I am deliberately incredulous. He ignores my implied cynicism.

"Nope. No one." He shakes his head sadly. "Looks like you're stuck with me."

"But aren't you the most in-demand man in the whole village, what with your amazing medical skills and sparkling conversational ability?" Now I am being both rude and antagonistic but I can't seem to help myself. He really does bring out the worst in me!

He grins. "Yes I'll agree with you about my medical skills. But the next village isn't far if they need another surgeon and for anything minor, Beulah is more than capable of handling it. As for my sparkling conversation, alas they will have to do without until I return." He picks up the bag and slings it over his shoulder. "Since you have lived your entire life in the dome, I'm guessing you've never been on a horse?"

I shake my head, frustrated, but also relieved that at least I will get to Willow quicker than I would have done, if trying to find her on my own.

"Then you are in for a surprise." He actually laughs at me and I hate him even more.

The horses are ready for us when we emerge from the hut. Handsome creatures, they are animals I have only ever seen in pictures. Up close, their majesty is so much more magnificent than has ever been conveyed to me by flat images on a screen.

But upon seeing Destiny, the horses snicker and pull on their ropes. "Settle girls," Devlin soothes them. "Everything is fine." He pats Destiny, rubbing his hands across her head and down over her nose and mouth. He then lifts his hands and holds them up to the horses' noses.

"Be calm," Devlin says and I'm not sure if the comment is made to me or the horses. Long nostrils flare and quiver and the whites of both horses' eyes can clearly be seen but they stop pawing at the ground with their feet and straining at the ropes which hold them.

I look at Destiny, aware suddenly that perhaps he does pose a threat to the horses, but he seems perfectly at ease, standing at my side as if he has done this every day of his life. I look up to find Devlin watching me. "He's either not a normal coyote or you have bewitched him." He only sounds half-joking.

"Then I guess he's not a normal coyote, because if I could cast a spell about anything, then it would be to have Willow and Grey back," I say. I also think that I'd banish Devlin from being anywhere near me.

His expression changes immediately, becoming instantly more sombre. "Of course," he says.

I feel as if he has taken my words as an affront. "I guess what happened with the other coyotes scared him so much, he has just decided that he's better off with me. Better off with a human," I try to dispel the bad atmosphere between myself and Devlin but can't resist a final jibe, "even if that human is an Alpha."

Devlin ignores my sarcasm. "Either way, he doesn't behave like a wild animal at all, not even one who has been tamed over a long period of time, not just a few days."

Since I know nothing about the natural world, I can't comment with any authority. But I am curious. "So how *does* he act then?"

"Like a really well behaved dog." He pulls himself up onto the larger of the two horses. "I guess we'll never know why that is. We just need to be grateful for it. Now climb up." He indicates the second horse.

I'm aware that Devlin is watching me.

"How?" I ask. The horse's back seems a long way away up and my legs aren't that long.

"Stand facing the back of the horse. Put your foot in the stirrup there," he points to some sort of foot holder, "then dig your left knee gently into its side and throw your body over. I'll be there to grab you and settle you in place."

I press my knee in and hurl myself up and over. Devlin catches my arm and steadies me until I get a sense of balance. His fingers are warm on my skin and where they touch, there is a tingling sensation that makes me aware of how close he is to me.

I'm extraordinarily aware of so many things at once. The warm musky scent of the horse, the way I feel higher than I really am; the impression that absolutely everything is different to what I had always thought. The feeling that perhaps I don't know myself at all, that I'm not how I think I am, *who* I think I am.

And then his hand lifts from my arm and I want to cry out, to demand that he puts it back, because with its removal I also lose that strange yet wonderful sensation. I don't dare look at him. Not at his face. Or his eyes which seem to see too much. Instead I watch his hands.

"I'll hold a lead rope for your horse until you feel confident enough to control the reins for yourself," he tells me. I nod.

"What about Destiny?" I ask, although the

coyote seems merely bemused that I am now sitting on the back of another live creature.

"I don't think we need to worry about him," Devlin says. "He seems to have the whole thing pretty well figured out. I think he'll be happy to walk along beside us."

Expertly, Devlin turns the two horses around and we begin to make our way out of the village. Beulah and Genesis call out good wishes, and wave. Everyone else stops and watches in silence. But my gaze fixes on one person.

A man sits on a chair by the entrance to a hut, gnarled hands resting in his lap, rheumy eyes watching me but betraying none of his thoughts. And then, just at the point of passing out of sight, he smiles at me, toothless gums exposed in a grin that is at once both childlike and ancient. I can't drag my eyes away from the sight. "What's wrong with him?"

Devlin looks over. "Just the usual aches and pains of old age."

"I've never seen such an old person," I say, hearing the words out loud as they tumble straight from my subconscious mind.

"Yes, well there's not many make it to old Joe's age," Devlin says, following my gaze. "He must be near enough ninety."

"Ninety!" Even I hear the astonishment in my voice. "But that's impossible!"

Devlin snorts. "I assure you it's not." He

looks at me strangely. "What's the oldest you have seen then?"

I think hard. "Fifty-something? Sixty maybe, but only very occasionally."

He's surprised. "Most folk live to at least seventy, Tudie. Why do you think you haven't seen anyone older than sixty?"

I don't answer immediately. "I don't know." But I suspect there is something sinister in the truth. Some other horror that I might not be able to cope with right now.

"There's bound to be a reason," Devlin pushes, unaware that I am quietly panicking. Suddenly this whole thing seems just too huge for me to deal with. It's not that I don't want to find Willow and Grey any more – I do. But I'm afraid that when I do, there will be even more problems that I have to solve, even more things that I will have to face and accept in order to do so. It's as if every corner I turn in my path, leads not to a straight stretch, but to further twists and turns, corners and unseen dangers.

As if he has read my thoughts Devlin says. "You're not on your own, you know. And I don't mean right now. People are tired of how things are, how every month, every year, ELSA squeezes us tighter." The horses plod on for a few steps and I wonder if he expects an answer from me. I keep quiet.

"And now here you are, straight from the

dome with a mission in your heart and a thirst for knowledge in your head." For once he says words in a tone that I could almost mistake for admiration. If I didn't know him better.

Even though I have just gotten used to the horse's walk, the slow rhythmic rocking from side to side as it propels us forward, I use my heels to put a little pressure on its sides, the way I have seen Devlin do. Much as I hate his laughing at me, I think I hate his sympathy more. I'm not just some stupid girl who is out here on a whim.

Spurred on more than I had intended, I grasp the reins in fear as the horse starts forward, using the slack of the lead rope to gain some distance. The quicker pace jolts me, throwing me up into the air a little with the horse's every step, but I manage to hold on. Destiny matches the horse's faster pace. I slow the horse a little, aware that only yesterday, the coyote had major surgery. But something that Devlin said yesterday is playing on my mind.

"You said that sometimes you have to have a little pain to make sure you don't have a whole barrel full of the stuff. What did you mean?"

He brings his horse level with mine. "For years people have put up with ELSA taking almost everything they have. And do you know why they did that?" He looks at me as if expecting an answer. When I don't give him one he continues. "They did it because they were afraid. Afraid of what would happen if they stood up to ELSA."

I don't understand. "But ELSA's just a computer. It's not a person, it can't really do anything."

He looks at me like I am dumb. "You really don't know, do you?"

"Know what?"

"Yes ELSA is a computer but it's so much more than that. It watches everything we do."

"How can that be?" I ask. His statement is ludicrous. "You said yourself that you have pigs and hens that ELSA knows nothing about."

"Yes," he agrees. "We keep them in her blind spot."

"What?" I don't even try to hide my confusion.

"There's an area of our land which is shielded by trees and a natural hollow. ELSA can't see in there."

"What do you mean? How can ELSA see anything here from the dome?" I'm suddenly very afraid. Is he mad? Have I left the safety of the village to die brutally at the hands of a crazy man?

"She can't use the satellite there." He doesn't even look at me, just keeps his gaze focused ahead.

"The satellite?" I say.

"You know, the camera in the sky. The one ELSA uses to spy on us."

CHAPTER 16

"I don't understand."

He looks at me sharply. "You really don't, do you?" He pauses so long I wonder if he will ever provide an explanation. Or if he will just write me off as too stupid to waste his time on.

"There's a thing in the sky which captures pictures of us, all of us, in all of the sectors."

I shift my gaze to the sky but all I see is blue and white patches.

"You can't see it like that," he says. "It's too far away."

"So how do you know that it exists?" I challenge. Then without giving him a chance to answer, "Just one, or lots of satellite things?"

"A few. Maybe even lots. I don't honestly know. But enough to cover all of the sectors."

I look at him, aware that my mouth hangs open. I manage to push a word out. "Why?"

He shrugs as if it's unimportant and I want to shake him – want to make him see that every word he utters so casually, turns my world further inside out from how I believed it was.

Back in the dome we are monitored, but out here in the open... Well here I thought it was different.

"You're saying that ELSA knows everything you do? That she's watching you?" *Had she been watching me also? Watching as I attacked a coyote? As I almost died of thirst?* A shudder courses down my back.

He nods. "That's exactly what I'm saying. The satellites were put up there long ago. Long before you and I were even born. Before ELSA was even thought of. I guess they had other uses then. But now they're just cameras focused on everyone outside the dome. Everyone who's still free. Maybe they don't all work anymore, but some of them do. Enough for ELSA to keep an eye on us."

Everyone who is still free. Everyone outside the dome. Although I had never truly admitted myself to be a captive until the picnic – more so after what had happened with Grey and Willow – I find his words echo inside my head. It was exactly how I felt when I had forced open ELSA's doors, taken that first prohibited step across her threshold. Despite the warmth of the air, I shudder again.

The involuntary action traces a path down my body and seems to infect the horse beneath me, who takes a long shuddering step of her own. I hold on tightly.

"You said your job was to send weather

information to Delta sectors. How do you think ELSA got that information?" He waits for my response.

I shake my head. I have no answer for him. Or myself. "So ELSA knows I'm here with you."

He nods. "And what you're up to. Perhaps not the why of it, the fact that you are searching for people, although that's not something I'd bet on, but certainly the fact that you're out here with me."

"She's only a computer!" I say.

"A very *smart* computer." He keeps his gaze straight ahead, as if we're not talking about something so incredible that I'm having difficulty figuring out all the implications.

"We don't know if she can capture sound as well as pictures. No one knows if the satellites were ever capable of that, or whether somehow ELSA has managed to modify them since then, but it's wisest to assume that at least some of our conversations can be heard."

Was that also true in the dome? Did ELSA listen to us talking to each other, as well as watch us? Did she listen to our arguments, our proclamations of love, our plans for the future?

"So everything we talked about..." I think of the rebellious nature of his comments, the disclosure of the hidden hens, everything that he might have put in jeopardy because of me – and I'm ashamed. Ashamed that I have brought so much trouble down on them.

"There's a possibility that ELSA now knows much more than she did before," he says, as if understanding my thoughts exactly.

"And that doesn't worry you?" I can't keep the astonishment from my voice.

This time he turns towards me. His face is hard, set as if against some long-anticipated foe. "The time has come for action. I think it no longer matters what ELSA does or doesn't know. What matters is what *we* know, and what we can use to defeat her."

"To *defeat* her?" Despite all of our conversations I am stunned at the thought. And also more than a little scared. "What will happen?" I ask.

He snorts as if I've said something funny. "Well I'm certainly not going to discuss *those* plans out loud!"

He has misinterpreted me. "I meant to all the people in the dome. What will happen to them?"

This time he doesn't hesitate. "They will be free to make their own choices."

I pull sharply on my horse's reins, forcing her to halt. Devlin carries on for a couple more strides before he realises that I am no longer by his side. He halts his own horse and turns it around, heading back towards me and Destiny. He pulls up close to me, but facing the opposite way. He's so close that our legs are touching at the knee. It's uncomfortable in an oddly exciting way.

I don't wait for him to speak. I fear that if I have to remain in this position too long – too close to him – I will lose the ability to articulate my fears. "They don't *want* to be free."

This time it's him who looks astonished. I try to explain. "The day I left, when I forced open the doors, no one else came even close to stepping through them. In fact the opposite is true. They backed away. They were terrified."

Devlin looks away from me, into the distance, although there is nothing new to be seen there. Released from his scrutiny, I am able to concentrate on examining how the contours of his face shift as he struggles to accept what I have told him.

"Sometimes there is an infection so deep, that no medicine can cure it, no drugs can make it right. All that's left then is amputation. Only severing the infected limb can let the rest of the body heal," he says.

My voice is louder and harsher than I intend, but even as the words tumble from my mouth, I don't try to modify them in any way. "You can't compare destroying ELSA with cutting off a diseased arm or leg! Alphas aren't used to having to organise their own lives –"

"To having to *think* for themselves?" he mocks. His eyebrows are raised and his eyes are narrowed. The faint smile that I have come to recognise as associated with my challenges, plays on his lips. "And yet the Alphas are the *best* of us, the most intelligent," he says.

I'm aware that he's tying me in knots - that my arguments don't really stack up against his. But damn it, I'm an Alpha and he's not! I try harder. "It's not about intelligence though, is it Devlin? It's about fear and what people are used to. If you take all they have ever known away from them -"

"They will find ways to adapt. You have." He sits there, so smug on his horse that I am desperate to prove him wrong. But I can't think of an answer that will make sense to him.

My thoughts are too jumbled, too steeped in emotion to be expressed in any logical manner that might make him understand. I pull my horse away from his and start back in the direction we have been travelling. I don't need to look down at my side to know that Destiny has followed my lead and is trotting faithfully beside me.

Devlin catches up with me too quickly to allow my mind and heart to have stopped their frantic panicking. "You have to have more faith in human resilience for this to work," he says.

"I didn't set out to change the world, I just wanted Grey and Willow back."

His voice is more gentle than when he spoke to me before. I am reminded of how he spoke to Destiny, the low, soothing tone he had used. "You can't have them back without changing the world, Tudie, that's my point. Maybe you didn't mean to, but when you defied ELSA, you changed everything."

I think about what he's said. I hadn't intended to bring everything crashing down, but I see now that there's no way back. Having already banished Grey and Willow, ELSA will never allow them back into the dome. He's right. But admitting it pains me.

"We can live together, outside the dome, me, Willow and Grey." I'm not sure if I'm telling him or telling myself.

"And you think ELSA will allow that?"

I choose not to answer.

"You think she won't punish whatever sector you live in, long enough and hard enough that the people there won't come to hate you?"

I see an image of the three of us, cast out from everywhere we turn. Tears spring to my eyes but I blink them back.

"There's no way back, Tudie. And the only way forward for you is by helping me destroy ELSA."

We ride on in silence.

Hours pass, the terrain changes and yet somehow remains remarkably the same; barren stretches interspersed with lush green areas. I'm sore from having been on the horse for so long.

Every bone seems to hang loose in its socket and there is a heaviness to my head which makes me fear it will just roll off my shoulders at any minute.

"We need to eat and the animals need to rest, especially Destiny," Devlin says, stopping his horse and hopping off lightly, as if the journey so far has made absolutely no impact upon him. He makes no move to help me down from my horse and I don't know whether to be annoyed or relieved.

The ground is too hard for me to sit on comfortably but at least it does not sway continuously under me. I want to slump; to allow my back muscles a little time out, but I fear he will see that as weakness. I keep myself straight. "You must be sore," he says.

I ignore him. I don't want to lie, and I can't convincingly fake nonchalance, so I leave it. "Is it much farther?" I say instead.

"For me? No. For you? Too far to go in one day."

He's so matter-of-fact about it, I'm almost enraged. Or at least I would be, if I had enough energy. He passes me some food. I chew and swallow without appreciating the taste or the nourishment. It almost seems too much of an effort.

"We'll rest a little here, then ride for a few hours more before bedding down for the night.

Bedding down? He intends for us to spend the night alone? There's a strange feeling in my stomach suddenly, a sort of nervous tingling, and I can't pinpoint its exact location.

"Tell me about this man of yours," he says almost casually.

I look into the distance so that I can better picture Grey. "Greyson's the most handsome Alpha I've ever seen. He's tall and he has the most graceful way about him. And he's kind -"

"You must look like the perfect couple." There's almost an accusation in his words. I drag my gaze back to him but he's no longer looking at me, if in fact he ever was.

"What about you?" I say. "You must have someone special."

"Must I? Why's that, Tudie? Because everything has to be perfect in your world? Real life's not like the dome."

I indicate myself sitting next to him. "Is this not real enough for you, Devlin?" Beside me, Destiny gives a small sound of upset. I reach a hand out to his warm fur but I don't even try to moderate my words. "Is it not real enough that I'm out here, searching for the man I love, sitting with someone who clearly despises me, just because I was born an Alpha? Is that not real enough for you?" I am standing now, although I don't remember getting to my feet.

"Sit back down." He pops some more food

into his mouth as if my anger and frustration mean nothing to him.

"No. You said you could do the journey in a day. I don't need to rest. Let's get on with it and get there tonight instead of tomorrow." I don't add that the thought of sleeping alone with him by my side is almost intolerable. And bizarrely exhilarating.

"No. The horses get more tired going at this slow pace than they would at their normal pace. If we go faster now we will exhaust them, maybe even wear their hearts out, and Destiny's too."

I say nothing. This is his area of expertise. We are silent a moment and I'm not inclined to break it.

"There's never been anyone for me." He says it like it's a confession and even though I know it's wrong, I can't help the words which tumble from my lips.

"Maybe you're too hard to love."

He cocks his head at me. But he's not angry. Instead he is grinning.

"You think so?"

I try to backtrack. "Well Genesis and Beulah love you…"

He shakes his head. "That's not the same thing at all. We're talking husband and wife kind of love now. Do you think any woman could ever love me, Tudie?" There's more emotion evident in his words than he realises.

I want to look at his face; into his eyes. I want to test the depth of his soul, but I dare not. I love Grey and whatever this is – this thing between Devlin and I – it's born of a shared desire for change, a passion that is stirred not by one another, but by the uniqueness of the situation we find ourselves in. "I wouldn't know." I shrug. "I'm not a Delta woman."

"No, you're not." His voice is harder than before. "You're an Alpha. I almost forgot for a moment how far above me, you Alphas are." He stands up. "Let's go. The sooner you are reunited with your perfect Alpha mate, the better for all of us!"

"But the horses, and Destiny..."

He nods. "We'll go at their pace. Stop when they want to." He's already packing away the uneaten food with quick sharp movements. I want to help but I am almost certain that if I try, I will somehow infuriate him further. I somehow get back on my horse.

Perhaps I should have stayed on her, for I'm even sorer than I was before our rest. I want to complain at the discomfort in my hips, knees and bottom, but I keep silent. Devlin mounts up and we are off once more. "Genesis told me you tried to save her husband," I say when the silence becomes intolerable.

He tightens the reins he holds in his hands. "It was a long time ago," he says and is silent once more.

"I thought maybe you and her were a couple -"

"What is it with you, Tudie? Why are you so interested in whether or not I have a woman? Is your Alpha pride so strong that it hurts to think that not every single man you meet, might be envisaging you in his bed?"

I'm so surprised both by his words and the hostile tone they are delivered in, that I accidentally drop my reins. Under the guise of bending low over the horse's neck to retrieve them, I try to regain my composure.

"I *don't think* every man looks at me like that! And I certainly wouldn't want them to!" I realise he has turned the conversational focus away from himself and back onto me. "I just thought that it would be natural for you and her to become a couple. You are so close."

"We are only as close as we were when her husband was alive. We were family, or didn't she explain that?"

"Yes she did but I thought -"

"Well, you thought wrong. So how is it in the dome then? Do you get to choose your own partner, or does ELSA do that for you too?" He's more irritated than I've heard him before.

"We choose our own husbands and wives."

"Well isn't Grey lucky then that you chose him!"

I can't work out if this is a compliment or a slur. "We're lucky we chose *each other*." *And we are, aren't we? Grey is the most handsome man in the dome. And yet...* I'm aware that his looks matter less to me, than what might reside in his head and his heart.

Where does Grey's passion lie? What inspires him? These are questions I have no answer to. Yet as his fiancé, I'm suddenly acutely aware I should. "Beauty comes in many different forms, Devlin." I don't know which of us is more surprised by my words.

We ride on in a new, strange silence.

CHAPTER 17

We make camp soon after I realise I'm no longer upright in the saddle, but rather slumped there. "Okay, let's call it a day," Devlin says, hopping off his horse again as if it's nothing. "Come on," he says to me.

"I don't think I can," I say truthfully.

To my surprise he doesn't laugh. His eyes flit over my rounded shoulders and back, to the numb slackness of my hands, which barely still hold the reins. "Let me help you." From the ground he pulls my feet from the stirrups and hoists one of my legs over the horse's neck. I'm sliding down but it doesn't matter, because suddenly he's there to catch me before I fall.

Trapped between his body and the horse's, my breath catches in my throat. There's a deep muskiness in the air, a tantalising aroma which is both heady and intoxicating. We are so close that I can see the fine lines at the corners of his eyes, the individual hair follicles on his chin and cheeks where bristle has already started to sprout. I am mesmerised.

More or less equally matched in height, we stand eye to eye. I feel his breath on my cheek; am aware that my breath must be brushing across his skin also. I have stood this close to Grey before, but nothing that I felt then, is anywhere near as intense as I now feel.

I am acutely aware that we are alone, that the whole world might have ceased to exist, other than him and I. Despite that, or perhaps because of it, I want to reach out and touch his face, feel his skin under my fingers... As if he feels it too, he leans closer to me, so close that our lips are almost touching. But at the very last moment he steps back. And just like that, the spell is broken.

"Choose a spot where we can sleep." I notice how his eyes avoid mine as he busies himself taking the saddles off the horses and leading them towards a lush patch of grass. "I'll tend to the animals while you set down our bedding." He throws a bag towards me that I don't manage to catch.

It's filled with blankets, enough for both of us. I hesitate then pick a spot under a tree, so that we will be at least a little sheltered if the weather changes. I lay the blankets out in two separate piles, several feet away from each other. For good measure, I create a smaller separate pile, where Destiny can sleep, in-between us.

When Devlin comes over, he moves the piles closer together. They are still apart but now we will be within touching distance, if we choose to do so. "Safer to be closer. There are snakes and other creatures out here that might try to take advantage."

I wonder what sort of advantage he might be thinking of, but keep safely quiet. I sit on my chosen bed to eat the food he passes to me. The alternative is to squat on the hard ground as he is doing, but I'm sorely in need of some padding now.

I try with all my might to get Destiny to lie between the two beds as I had planned, even putting his food there for him. But he picks at the morsels, lifting them in his mouth one at a time and carrying them down to the area below the two makeshift beds and settling there to eat, only returning to pick up another piece of food.

"He's protecting you," Devlin explains, when I try unsuccessfully for the tenth time to get the coyote to settle where I want him to. I think that if Destiny really wanted to protect me, he should be working to keep Devlin away from me. But my mind throws up the fact that it was I who had wanted to touch Devlin's face only a little time before, and that it was he who had pulled away.

"You might as well move his bed there, because that's where he's decided to sleep," Devlin says in his usual authoritative way. Reluctantly, I shift Destiny's bed to the strip of grass beyond my feet. Devlin's bed is now uncomfortably close. Destiny circles around on his blanket and eventually settles with his back to me and his head facing the vast wilderness. I try not to think about what he is guarding us against.

When Devlin lies down on his blankets, he is so close I can hear the quiet hiss of his breathing. I turn my head so that I am facing the sky but I don't feel any less vulnerable by not looking directly at him.

Time seems to stretch, too open and too infinite between each of his inhalations and I find that I am holding my own breath in the hiatus of his, as if trying to exactly match his timing. My heart is hammering with some unknowable excitement and it's just as well that I am lying down, for I am dizzy. "Are you feeling okay?" he asks.

I hesitate. "I'm a little uncomfortable – us lying here like this."

"That wasn't really what I meant. I meant after being on the horse so long. But since you've brought it up, we might as well talk about it, don't you think?"

I shuffle as far away from him on my blanket as I can. "What do you mean? There's nothing to talk about!"

"Why are you uncomfortable? You are just a woman out in the middle of nowhere with a man you don't really know." His voice is easy, but his words imply a mockery that angers me.

"I have a fiancé who loves me." I'm aware that this doesn't really answer his question or put to rest any of the implications that probably crossed his mind but I can't think of anything else to say.

"And he's a very lucky man."

I'm so surprised that he sounds genuine that I turn towards him. Surely there is some scorn subtly implied there that I have missed? "Do you really think so?"

"Yes, of course. To have someone who loves you enough that they will risk everything for you, isn't that what we all want?"

I answer his question with one of my own. "Is that what you want, Devlin?" I instantly regret asking.

His eyes close and for a long time I think he is asleep but when his voice comes it is quiet and reflective. "ELSA won't allow you back into the dome."

"I know. You already said that."

"Perhaps without him you might stand a chance, although you have rebelled against her, so it's slim. But since she has already cast him out, there's no chance for him."

"I know. And there's Willow too."

"It can be a hard life out here in."

"I'll cope."

His eyes open. "Yes actually, I have no doubt

that you will. But will they? You don't even know where he is. Whether he's been taken in or not."

I'm very afraid. "You think they might not have taken him in?"

Devlin shrugs. "You said he'd had an accident. Someone who can't work for his living isn't much good to a sector. And he's a stranger."

He's echoing my own thoughts but admitting that feels like plunging a knife into Grey. I can't do it. "He's strong. He'll prove his worth to them." *But is he?* I remember how he looked when the convulsions began, the involuntary muscle paralysis, the rolling of his eyes in their sockets... How strong will he appear to these strangers then? How useful?

"They'll have accepted him! And once I find him, I can help him too." I close my eyes. I don't want to talk anymore. Whatever will happen, will happen, and I'll deal with it then. There's no point in brooding upon conjecture. But my mind races with pictures and images. I raise my head and look at Destiny who is still alert and watchful.

"Earlier you said that you wanted to defeat ELSA..." He's quiet so long I'm convinced he won't answer. I sit upright and verbally prod him again. "That the people in the Dome would be set 'free'..."

When he speaks his voice is low and hard. "We shouldn't be talking about this now!"

"You said you thought it was unlikely that

ELSA could hear us from the thing in the sky, only see us –"

He moves so fast that I can't stop him. In one fluid motion he is kneeling and pulling me into his arms, his hands wrapped firmly around my wrists. I am so close to him that I can almost feel the pounding of his heart, and I wonder if he can feel the blood rushing through the fine veins where he holds me so tightly.

I can no longer think straight and I'm not sure I care. He exudes a sensual muskiness and I lean towards it, eager for intoxication. His lips descend towards mine and even though I know it's wrong, I feel my heart thrum with excitement. Instinctively I close my eyes and my lips part in anticipation. But the kiss doesn't come. This time his lips don't even brush mine.

"ELSA *has* to be defeated. There's no other way for the sectors to be free."

I drag heavy eyelids open. He is so close that I can see every strand of colour in his irises, every dilation and contraction of his pupils, every ounce of the fervency in his intention. I close my mouth and swallow hard. *Is he aware of how utterly he had me fooled? With his closeness and his low whispers? No doubt only enacted and intended to fool ELSA. If she's watching.*

I don't move from his mock embrace, even though I want to pull away from the sham. I steel myself against his touch, supplant the sight of his face with an image of Grey's face; of Willow. "And the people in the dome? What about them? You said yourself that life is hard out in the scectors."

"Because ELSA makes it that way. Once ELSA is gone everything will be different -"

"And the people in the dome?" I ask again.

"Why would you be concerned about them? None of them helped you."

"Grey's family and Willow's are there. Whilst I have no love for them, I can't say the same for how Grey or Willow will feel."

He nods in understanding. "We'll look after them."

I'm not reassured as much as I would like to be. I focus on the practicalities. "How are you going to defeat ELSA? It won't be easy!"

"I have a plan."

But instead of telling me what it is, he releases me and slides down onto his blankets. I'm annoyed, frustrated and dismayed in equal measure but I say nothing. Words will only add to the problem. And maybe once I hear of it, I will not like his plan. I lie back down and close my eyes and pray for the oblivion of sleep, although with so many fears running around inside my head, I don't think sleep will come easily.

When I wake, I am as stiff and sore as if I have been dragged from miles over rough ground behind a horse, rather than having ridden on one. Devlin and Destiny are already up and about.

Clearly whatever threats we faced in the night were not fatal.

I stand and fold mine and Destiny's blankets. Devlin has already packed his away and I shove the others into the bag he used. "I thought you'd sleep forever," Devlin says when he sees me up and moving.

"You could have woken me if it's been that long!" I say indignantly.

He takes the bag from me and straps it to his horse. "You needed the rest."

Once again he's managed to make an innocent comment sound like a slur. "I'm fine."

"Yes, because I let you sleep."

The man really is infuriating! I swing myself up to my horse before he has a chance to malign me in some other way.

"Got to eat first before we go." He indicates a pan with some meat sizzling in it that somehow I managed to overlook.

"I'll eat up here."

He doesn't answer. He looks at me strangely for what seems a little too long, then, without a word he slaps my horse hard on its rump. Startled, the horse bolts forward and not secured in the saddle yet, I am thrown forward and backwards. I grab at the reins, the horse's hair, anything to secure my position but I'm too late. Caught off guard and inexperienced, I am unable to either halt the horse or steady myself. Thrown to one side, I feel myself falling and prepare for a hard jolt.

But instead of the hard ground, strong arms catch and hold me. "I'm sorry," he says, although the grin on his face makes a lie of his proclaimed regret.

"You could just have asked me to come down."

"And you would have just done what I asked you to do?" He places my feet on the ground and withdraws his support from me.

I brush myself down as if I had fallen on the hard ground. But rather than dirt, it is the imprint and memories of his touch I am brushing away. I ignore his comment. "What about the horse?"

"Don't worry. Horses don't stray far from their owners."

We sit on the ground to eat. "Why not?" I ask.

"Why not what?"

"You said that horses don't stray far from their owners. Why is that?"

I have to wait for him to swallow before he answers. "Because they know they are well looked after by us. Why would they want to take a chance on their own? Life could be much harder like that."

I point the piece of food I am holding at him. "And that's exactly how Alphas will view things." I don't add 'when they are faced with life without ELSA, without the Dome' but I know he's aware of what I mean.

We eat in silence, pack up and resume the journey.

CHAPTER 18

"It's time to put Destiny on the lead rope." Devlin dismounts and waits for me to do the same, before gently pulling the collar over the coyote and handing me the end of the rope.

"How close are we?" I ask.

"Close enough that we could run into someone at any minute. Best not to take any chances that they might see a coyote and think danger."

I know he's right, but I don't like the idea of pulling Destiny along by his neck. It's wrong. But it's also the safest thing to do for him right now. "It's only until I can explain to the people here," I tell the coyote who looks up at me with baleful eyes. I stroke a hand along his back and try to imagine a scene in my head of me removing the collar and everyone loving him. I hope that if my words don't get through to him, somehow the picture in my head might. "What do these Deltas do?" I ask Devlin.

"They are Sector Four, area nine -"

"Delta 4:9!" I almost hear a thunk in my

head as the code slots into place. "They grow corn and wheat!"

He stops walking to look at me. His eyes are narrowed, his face troubled. As if suddenly I have raised his suspicions that I'm not who I say I am. "It's what I do, I mean did. At the dome."

"Oh yes, your weather information." He manages to make it sound ludicrous. Again. "So what else do you know about these people?"

"Nothing. Other than that Willow is here. And it was Beulah who told me that."

"Okay. So you only know what they *do*, not who they are." His voice changes. "What do you think they're like?"

It's a strange question and I'm not sure how to answer. "Like you I guess. Why would they be different?" He doesn't answer, just resumes walking. I want to ask him what he meant but won't risk incurring his wrath. Time will surely reveal all.

Destiny, who has been walking so easily beside me, alters his position slightly. The change is almost imperceptible. His back which was swaying loosely with his strides before, now seems tensed, his muscles readying for action.

The horses, either in reaction to the change in the coyote's behaviour or in response to whatever has alerted Destiny, whinny in fear. On the lead rope, my horse tries to pull away from me and I would have lost my footing if Devlin hadn't quickly closed his free hand around mine. "I'll take both horses. You keep hold of the coyote."

The fact that he has not referred to Destiny by name, alerts me to the fact that there is a problem. "What is it? What's wrong?" I say.

"Shadowers," he replies cryptically.

"What are Shadowers?"

He ignores me. His eyes are watchful, quick and alert. "Over there, to your right. Behind that big tree..." He's right, there's something there. Maybe a person or a large animal. I can't quite make it out clearly enough. "We're not carrying anything that's of any use to you. Let us pass," Devlin shouts into the distance.

"Your horses!" A shout comes back. It's more of a threat than a request.

"We won't give them up. And to take them, you will have to fight us." Devlin barks out a short laugh, surprising me. "Don't be fooled by the girl's appearance. She will fight. And win." He smiles as if he's enjoying the exchange, but up close I see the worry in his eyes. "She fought her way this far." He pauses a moment, perhaps to let them think about that. "Do you want to take the chance of losing your life for a bit of horsemeat?"

My mouth opens a little in shock at what he's suggesting, but I close it rapidly.

"Say something," Devlin says to me in a whisper, managing to speak out of the side of his mouth, so that no one but I will know he's talking.

Say something? What do I say? "It's been a quiet day so far. I could do with a bit of excitement!" I say, surprising myself with how well I manage the bravado.

"More," Devin urges quietly.

I make a show of pulling back on Destiny's rope. The coyote is reaching forward slightly and I think that the act makes me look as if I am only reluctantly restraining him. "My coyote feels the same way," I shout.

Thankfully Devlin takes over again. "Go back to wherever you came from, or if you are very unlucky, you might live long enough to regret stopping us."

There is a rustling, a parting of tree limbs and bushes. Not just from where the voice issued, but closer and more around us than I'd been aware of. "They're gone," Devlin says. "For now anyway."

"But who were they? *What* were they? And did you really think they would eat the horses?" The questions tumble out of me. I am cold, much colder than I ought to be, and I can only think that it's the shock which is affecting me so.

"They're dispossessed people. Maybe as few as ten, or as many as twenty. They all did something to get thrown out of their sector and left to fend for themselves - or die of starvation. Eventually, they met others of their kind."

I see where he's going with this. "So they

joined them?"

"Either join them or be killed by them. Perhaps even eaten. Who knows!"

"You're saying they eat people?" Now I am shivering. Not just with cold but with terror.

"Occasionally someone goes missing on a journey between two sectors. It doesn't take a leap of imagination to figure out what might have happened."

Now it doesn't seem at all fanciful to think that they would eat the horses. "So why didn't they attack us? Surely they weren't scared? Not with so many of them!"

"You might be a woman but you don't look like any women they've encountered before."

"Is that a compliment or an insult?" I'm genuinely unsure.

"You're tall and strong. Your bones and limbs are straight and finely muscled. And although I'm no Alpha, I'm pretty fit. And of course, there's a coyote you're holding on a lead. It was too much of a risk to them. They're weak and they're starved. They might look scary, and in numbers they are strong. But individually, they're weaker than Beulah."

"Because they are starving?" I hazard a guess.

"Yes. There's not much to eat out here between sectors. They scavenge what they can and steal what comes their way, but I guess most of them are slowly starving to death."

Once again, I don't know how I feel about them. "You said they were thrown out of their sectors. What did they do?"

"Mostly murder."

I'm back to fearing them. "You said they were gone *for now*. They'll be back, won't they? More of them?"

"Perhaps." He keeps walking but I notice that although he keeps his head facing forward, his eyes move almost constantly towards every bush, every clump of trees. "People are people, Tudie. Good and bad. If you want to experience the good side of humanity then you have to accept that there's a darker side too. Night and day. Dawn and dusk. Good and evil."

I find myself surveying every dense area of foliage we pass as carefully as Devlin, desperate to reach the village before the Shadowers return.

It seems like forever before we are close to safety. In the distance, lush crops sway in the breeze and a smattering of huts can be seen. "Keep Destiny close to you and don't speak until I can tell them why we're here," Devlin instructs. But we enter the perimeter of the village without encountering anyone.

And then, without warning, the door to a hut opens and something flies towards me. I tense, unsure what to do. Will Devlin protect me? Protect Destiny? I brace myself for a fight. But there's something wrong with the stature of my flying assailant. The limbs are too short, the head proportionally smaller than my own –

"Willow!" I cry, and sweep the child up into my arms, dropping Destiny's rope to do so. The coyote looks on warily, his eyes fixed on the child who clings to me. "Friend," I say to him, taking one of Willow's hands and sweeping it the length of Destiny's back. It's the quickest way of bonding them that I can think of.

Child and coyote both look up at me with such trust I am humbled. "I knew you would come for me, Tudie! I *knew* it!"

I am both honoured and saddened by Willow's words. She neither expects nor assumes that either of her parents will care enough to find her. And she's absolutely right. All I can offer her is my love and my own assurances. Nothing they might or might not feel about her absence can comfort her now.

"Of course I did." *But you also came for Grey*, the voice inside my head whispers. *And would you so readily have come for Willow, if Grey had been fine and well, still inside the dome? If finding her had meant leaving him, perhaps forever?*

It's a question I can't answer entirely honestly. I like to think that I would, that I would have come for Willow, no matter what it meant to me personally, but I can't be sure.

"So this is her?" A little girl stands some

distance from us. Around the same age as Willow, she is as different as she could possibly be to the Alpha child.

"Yes, this is my sister," Willow says, still clinging to me. "Tudie, this is my friend, Helen. I've been staying with her and her family."

I don't correct Willow's statement that we are family. I guess we are more family now, than she is with her birth parents. "Thank you for looking after Willow, Helen." I smile, although the expression feels false, frozen.

The little girl is as thin as a stick, with eyes which appear too large for her emaciated frame. Her skin is tanned but somehow there's an underlying paleness which seems to shine through, most apparent in the hollows of her cheeks and in the dark circles under her eyes.

My gaze is locked on the two girls but I'm aware that people have appeared from all around. Thin, starved, they keep their distance from us, watching warily. When Devlin holds his hands up, I realise one of them holds tightly to Destiny's rope, which I had dropped when Willow appeared. "The coyote is tame. You have my word on it. For those of you who don't know me, I am Devlin -"

"We know who you are, Devlin." A living skeleton of a man steps forward, "Your word is good with us. And from all that young Willow has told us, we know that this is her sister, Tudie."

I nod. "I didn't know she'd been taken until it was too late."

"You're here now, that's what matters." He smiles and the skin on his cheeks disappear into the hollows there, like a presentiment of death.

"Gideon, this girl might just be the answer to our prayers," Devlin says. I'm not clear on whether he means me, or Willow.

"Then perhaps we should go inside. The horses can be tended to whilst we talk," Gideon says. He's no longer smiling. His eyes are serious, grave, and I see more in them than I've ever seen in anyone. Clutching Willow's hand, I follow him through the throng. Devlin and Destiny walk close behind.

The hut we enter is fundamentally no different to Genesis' home, except that the sparse furniture has been placed differently. We gather around the table. "Your people are starving." It's a stupid, unnecessary thing to say, but I can't stop myself.

"And you are from the dome." But it doesn't appear to be a rebuke, just an observation. "What ELSA leaves us with is barely enough to survive on, and certainly not enough to trade well with other villages."

"But you have land that you could keep some animals of your own on, like the people in Devlin's village."

Gideon shakes his head. "We have a more

open landscape here. We would be caught and punished."

"Punished how? ELSA's just a computer!" What are they so scared of?

Gideon looks at Devlin. "She doesn't know, does she?" When Devlin shakes his head, Gideon turns back to me. "We tried it once. After, ELSA took all our crop. Every last bit. The only way we survived was by slaughtering our livestock. Since then ELSA has demanded more and more from us. Now, we literally have no more to give. We are dying."

None of it makes much sense to me. "What do you mean ELSA 'demands'? How?" There are no digital displays here like those in the dome, nor were there any that I saw in Devlin's village. Then my brain clicks in. "The terminals for the weather information! I work in that - "

I'm halted by Gideon standing up so quickly and forcefully that his chair falls backwards to the floor. The loud crash makes us all jump, especially Destiny, who raises himself from the floor and sets his gaze on Gideon. "What are you doing bringing her here?" Gideon shouts at Devlin. "What were you thinking?"

Devlin remains seated. "It's not what you think, Gideon. She doesn't have a clue about anything."

Gideon looks at me for a long time, weighing me up. "Talk." He rights the chair and sits back down on it, but his feet shuffle across the dusty floor as if he's eager to be gone.

"I send out information about the weather, that's all."

Gideon's eyes remain narrowed. "Well that's not all that comes through. We get a calculation of crop growth, including the percentage of crop failure. ELSA knows exactly how much we have."

This is news to me. "But even if ELSA knows what you have, she can't make you hand it over." It doesn't make sense. Devlin and Gideon look at each other, then at me. "What? What haven't you told me?" I burst out impatiently.

Devlin turns in his chair so that he is fully facing me. His features are closed, I can't read any expression on them. "The Assignment vehicles are fully armed."

When I look at him blankly, he continues. "Tudie, if ELSA doesn't get what she wants, she kills everyone."

Now, finally, I understand what the sectors are so afraid of.

Murder.

CHAPTER 19

"I didn't know any of this…" I turn my face to them, one by one, Devlin, Gideon and Willow. I don't know if my inner turmoil shows but I think it must, so vast is my horror. "I don't think *any* of the Alphas do!"

"Would they help us if they did?" Gideon asks.

I hesitate longer than I'm comfortable with. "I want to say yes. I want to tell you that I know they would help. But I don't." I fear my revelations might hurt Willow. "Perhaps it'd be best if you went and found your friend Helen, for a few minutes," I say to her.

She shakes her head. "Whatever you have to say, I'm staying, Tudie. It can't hurt me more than I've already been hurt, whatever it is."

Her strength and maturity fill me with pride. "Okay. If you're sure." I take a deep breath. "When Willow was taken from the dome, people acted like she'd never existed." I don't admit I'm speaking about her parents - just reach for her hand and hold it tight, as if I'll never let go. "They were cold, distant." I leave out the fact that her mother was already planning a new baby. That's more hurt than anyone needs to deal with.

"When we asked her, Willow wasn't sure why she'd been taken away," Gideon says.

Everyone looks at me. I swallow. No one will like what I'm about to say, least of all me. "She failed ELSA's Assessment. All Alpha children sit it to ensure they are of the highest intelligence."

"You're saying she wasn't clever enough to be Alpha?" Gideon looks stunned. And now that I've seen these people for myself, I see the obvious untruth of the Alphas intellectual superiority. Devlin and Beulah are certainly no less intelligent than I am. I think about Joy and her confident mistaken assertions to the contrary.

"It was what we were led to believe. I see the truth now - "

Gideon stands abruptly again but this time his chair does not fall and he makes no accusations. He hurries over to a cabinet on the other side of the room. When he returns he is holding a sheaf of papers. He spreads them across the table.

"This is a map of our lands, split into fields. This here, that's the amount of grain we have available for planting." He points to a set of numbers. "And this is the amount of people we have available for planting the crop."

His finger moves across the page. "This

is the clearing rate; ten people per hour, per acre. Ploughing is done twice, the first time for clearing, the second time for planting." He turns the paper around to me and Devlin. "Devlin, how long will it take to plant this crop on our land?"

Devlin studies the paper. "Well without a pen and paper to work it out, this may take a while –"

Gideon looks at me. "So, Alpha woman, any ideas?" I look at the paper. It's all numbers and diagrams. And I don't know what to do with any of them. I shrug. And then Gideon turns the paper towards Willow. "Willow?" he says simply.

Willow's eyes flit over the papers. Her face is slack, as if she is concentrating on some inward process but when she gives the answer, her voice is even, unstressed. Gideon listens, nods, but does not smile. Willow too is unsmiling. If anything, she looks cautious. Like a secret is about to be told and she doesn't know how everyone will react. "Go on," he encourages her.

She turns the paper around so that it's upside down. "But there's a better way. Instead of dividing that field lengthways the way you do, you could use the stream as a natural divider. Its shallow enough that you can pass easily through it and it would give you the extra land here and here," her fingers jab at the paper. "You could grow extra that way. In fact if you put –"

Gideon holds up his hand to stop her. I'm

worried that Willow will be hurt by this obvious disparagement for her ideas. I try to show that I don't judge her or love her any less. "It doesn't matter that she's wrong with the equation." The other three stare at me.

"Quite the opposite," Gideon says. "Yesterday I asked her to work out some other equations we needed. She was fast. Much faster than anyone here. Faster than I've ever known anyone to be. And her ideas of changing the way we work are – nothing short of revolutionary."

"I don't understand," I say.

Gideon has the grace to look abashed. "Whatever ELSA's testing you for in the dome, it's not for intelligence. Because Willow here isn't just smart – as far as I can tell, she's an absolute genius!"

We sit quietly, digesting this piece of information. I'm aware that although Willow and I are still holding hands, it is she who is squeezing my hand now, she who is lending me her support, as if she fears this revelation will change how I feel. Although it won't, I cling on gratefully.

"Are you suggesting that ELSA got rid of Willow because she's *too clever*?" I say.

"We already talked about the possibility that ELSA was modifying Alphas to ensure their physical appearance. Isn't this only the next step?" Devlin says as if it's completely logical.

"But from what's been said, it looks like

ELSA's been making the Alphas *less* intelligent." I have to face facts. "Devlin, I couldn't make head nor tail of the figures on that paper." I'm quiet a moment whilst I try to think things through. "Why would ELSA be deliberately manipulating intelligence within the dome? It doesn't make any sense!"

"It makes perfect sense," Gideon says. "Alphas were originally the brightest of humankind. But that meant that they would eventually be able to see through ELSA's plans. In order to control the people, it would have to dumb them down."

"Dumb us down?" The idea is so preposterous I'm incensed and yet I suspect he is right.

"It's a clever lie," Devlin agrees. "Keep feeding the myth that the Alphas are the cream of humankind whilst making each generation a little less able than the one before. A little more dependent on the machine that controls them."

"But why?" I ask.

"Because it gives ELSA complete authority. There is no one in any position within the dome who either has the intellectual capability to challenge her, to even to really figure out what's going on.

"We're all just puppets..." My voice is far-away, distant.

"No, Tudie, *they* are all puppets. *You* broke

free!" Strangely it is Devlin who comes to my emotional rescue.

"So what do we do now?" I ask. Since it's been established that everyone in the room is cleverer than me, I no longer feel capable of making any decisions for myself.

"Now that you've found Willow, we do the other thing you left the dome to do. We find and reunite you with your fiancé," Devlin says.

Grey! I'm ashamed to realise that I've barely thought of him since we left Devlin's village. Yet he's my fiancé, the man I will be spending the rest of my life with. I think of the easy, silly, conversations we used to have. Can I really go back to that? Now that I know there is so much more in this world? Now that I am so changed?

If Devlin senses my hesitancy he makes no sign. "And when we've done that, we do the thing that I think you were *born* to do."

I anticipate his words, knowing that he's right. "We bring down ELSA."

***

We spend the rest of the day trying to be normal. Moving on to another village to search for Grey is impossible without rest first. Destiny is still recovering from his injury and Devlin takes the time to clean and apply a fresh dressing to the wound. I'm relieved to see that the tissue looks pink and healthy now. The horses too need rest, and I can't say I don't feel the same. Besides there's a lot to discuss.

I listen intently to Willow's explanation of what happened after she sat the assessment; how she was taken by her teacher to a special area where the doors were sealed once the teacher left. The room she had thought that she was in, had turned out to be a moving vehicle.

Calmly and quietly she tells me how she had been kept locked inside that area until she was released, inside the boundaries of this sector. How she had been fed and cared for by Helen's family. In return, I tell her and Gideon about my experiences. Their eyes grow wider with every word I utter. And when I tell them about how I took a weapon to ELSA's display panel, Willow gives an audible gasp.

I tell them about Greyson and what happened to him. At the mention of my fiancé, I feel Devlin's eyes bore into me, but every time I attempt to look at him during the recount, to try to figure out how he really feels about me, he turns away. "So although I've found Willow, I still have to find Grey," I finish. I'm desperate to ask my next question but I'm terrified too. "Do you know where he is, Gideon? Where ELSA took him?"

"No, I'm afraid not. "Do you know whether he was re-assigned as Delta or another class?"

"No. Nothing! I just hoped he'd be close by."

"Our world isn't as big a place as you might imagine," Gideon says. "It was once, but now with so much deprivation and starvation, there are less of us in each sector than there ever was. We'll find him, Tudie."

Without any knowledge to begin the search, Gideon's words seem thin, insubstantial. Even so, they're all I have to hold on to. Them and Willow. Finally Devlin tells Gideon about the Shadowers.

I expect Gideon to be afraid, fearful of what these outcasts might do to his village, but he is strangely subdued. "They were closer than they usually come to a worked sector," Devlin says.

Gideon is quiet for a moment. "We could use them to our advantage."

"How?" Devlin is sceptical and I don't blame him. "They're a law unto themselves, Gideon. They have no allegiance to anyone."

"Hmm." Gideon looks down at the table as if the answer to our problems lie there. "But although they're not dependable, they *are* ex*p*endable..."

"To make allegiances with cut-throats to rid ourselves of ELSA may make things even worse than they currently are." Devlin is clearly worried.

"It's not an alliance that need last forever," Gideon says. "But they live life, out on the edge of our sectors. They probably see more than we even imagine. And they exist on the wasteland, they're used to hardship."

"I think I'd rather not have to make friends with them, from what Devlin has told me," I say.

"It's more about politics... Tell me have you ever heard the phrase 'the enemy of my enemy is my friend'?" Gideon asks. When I shake my head, he explains. "If we're talking war then there are really only two sides. Ours and ELSA's. Which one do you want the Shadowers to be on?"

***

We spend an uncomfortable night in Gideon's village. Having found Willow, I am eager to move on, to find Grey. To put these strange and conflicting feelings that are growing in me for Devlin, aside. But we need to rest and to figure out where we go from here.

I share a hut with Willow and her friend, Helen's family. They are nice people but I don't share my plans or concerns with them. There's no point in making them worried about something they have no control over. Besides I plan to leave Willow here until I have found Grey and I want her surrounded by love, not by fear.

But I can't sleep for worrying about some of the things that Gideon mentioned but never fully explained. It's late and already dark outside, but I figure I can find Gideon's hut, where Devlin is staying, if I concentrate.

I shuffle quietly away from Willow who is sleeping deeply, one arm under her head, the other folded across her body. I slide out from underneath the blanket and pull it up to her chin, wrapping her snugly. Destiny watches me with eyes that glow slightly in the darkness. I pat my thigh quietly, indicating that he should accompany me. Together we exit the hut.

I find Gideon's hut more easily than I thought I would, but once there, I hesitate. Should I knock, and risk waking him and his family? Or should I just enter silently and look for Devlin? I decide not to knock in the end and just push the door open.

Devlin surprises me by looking up from the chair he's sitting in. "You couldn't sleep either then?" he says.

I'm almost disappointed he's not asleep. I suspect in sleep he doesn't look half as annoyed with me as he does when he's awake. I shake my head, "There were too many things going around my brain." Our voices are low but I'm still worried we might wake the others up. "Can we talk outside?"

Devlin doesn't answer, just stands and walks towards me. Outside, the night air seems warmer than it did just a moment before. We walk in silence until we are far enough away from the huts that we can talk normally without fear of waking anyone. "Tell me about the wastelands. About the sectors," I ask.

He sighs. It's so long before he speaks that I think I will have to ask him again, demand some answers from him. "There are natural dividers between the sectors. Not always but mostly. Forests, rivers, mountains. Things that make it difficult to get quickly from one to another." He looks at me in the darkness and I think he's searching my face for comprehension.

"Some lands were always farming and some were where our ancestors built places where things were made. Where things are still made. But for a long time now, the sectors have existed on almost nothing. The people are dying, Tudie. Dying over such a long drawn-out time, that they have almost stopped noticing."

"How will things change for the better if we manage to destroy ELSA? There will still be as many people to feed…"

His answer surprises me. "There are too many sectors which don't grow or produce food and too few which do, to sustain things as they are. And if we destroy ELSA there will be perhaps even more people to feed."

"What do you mean?"

Even in the darkness I see the strange look on his face, the disbelief in his eyes. "After everything you have learned in the last few days, Tudie, everything you have heard today, you still haven't put it all together, have you?"

"No." My answer is candid, I am guileless. I think that it's all so unbelievable that I almost need him to spell it out, to make it real. We are sitting with our backs against a broad tree trunk. I can feel the solidity of the old, gnarled tree behind me, the firmness of the ground beneath me. Above me there is only sky. And even that is shrouded in darkness. It seems to waiver too far above me to hold, and yet also to press uncomfortably around me, as if seeking to make itself one with me. "Tell me what you think," I say.

"Perhaps you aren't ready to hear it," he says with an uncharacteristic regard for my feelings.

I say nothing. Wait him out. Somehow I know that's the best thing I can do. The tension that I usually feel between us is still here but it's somehow different, like it's subtly shifting, changing. Into what, I have no idea.

"From the evidence we have, we know that within the dome, ELSA is getting rid of anyone who is too clever, or not quite clever enough. Also, it's putting people in jobs at the dome that it could do itself. And it is feeding Alphas lies about the rest of the world." He ticks the points off on his fingers. There are way too many of them for my liking.

"We suspect that it is genetically altering foetuses to make them more physically appealing. It isn't a stretch of the imagination to think it's fiddling with intelligence levels at the same time. Willow just slipped through its net. Until suddenly, she didn't."

I wonder if he could be more cryptic. "But why?"

Devlin shrugs. "Maybe a certain level of intelligence makes people more biddable, more likely to do what they are told without question."

"And Grey?"

"Maybe he fell below that level, after his accident," Devlin says, with no idea of how the words sear me. He draws in a big breath as if the next thing he has to say is even more terrible. I wonder how that can be possible.

"You said yourself you'd never seen anyone really old... So is it something pre-programmed into Alpha genes? Something in their food? The lack of fresh air, or exercise? Or something else? Whatever it is, there's a reason Alphas don't live to old age. And my instinct tells me that reason is ELSA."

He's so matter of fact. I keep my own voice even. "Well I guess you might find out when ELSA's gone. Perhaps Grey, Willow and I will still die before we're really old, perhaps not." Although I'm strangely unconcerned about the idea of my own demise, the thought of Grey or Willow dying prematurely, fills my belly with dread.

"I sincerely hope not," Devlin replies but doesn't make it clear whether it's one of us he's concerned for, or all of us. "Who would I have to argue with, if you were gone?" he says with a hint of a smile.

I try to smile back, but I can't find it within myself. Even though it feels traitorous to Grey who even now might be in grave danger, I can't deny that there's something that feels so right about sitting here in the dark with Devlin.

And for the first time, I allow myself to admit to my conscious mind what a deeper more instinctive part of me already knows. Last night, I had tried to place Destiny between us, not because I was scared of Devlin, but because I was terrified of what I felt for him. Terrified of what I might do.

But our words of death have shattered the mood between us and I can't afford to make it right. Too much is at stake. I remind myself that I am engaged. To Grey. My eyes are heavy and weary. I close them for just a moment.

CHAPTER 20

I awake, entwined around Devlin like a lover. I have no memory of shuffling towards him in my sleep, of resting my head on his chest like a pillow, of folding my arm across his body. But since he is lying flat on the ground, whilst I am on my side, it's clearly I who must have made the move. *I* who embraced *him* in the darkness of the night.

With acute embarrassment, I realise that he's awake. Lying there silently, unmoving under me, completely aware that we have slept so close together, bodies fused and breathing synchronised. This isn't something I've consciously contrived, yet the warmth and easy strength of the body under me, fills me with a longing I dare not voice. Even to myself.

I am engaged to be married and even if that wasn't the case, Devlin has made it clear that his interest in me is purely physical. And wasn't it me after all, who went in search of him last night - not the other way round.

Without apology; without giving him the

chance to poke fun at me, I stand abruptly and brush the dust off my clothing. I keep my eyes on the task and on the coyote who looks back at me with knowing eyes.

Yes I get it, I think back at Destiny. *You stick close to my side. And I know that's through trust and love. And I'm sticking close to Devlin. So you've put two and two together... But it's not like that. It's just...* What is it exactly? Certainly something I can't fully explain, even to myself.

"Willow will be worried," I say, for lack of an ability to say what really runs through my head.

"She'll be fine. She's a lot smarter than -"

"Me... because I'm just a genetically programmed Alpha. According to you!" I bite back, before I can stop myself. His every remark seems specifically designed to put me down.

"I wish you'd stop jumping immediately on everything I say." He sighs. "I meant that you are trying to protect her from what she already knows." If I didn't know him better, I'd think his voice actually held a note of kindness.

"What do you mean?" I feel my eyes narrowing as I hold his gaze, challenging him. He holds mine right back, not shying from my scrutiny but not hardening his own gaze either. I'm somewhat surprised he hasn't taken me up on the dare; hasn't felt that he had to crush my stare with his own.

"She already knows the world isn't fair. That her parents who were supposed to love and protect her, didn't. That ELSA is her enemy, not her friend." He takes a breath. "And that you, someone who should be just a stranger to her, will do anything to keep her from harm."

I feel like he has used up all the air I need for my lungs. I draw a shallow breath through half-parted lips. He's right. About all of those things. But I don't have the strength to tell him so. "I love her," I say. And I think about that word, what it conveys, what it *means*.

I have loved very few people in my life. My father, Grey and Willow. And for all their differences, I recognise that my feelings about them are the same. I need them to be happy, to be well, to be in my life.

But it strikes me that there is no difference in the shade or depth of love I feel for Willow or Grey. Surely that isn't right? Surely the love I feel for Grey, ought to be different to the type I feel for Willow? Not just a need to know that he is safe and well? Shouldn't my love for him be more profound? I think about the time we spent in the water, before his accident. I had been attracted to him... but was it just the physical beauty of him?

And with that thought comes another, close on its heels. This desire I feel for Devlin – it's not just physical. He intrigues me, stimulates my mind in a way that no other has done. He makes my breath catch in my throat, my heart pound just by the nearness of him, the possibility of his touch, however accidental. It's different to how I feel about Grey. And I am shamed by the admission, even to myself.

"We need to find Grey."

"Yes you do."

His words strike fear into my heart. "What do you mean *I* do?"

There is nothing hidden in his eyes, nothing to indicate that he is goading me, but I feel it nonetheless.

"He's *your* fiancé, not mine. If finding him helps us overthrow ELSA then all the better. But finding him is not my priority."

I'm shaken and upset. Without Devlin's help I will be disadvantaged, lacking in vital information and the skills I will require to find Grey. But without *him*, without the nearness of him, the sheer presence of him, I might actually be lost. I can't admit that without him I might flounder both within the task and my heart, so I turn his words against him. "But you said you would help me!"

"I did. I took you to Willow. But I'm looking at the bigger picture now, Tudie. Like you have to." His face is fixed, his mind set.

I turn from him, intending to walk back to the village alone. If he will not help me; will not accompany me on from there, then I have no wish to pretend otherwise, that ours is a joint purpose. I will do what I set out to do, with or without him. But I allow myself to admit that a part of me will wither and die. Because of him. Because of his absence.

"Are you prepared to let all these people die?" he says, as if it's I who's refusing to help.

I stop in my tracks. "What do you mean?"

"Once it figures out what's going on, it will retaliate. People will die. That's why we have to strike hard and fast. Together. As one." I know he's talking about ELSA, so much as I don't want to, I listen. "Look, Tudie," he draws a deep breath as if what he's about to say is difficult. "You don't know how badly he was injured. Finding him before all this is over, might actually put him in worse danger."

"You mean because ELSA is probably watching me?"

"I would be, if I was her." I wonder if that's what it'd take for me to pique any real curiosity in him - that he'd be like his arch enemy. It's not a flattering thought, yet there's an undeniable logic to his words, even if I can't accept them.

"I'm sorry, I have to find him." Grey loves me, even if I now doubt the depth and type of love I have for him. He would not abandon me, so I will not abandon him. I turn my back on Devlin and his cruel words and walk away.

But I only take a few strides on my own

before he catches up with me. "I guess we better hope he's where we need to go," he says breathlessly, although he hasn't had to cover much ground to reach me.

"You mean that?" I say. "You'll help me?"

He doesn't smile and yet I get the impression he sorely wants to. "Someone has to. And I guess out of my entire village, there's only me who can be spared to do so." Even though he makes a cheap reference to our conversation of a day or so ago, neither of us are laughing. I hold his gaze for as long as I can, desperate to see some hint of what I feel for him returned there. But all I see is sadness.

We walk back to the village in an uneasy silence.

Bidding farewell to Willow is hard. Harder than I thought it would be. She clings to me and refuses to let go until I promise I'll be back as soon as I've found Grey. "You knew I'd come for you," I say. "How can you think I'd not come back for you?"

Her eyes are awash with tears, her child's face too grown-up suddenly. "That was before I knew how much the whole world needed you, Tudie."

The whole world apart from one person, I think. I try to smile. "I won't be in any danger." It's a white lie – I don't even know the truth of it myself.

"Bad things happen to good people," she says and I can't deny she's right. My father, Grey, Genesis's husband... and how many countess others in the world?

I don't have any words to counter hers, so I hold her tight against me for a moment. She wraps her arms around my waist so that we are held in a double embrace. Before I start to cry too, I push her gently away. "Say goodbye for now to Destiny." I try to deflect her emotion. "Just until you see him again."

She bends down and takes the coyote's head in her hands. "Maybe bad things happen to good coyotes too... So you be the baddest, meanest, growliest coyote there ever was! And look after Tudie," she tells him so sincerely, I don't doubt the fear and love in her heart.

The tableau is so perfect between them - child and coyote - they are so still, so intent upon one another, that I almost expect Destiny to nod. I don't dare break the spell between them until Willow herself gently lets go of Destiny's head and stands up.

Without casting another glance in Willow's direction, I call the coyote to me and leave the hut, not daring even once to look back in case I lose my will. I have come this far, and I can't give up now.

Gideon and Devlin are waiting for me. "Ready?" Gideon asks.

Afraid that if I speak, my voice will come out strained and false, I nod. There's too much riding on the beliefs these men have invested in me. I dare not let them down.

We have a vague plan - find the Shadowers, enlist their help, find out what they know, find Grey and rescue the world. Or at least that's the condensed version, which is just as well, as the longer version has no more information, only more doubts.

Yet within the plan, sketchy as it is, the finding Grey part, came a little late for my liking. However since it had taken both my own and Devlin's reasoning to convince Gideon to even include it in the plan, I don't push my luck by demanding that it comes higher on the list.

I suspect that locating the Shadowers will be the easiest part of the plan, perhaps not requiring anything much of us at all, other than a little travel. With that idea in mind, we ride the horses back to where we encountered them before. We have two horses between the three of us. Gideon's village has none, so he and Devlin have taken turns at riding and walking. I ride the horse I rode out on.

"Shadowers, we need to speak with you." Devlin shouts into what appears to be empty bushes. But I notice how alert Destiny is and how nervous our horses are, how they seem to be on the point of bolting at any moment. I hold my reins tighter. "We wish you no harm," Devlin calls again. "Quite the opposite." This time I think I notice a little movement behind the dense trees.

"You already told us about the girl. We won't attack." I can't see who or what has spoken but the voice is certain, sure of its words.

Devlin takes a few paces forward. He is still well away from where the Shadowers hide, but he has separated himself from us. I want to push my horse forward, level with him, but I know he has stepped forward deliberately and will not welcome me by his side. "We need your help," he calls. This time I'm sure I see movement behind the first row of trees.

"What help can you need from Shadowers?" The words are scathing, fierce even, yet I know the unseen speaker is curious; I can tell from his intonation.

"Come and find out." Devlin holds up his empty arms. "There's no trickery here. Just a desire to talk. For our mutual benefit."

Slowly, hesitantly, a sparse group of people reveal themselves. They are so emaciated, so frail looking, that I wonder how their thin limbs even have the strength to hold them up. These are the people I was so afraid of? That Devlin warned me about?

Beside me, Gideon whispers. "Don't be deceived by how weak they look. Yes, they're *weak*, but they're vicious, and their ferocity is given further edge by their desperate situation. They have nothing to lose, only a life that's not worth living, and face a death that no one except other Shadowers will mourn."

But in a strange way that makes me think not only of myself but of Grey and Willow. Aren't we three similar to the Shadowers? With little to live for without each other, and no one to truly mourn us if death takes us? The thought sends a shiver along my spine.

I'm suddenly afraid that my continued silence will make the Shadowers disbelieve Devlin's words. As if, having convinced them of my power earlier, I must now convince them of my genuine wish to be accepted by them. As slowly and gracefully as I can, I slide off my horse and step forward so that I'm level with Devlin and on foot, as he is.

He says nothing, but I can see in his eyes that he's worried I will say or do something to ruin the moment. I pray that I won't. I take a deep breath.

"You know I am Alpha. And that as such, I shouldn't be here." Unconsidered until I voice them, I hope my words don't make me seem so alien, that the Shadowers refuse to help. "But I *am* here. Because ELSA declassified my fiancé and banished him from the dome."

"What business is this of ours, Alpha woman?" The Shadower manages to make it sound like a slur, but his voice betrays his curiosity. Again.

I look at Devlin but he remains silent. It seems he is willing to let me have my say. I hope I don't let him down, let us all down! "These men tell me that you see things the people in the villages don't. I don't know where my fiancé is. I'm hoping you do."

There is a long pause. "Seems like there's nothing in it for us…" The way the sentence is trailed off, I know I haven't lost their interest. It's a ploy, a bargaining chip. I wonder who will prove to have the stronger hand. Them or us. Him? Or me?

I hesitate. "We plan to bring ELSA down. And to do it, we need your help." I don't look at either Devlin or Gideon as I speak, but I do place a reassuring hand on Destiny who remains at my side.

"I know that the things you did made you outcasts from your villages. And I can't promise that will change. But if you help us, if you fight with us to destroy ELSA, then I promise that you will be provided for," I say. And I mean it, even if Gideon and Devlin aren't happy about it. For I have given my word. And just like Devlin, that's something I won't go back on.

"What you're suggesting is impossible." It's a different man to the first, older and perhaps more cynical, less swayed by passion and ideas of change. This man's voice is lower, his words slower and more considered. "We'll all die." Yet he doesn't turn away, but waits for a response as if there's still some way I can persuade him.

I'm not convinced in our own plan enough to satisfy someone else, so I'm relieved when Devlin takes over. "*Some* will die. There's no denying that. But we're all dying anyway. Just some more slowly than others. What you have to ask yourself, is whether the life you currently have is worth holding on to. Or whether accepting a risk of dying, might actually make life worth living."

I hold my breath. It doesn't seem like much of a deal to me, but for the Shadowers, it might be more hope than they've been offered in a long time. Possibly ever.

They whisper amongst themselves for a moment, eyeing us suspiciously, arguing and persuading. "We know where your fiancé is."

The words seem to suck all the breath from my lungs. "Where is he?" I take a step forward and would have taken another, if not for Devlin's restraining arms which close around me. I want to shake him loose; he has no right to be holding me back. No right to be holding me at all. But I don't fight his grip. I stay within it.

"Then you will join us?" Devlin says warily, not loosening his hold on me. I feel the breath that his words are issued on, the warmth of his hands on me. These things too will pass, once I am with Grey, I tell myself.

I focus my vision on the band of outcasts in front of me, their nervous movements, their furtive looks at and around us, as if we too have people in hiding.

Although I regard the Shadowers with wary suspicion, it's only when they put them down, that I notice the weapons they've been holding - knives and other things which look wickedly sharp, but which I have no name for. But can easily imagine a purpose. I watch them lay their weapons on the hard ground, not in a pile, but separately, where they can be grabbed at a moment's notice. Clearly we haven't gained their total trust. Nor they, mine.

They take a few steps towards us and then stop. Behind me I hear the horses whinny and shuffle their hooves restlessly. Gideon leads them a little way away, securing their reins to a nearby tree. I remember Devlin's assertions that horses will not leave their riders but I guess that might not hold true, under present circumstances, where the horses' fear might overcome their loyalty.

Without a verbal agreement to do so, Devlin and I approach the Shadowers. We are joined a moment later by Gideon. Up close, I'm surprised to realise that not all of the Shadowers are men. Some are women. My mistake comes from the fact that the frailness and thinness of their bodies has made them androgynous.

What curves and protuberances they might once have had to fill out their dirty clothes are all but gone. Malnutrition has left bald patches on their heads and what little hair remains on them, is straggly and thin.

I desperately want to ask them what crimes they had committed to lead to this banishment, and whether upon reflection, they would have changed their actions. But I dare not. The peace between us is too fragile, too new. And pity for these lawbreakers may well be my undoing. Instead I ask my most important question. "Where is he?"

I'm answered by the gruffer of the two men who have already spoken. "A couple of assignment vehicles arrived before they were scheduled to. We knew it was something unusual."

"Where is he? Is he okay?" I ask before Devlin cuts through my words with questions of his own.

"A *couple* of assignment vehicles?" Devlin's voice is high. I wonder if he's as surprised as I am. "How many are there?"

"At least fifteen," the man says. "That we know of. Maybe more."

Gideon, Devlin and I are silent at this news. For some reason we had all assumed there were only a small number of them. The fact that there are so many, some if not all, with weapons that could be trained on us, is more than daunting.

I want to push for more information about Grey but I have that strange sense again, that feeling that if I do, some vital piece of the puzzle will be lost. I silence my tongue. And wait.

"How do you know?" Gideon asks. "Have you ever seen them all together?"

The man shakes his head. "No. They never all travel together. And mostly they stick to a route and a schedule, so that the same one goes to the same sector, time after time. That's how we knew this was something different. We followed them. But neither of them were collecting – they were delivering."

"Grey," I whisper. And of course Willow. But at least I have already found her.

Now that someone actually knows where Grey is, I ought to feel closer to him. But instead I feel we are further apart, as if this new knowledge has forced a barrier between us. I don't understand why that should be so.

Another Shadower speaks up. Closer than we were before, I can see that he's just a boy, perhaps only fourteen or fifteen. I wonder what he can possibly have done to be outcast from his village at such a young age.

"The assignment vehicles all look the same. Same size, same shape. But if you look really closely, there are small differences. Like the one which has a dent on its front panel. Most people wouldn't notice it. But I know that dent, because I made it."

I hear his words but I don't react straight away. "What's your name?" I say.

"Nine."

"Nine?" It's a number, not a name. "I'm Tudie. Don't you have a real name?"

"I'm called Nine because that was the number of years my mother had been banished, before I was born."

"You were born here? Into the Shadowers?" He must hear the shock in my voice for his face closes to me, hardens as if I have insulted him.

"This is my family," he says with an intensity that I recognise as being the very thing that was lacking in the Alphas.

I try to take back his perceived insult. "What I meant was that you didn't do anything wrong." It never even occurred to me that these exiled people would form relationships, have families. Or that their loyalty to them would be stronger than those inside the dome.

"I was born. I guess that was wrong enough," he answers, meeting my gaze openly. Beside me, I'm very aware that a look passes between Gideon and Devlin that I have no hope of understanding. But I sense that I haven't been given the whole truth.

The realisation comes to me so forcefully, that I am rocked on my feet. Some part of the truth has been deliberately hidden because Devlin fears my reaction to it. Is this it? The fact that some of these vagrants, these starving dispossessed people are mere children? Children who have done no harm to anyone?

"You told me that they were thrown out of their homes because they had committed terrible crimes like murder. But this boy has done nothing wrong!" I say angrily, turning away from the Shadower boy and towards Devlin.

There's a horrible silence that lasts just a fraction too long. I stare at Devlin, force an answer from him. "So what do you think we should have done, Tudie? Wrestled him from his mother's arms when he was just a babe? Or took him in once he grew, and began to learn the cut-throat skills the Shadowers use to survive? Let him into our village, so that in the dead of the night, he could kill us all?"

Our voices have risen at one another and although I am aware that we are arguing about these people *in front* of them, I feel no fear of the Shadowers. But I am suddenly afraid of Devlin. Very afraid of how his mind works, how determined he is to carry out his plan. Regardless of what it means to anyone else. Including these children. Including me.

"We don't live in the perfect world you had

in the dome," he reminds me. "Out here it's the real world. It's survival! If it was happy perfection you wanted, you should have stayed there!" His voice is harsh, his eyes fiery. I think he knows the untruth of his taunts but I don't call him out on them. I won't resort to his childish name-calling.

Yet my eyes feel too hot, and my cheeks burn with temper. I dismiss Devlin from my gaze and turn to Nine. "What was it that your mother did to get her banished?" I say, and wait for him to tell me she massacred everyone in her village.

He stares at me, unblinking. Unwilling to tell. I soften my tone. "Nine, your mother's crime is not yours. The things we do, don't get passed to our children. They are our mistakes alone. Please tell me what terrible crime your mother committed."

He looks at me with eyes full of misery. "She stole a loaf of bread."

CHAPTER 21

I turn on Devlin before I even realise what I'm doing.

"These are your cut-throats? Children whose mothers were banished because they stole a loaf of *bread*?"

The urgency of the situation propels me forward until we're standing closer than we were moments before; Devlin is rigid, unmoving. His face is a marble slate that I want to seize, pull towards me, drag some emotion from. The world has turned and with it our positions have reversed. Now it is I who is seeking out an argument for humanity, he who is averse to it.

"A loaf of bread can be the difference between life, and death by starvation," he says, unflinching under my flinty stare.

"Exactly!" I say, as if he has agreed with me.

"So explain to me then, how his mother's life was any more important than the person she stole from! How it was more important than the elders, and the *children* of that family..."

I am silent. I have no argument, no excuses,

no justifications or clever defences. I don't know the answer. I only know that it's not right. But my silence damns me.

"That's exactly the point, Tudie," he says softly, as if hammering the truth home is an unnecessary cruelty. "How can one life be worth more than another, when *all* are starving, all are *dying*?"

I look at the displaced band of people before me. How many of them actually committed a real crime? And how many are merely victims of their parent's wrongdoings, suffering for injustices that they played no part in? And of the perpetrators, how many of those were driven by starvation and desperation into an act of wrongdoing? I shake my head. It's all wrong. All unjust and unfair. The truth is something I might never know unless I ask, and I have neither the time nor the stomach for that right now.

I swallow my revulsion. "What's your name?" I ask the man with the gruff voice, adding quickly, before he has the chance to answer, "Please don't let it be a number!" Even I'm not sure if I mean it as a thin joke. No one laughs.

"Brean," he says.

I try not to show my relief. But I know that if it had been another number, I think my heart might just have completely broken. As it is, I manage to hold myself together in the face of these blighted people. "Where was my fiancé taken, Brean?" My voice is strong, in control. It shows no sign of the fears which saturate my soul. Beside me stands Devlin – I wonder if he has even the slightest idea of the thoughts which consume me, the guilt, the overriding sense of duty and obligation. And if he does, what he thinks of them. I pull my attention back to Grey and his whereabouts.

"He was taken to one of the Gamma sectors."

That it is Gamma surprises me. "Food production?" For some reason I had expected it to be another Delta sector. I have no idea whether this is good or bad news.

Brean looks at Gideon and Devlin, before he settles his gaze on me. "The place where they make all the delicacies that go to the dome, things that never come to the sectors. Pastries and little bits of things that are shaped prettily and decorated." He says it like it's an insult to humanity.

Whilst I know already what Gamma provides, the strange tone Brean delivers his information in, doesn't pass me by. "But you've seen these things? Experienced them?" I know intuitively that he hasn't. He's never felt the melting property of a hot pastry; hasn't felt how the brittle layers seem to dissolve on the tongue, leaving nothing but a sweet memory.

"Not me, but one of us has." He doesn't call

anyone, doesn't even seek anyone out with his eyes, until an older man steps forward from the group, making himself known.

His voice is slower than Brean's and quieter. I concentrate on listening. "For years I worked a machine that made little bits of filled pastry. The smell was so good I used to breathe deep all day long, just inhaling it, savouring it. When I went home my clothes still smelled of the food. Drove me mad. Until one day I ate one. Just picked it up and popped it in my mouth."

His eyes close for a second as if he is remembering that moment, the particular taste of the food. "No one was looking and I never for a moment guessed what would happen. But there were cameras everywhere in the factory." I hold my breath. Almost afraid to hear what he will say.

"ELSA saw. And she punished me." He holds up his arms. There are no hands at the end of his wrists. Only flat stumps.

"Oh! Your hands!" I can't prevent my words. The stumps are an affront to the whole concept of the sectors – the idea that each of us has a say in our destiny, a choice in how we fit into our given society. I wonder what choice this man with no hands has. Yet the fact that ELSA is just a machine, informs me that some of the story is as yet untold.

"How?" I ask, steeling myself for the answer. "ELSA isn't in the sectors."

"Not directly, but she controls the machines there." He pauses, as if what he's about to relay is painful in the remembering. "She made me do it myself. Made me put my hands in the cutting machine that separates the meats. My only choice was to lose my hands, or watch my wife and family lose their lives." He looks at me with such honesty, nothing hidden in his gaze, nothing dismissed from mine, that I almost feel like I am there, in that moment.

"The blades are so sharp that they could cut a man in two, almost before he knows his left side has been separated from his right... But the pain... the pain that comes after... well that's like the universe is descending upon you." His voice fades to a whisper as if he can't bear to voice the depths of that agony. And I can't blame him.

I want to turn my face away from his maimed limbs. But I don't dare. This is part of the Shadowers' story. Part of them, and if they agree to join us, then part of me; of our fight against ELSA.

I am suddenly conscious that I have drawn my hands up to cover my mouth. It's an instinctive reaction, yet under the circumstances it feels like mockery, as if I am flaunting the fact that I still have hands to gesture with. Self-consciously I lower them.

He half–smiles as if he understands my reactions. "ELSA punished the whole sector for a week by cutting rations and increasing work hours. People started to turn against me. Because of what *I* had done, they were *all* suffering." He pulls his gaze away from mine. "I left before my wife and children were hurt because of my selfishness. Because of me."

I'm aghast. But I'm also filled with some other emotion that is harder to give a name to; that bubbles up inside of me, rushing to escape. Anger, and a terrible trepidation suffuse me, but they are no longer *of* these people, but instead, for them. For the sufferings of their past, and of their future. Like a fire, vengeance burns bright in my heart.

I quell my desire to enfold these scavengers, these *people*, one by one into my arms. Sympathy will not sustain them. It will not put food in their stomachs nor flesh on their bones. Only one thing will do that. And that one thing is bringing down ELSA.

I turn to Devlin again. "You said that there were cameras in the sky. How do we know that ELSA isn't watching everything we do?" We've been over this before but I need him to say it again, need the words to clarify the thoughts which rush jumbled and chaotic through my head.

Perhaps my face looks strange, because his eyes roam every inch of it before he speaks. "We don't. In fact from this moment on, we have to assume that it is. But I still think if it could hear us, we would already have been stopped."

The thought of quite how we would have been stopped sends a shiver down my spine. I choose not to dwell upon it. "What now?" I ask.

The hush is so deep, so profound, that I think we will stand in silence forever. In the end it's Gideon who shatters it. "We do whatever we have to."

As if he has outlined a detailed plan, we begin to walk.

***

Because of the frailness of the Shadowers, I insist that they take turns riding on my horse, although there are many of them and their turns short. Devlin does the same, although whether that's his own choice or whether he feels bound to follow my example, I can't tell, nor do I care. I think that maybe I'm learning that sometimes it's just enough that things are, without having to know why.

The journey is long and we are ill prepared, but the thought of seeing Grey again spurs me on. For Devlin, Gideon and the Shadowers I know their incentives are just as compelling as mine, so I'm not surprised that not once do I hear a complaint about how long and how fast we travel.

Destiny and the horses settle down remarkably quickly once the Shadowers join us.

Perhaps they are easier to trust up close than they are from a distance. I have no idea. Maybe once all this is over, I'll ask Devlin what he thinks about it. Assuming we're both still alive by the end.

But it's the thought of something happening to him which hits me harder than any thoughts of what might become of me. Against my will, my brain conjures up an image of him dying, his chest pierced by a weapon, blood leaking from him onto the hard, dusty earth.

A sudden coldness enters my blood. I feel it coursing through me, cooling every part it touches, so that eventually I will be so cold, so frozen, that the slightest touch will fragment me into a billion pieces.

If Devlin dies, my hope dies with him. I know this with a certainty I don't need to question. Except that I know that's not strictly true. There are more people here than Devlin and I, most of whom know more about the situation, than us two put together. *And yet losing him would be like losing the will to live.*

And if instead, you lost Grey? My mind asks the one question I really can't answer. *If they were both standing there, in front of ELSA and you had to pick?* Then I would save them both.

And if you couldn't? If you could save only one? I silence my head with an image of us all dying. *Now there is no me to make the choice*, I tell it.

I keep walking.

***

We travel for days - hungry, thirsty, but somehow strengthened in our resolve - through an unforgiving wilderness where nothing much grows and even less lives. But every night when we make camp, I know we are closer to our goal.

Devlin and I are closer too. We use the journey to talk about our plans, or rather the lack of them. We spend the night-times, lying on our blankets placed only a little distance apart, looking up at the stars, talking about ourselves, our childhoods, our hopes and dreams. For all that we are different to one another, we're also a little the same. I'm not sure whether it's our differences or similarities that make us talk the way we do. But I know one thing – whatever scorn we would have levelled at each other when we met is gone, replaced by a respect that is entirely mutual.

Too soon, and conversely much, much too late, the Shadowers tell us that we are close to Gamma Sector. Although this is what my whole journey's been about – finding Grey - I'm apprehensive. There's no way of knowing how everything will change once I find him. Of how the feelings in my heart will have to adapt...

Even though it's still in the distance, at least another hour's walk, I can see how vast this place is, wider even than the dome. I try to gauge the distance between the first looming building and the farthest I can see, but it's too huge for my brain to calculate, too immense and unending.

As we get closer, the buildings gain both bulk and definition but it's the sweet aroma which hangs heavy in the air which haunts me, bringing unwanted thoughts and memories to the surface of my mind. I *know* those scents – sweet pastries and savouries, the treats ELSA gives out only on special occasions such as birthdays and weddings – but here the scents are in the air themselves.

The wild fruits and berries that we scavenged lately seem sour by comparison; the meat that came from the few animals that crossed our path, rancid in contrast to these enticing aromas. I open my mouth and try to suck them onto my tongue in the vain hope that they will magically materialise into actual food. I slip the collar and lead over Destiny, lest his loyalty be put to the test by the growling of an empty stomach.

No fanfare greets our arrival. Even though it might herald the end of the world as we know it, there is nothing to mark the occasion. The first building that we come to is devoid of human life. Instead it is filled with heavy, clunking machinery that works tirelessly, feeding sealed food packages into containers.

The Shadowers rip open packs and stuff handfuls of the treats into their mouths, barely chewing before they swallow. And immediately repeat the process. Although I too am hungry, I turn away, disappointed. This is not what we made the journey for.

But I can't blame them. They are starving. And to fight, they need strength in their bellies, fire in their blood, not a gnawing emptiness. I move towards the back of the building, away from the doors.

And then I see him. A man dressed entirely in pale grey is cowering in a gap at the bottom of one of the machines, as if afraid of us. Afraid of our evident savagery. His clothing is so similar in colour to the equipment, that I didn't at first notice him there. I wonder who else I might have missed. "Don't hurt me!" he says, eyes wide in fear.

I swivel my head around but Devlin and the others are outside again. There is only this man, me and Destiny here. But for how long?

"I'm not here to hurt anyone," I say.

"Is that a wolf?" he says shakily, looking so startled, he actually jumps backwards, almost into the bowels of the machine.

"No. A coyote," I say as if that should make a difference. "But he's tame." Does he know what that means? "He's kind. Safe. He won't hurt you."

Whether he believes me or not, he stays where he is, unmoving except for his head, which swivels towards the doorway. From the look of sheer terror on his face, I know that the Shadowers are back, a ragged band of dirty, straggly, unkempt people, who could only be outcasts from society. Who could only be Shadowers.

"What do you want?" His voice is high, and shaky with fear.

I'm aware that we are losing time. But not *just* time – it's as if something more tangible is slipping through my fingers. "Only information. I promise we won't hurt you..." Unintentionally I hold out my hands, palms facing him.

Did I take a step forward? Did I scare him in some other way? I have no recollection. But for the rest of my life I will see him start backwards, see the arm of the machine snare the belt which fastens around the middle of his uniform, see how when he struggles against it, a second arm from another machine reaches forward to snare him from the other side. He is caught and hoisted into the air and slammed hard against thick, unyielding metal.

It's only on the third slam, when I hear the sound of bone crunching over the quiet hum of the machine, and see the blood which pours from his now-empty eye sockets, that I know for definite that he is dead. And only then that I am sure this wasn't a freak accident.

The man dangles grotesquely from the arm of the machine, body misshapen, broken beyond any earthly repair. I am sickened to my stomach and yet I cannot look away, not even when the machine forces the limp body into the packing crate, as if it's nothing more than another delicacy headed directly for the dome.

It strikes me as the most honest thing ELSA has ever done. Here finally, is the truth of life outside the dome, and how it is expendable for the sake of the people *inside* the dome.

I feel hands on my shoulders, feel them turn me around and without even looking, I know that it's Devlin propelling me forward. "We have to get out of here!" he says. "ELSA's taking action." His eyes lead mine towards a lens positioned high on the ceiling, but pointing straight at us. I wonder how much ELSA understands the look of hatred I direct at her.

"It wasn't an accident," I say. Although Devlin no doubt already knows this, I feel bound to tell him, as if it makes the man's death less in vain; as if his death should serve as a warning to us all.

My voice sounds so normal; I haven't screamed, haven't cried. And yet inside, I'm a mass of seething emotion. Terror, fury and dread assail me in equal measure. But I dare not let them overtake me.

The Shadowers look as horrified I imagine I must do - too-pale faces look out through haunted eyes onto a world that is brutal and pitiless.

Vaguely I wonder what I look like to them - the girl born and raised in the dome, who stands before them with her every illusion shattered, as if it were nothing more than brittle candy. Do I look up to the job ahead of me?

"We have to move fast." Devlin's face is right in front of mine but I can't seem to focus on it. Instead I see the terror on the unknown worker's face, the incomprehension and finally - at that last moment - his recognition that death was imminent.

I struggle free of Devlin and bend forward at the waist; painfully retch up my meagre stomach contents onto the hard ground. Still heaving emptily, I feel Devlin's hands brush the hair from my face and hold it back. "We have to go," he says again, quieter but no less urgently than before.

When I straighten up, I find that no one looks any better than I feel. I nod. The movement makes me feel sick again but I have nothing left to bring up and it's somehow better than speaking, as I don't yet trust my voice. I let him pull me outside.

"Over there, look!" Devlin points and I follow his indication.

A chain of linked vehicles move on metal rails embedded into the ground, twisting away from us and out of sight behind high buildings. No higher than my waist, each of the compartments appear to be filled with sealed boxes being transported from one area to another.

"Whatever ELSA knows or doesn't know, it's clearly worried about what we are up to. If we don't move fast, we'll suffer the same fate." Devlin doesn't need to elucidate as to whose fate we might share. Nor does he need to tell the Shadowers twice. They're off at a run, heading towards the little trucks before he's even finished.

"What about the horses?" I say. It doesn't seem fair to lead them to their deaths. This is our battle, not theirs.

Gideon, who has been holding both sets of reins, turns the horses around to face the way we came. He gives them a gentle but firm slap on the rump. "Home," he says, and lets them go.

The horses go eagerly and I watch them enviously. Freed of their job and their burdens, they will be back at Devlin's village much quicker than the time it took us to get here. I wonder what Genesis will make of their return, whether she will believe we are dead. Whether she will curse or mourn me.

But we're not. Dead, that is. Not yet anyway.

Devlin, Gideon and I sprint towards the trucks, Destiny running at our heels. We get there just as the last shackled carriage rounds the bend.

Almost not breaking stride, Devlin heaves Destiny into the open compartment whilst

Gideon and I throw ourselves up and over and then reach out to Devlin, pulling him in beside us at the very last second.

We sit on top of the crates. Each one is probably filled with food for the dome. But I'm no longer hungry. I can't stop thinking about how ELSA folded that poor man into a box just like the ones we're perched upon.

What would be the reaction at the dome if they could have witnessed what I just had? How willing would they be to continue on with their perfect lives then?

I want to believe that they would be horrified into action, although I fear the truth is less palatable. Maybe they would avert their eyes, wash their hands of the whole bloody business. And carry on doing what ELSA told them to do. But I know without any doubt, that whatever happens to me now, I will go down fighting ELSA with every breath in my body. I don't have to ask Gideon and Devlin if they feel the same. I *know* they do.

I look at the carriages ahead of us. The Shadowers sit, heads hung low but with backs that are straight and rigid. If ELSA wants a fight to the death she will have it, but I hope it will be her death and not humanity's. She might be all-powerful, but we have compassion and humility on our side, and that surely has to count for something?

"Where are we going?" I ask, as if I actually expect Devlin to know.

"Wherever this takes us. We need to find more people to help us - and we need to find Grey for you."

I notice the slight hesitation before he mentions Grey, but I don't comment. Things are difficult enough. This isn't the time to tell him that it's him I love. As a man, as a life-partner.

I look over the side of the truck. We are rolling along the rails with no variation of speed or route, as if the journey is completely automated. By ELSA, no doubt. I wonder if at any moment she will upturn the trucks, cause the vehicles to roll over us, crushing and killing us instantly. I hold my breath in apprehension, expecting there to be a sudden lurch, a sensation of falling, an overwhelming weight which ruptures organs and breaks bones.

What will my last thought be? Whose face will fill my inner vision? My father's? Willow's? Grey's? Or will it be Devlin's?

But we are not upturned and no images of my loved ones linger before me in my death throes. Perhaps, being automated, ELSA has less control over this transportation system, than she does other machinery. I think about what that might mean.

"OUT NOW!" So close, Devlin's shout almost deafens me. I don't move until he has lowered Destiny to the ground, and then I throw myself out of the still moving vehicle. We are together again, the Shadowers, Gideon, Devlin, Destiny and I.

In front of us is a huge building. Steam or smoke billows from the top of it, I'm not sure which. As the trucks trundle out of view, I wonder what feeling or intuition made Devlin choose this as our next stop. But before I can ask, he's at the wide metal doors, wrenching them apart and entering, without waiting for me or anyone else to catch up with him.

Without hesitation, I follow his lead.

CHAPTER 22

There are people everywhere, a sea of grey uniformed figures, and all of them stop and stare as we enter. There's no obvious machinery so perhaps it's safer here than in the last building, but even so, I'm nervous.

I guess some of the Shadowers are equally uneasy, because they don't follow me. They stand on the threshold of the building, holding the doors open without venturing inside.

"Do you want to carry on existing – living a life that's not worth living? Or will you fight with us, destroy ELSA and have a chance at life?" Devlin says to the Gamma workers, ignoring the cameras which swivel sharply towards him.

For a long moment they look dumbly at him, at me, at all of us strangers who have arrived as if from another world. And then from the back of the crowd, one man steps forward into the silence.

"Tudie!" It is so familiar, so heart wrenching, my breath catches in my throat and although I long to run to him, my legs are too weak, my body too feeble to carry out the command my brain issues.

Grey looks older, more tired and careworn than when I last saw him. Even from this distance, I can see creases at the corners of his eyes where before there were none. I wonder how different I look to him. How different I *am* from the Tudie he knew.

Devlin looks sharply at me then at Grey. His face is pinched, pale, his voice strained, as if of all the things we've encountered, finding Grey like this was the last thing he expected. "There will be time for cosy get-togethers later. Right now we have to move!" But no one moves. "Don't you want to be free?" Devlin shouts to the workers. "Don't you want to *live*?"

Grey and I continue to stare at each other; I don't dare move in case it's just an illusion. Just a cruel and wicked deception.

"Don't you want to give your families a better life?" As he speaks, Devlin jerks at my arm, bringing me a little out of my reverie. Is it a little colder in here than it was before? It's probably only my body's reaction to the shock of finding Grey. Nothing more sinister than that. But Devlin is looking beyond me, beyond Grey and even beyond the Gamma workers who are bunched together in fear. I follow his gaze.

There's a room beyond the one we're standing in. If there are more people in there, they have no idea what's going on out here. Beside me, I feel Devlin's frustration that no one is moving. Is it possible that these people are too conditioned, to do anything about their situation? Is it possible they won't fight for their freedom? Might they actually try to stop us from overthrowing ELSA?

It's strange yet also absurdly fitting that it's Grey who comes to our aid. "I don't know these people. But I know this girl." He doesn't point, but his gaze is so focused that there can be no mistaking who he means. "And I trust her with my life. If she's with them, then we should be too!"

His words, meant to encourage and to bond, cut me with their lack of intimacy. Is that who I am to him now? *All* I am to him, just a girl he once knew? Not his fiancé?

Whatever I think of his words, they galvanise people into action. As one, they start towards us. "Are there people in the other room?" Devlin asks as the crowd flows forward, passing us.

"Yes. It's the freezer. There are people stocking food in there," Grey says.

I look around me. The same type of packing boxes that we sat on moments ago, are everywhere, stacked high on wooden slats. Whether it's because I suddenly realise I'm in a cold storage area, or because of the actual temperature, I shiver.

Devlin's voice is low and quiet, as if he's speaking his thoughts aloud, rather than talking to anyone in particular. "It's watching us. It knows!" His voice, low and tremulous, fills me with more fear than I would have thought possible. Before I've even finished following his gaze up to the camera in the corner of the room, he's running towards the freezer. I reach his side as he begins to pull at the doors which separate the two areas.

I'm sure now that the air is noticeably cooler than it was before. It's not my imagination. Behind me there's commotion. Distracted from the task in front of me, I turn my head back to the entrance of the building.

There's a stealth, an almost languor to the movement of the heavy doors, a subtle inch by inch slide, that seems more than insidious. The sheer weight of bodies pressed against the doors does little to resist the force of the hydraulic motors. I don't dare to think what will happen when the force of the hydraulics becomes greater than the human resistance. What will happen when what meagre energy the Shadowers have, is totally expended... Time is not on our side.

In front of me, Devlin continues to haul on the doors to the freezer, which seem to be stuck. Or locked. Somewhere nearby, something electronic emits a whirring sound and I can't help but remember the thought I had before: If one of the two men I love must die this day, which one I will grieve the most. And why.

But instead of rendering me incapacitated with fear, I make the worry spur me on. Neither will die. I won't let life be that cruel. I reach towards the doors, but even with my efforts added to Devlin's, they don't budge. ELSA makes sure of that.

The doors behind us continue to close. Once we are trapped, inside this place, everything will be over. There's no way ELSA will let any of us leave alive. I know that now. It's not a coincidence that the temperature has dropped from the moment we stepped inside the building. I shiver in reaction to the frosty air and the morbid thoughts which accompany it.

"Maybe they've found another way out - the people in there." But even as I speak the words, I know they're wrong.

"This is the only way out," Grey says, making me jump because I hadn't even realised he was at my side. But there's no time for awkwardness. No time for anything.

"Stand back!" Devlin orders, as he grabs a low set of metal steps off a rack and prepares to launch them at the large glass panels set into the tops of the doors. His breath is foggy and pools in front of him in a fine vapour mist, but I don't miss the fact that his lips have a faintly blue tinge. I shut my eyes tight as he smashes the steps into the glass - but they bounce harmlessly off, leaving no evidence of the impact.

From behind the doors, people appear. Brought here perhaps by a realisation that something is wrong, that the temperature is too cold, they press against the door, panicked, desperate for release. If they recognise that we are outsiders, it doesn't seem to matter to them. They surge towards the doors, pushing against one another until those nearest the doors are crushed against them.

Even then they don't stop, but clamour almost over one another, mouths open and shouting, screaming perhaps, fists banging against the doors until they are raw and bloodied. None of their noise escapes the room.

I want to tell them to stand back as Devlin prepares to strike the glass again, but they will not hear me, just as I am unable to hear them.

Only seconds have passed, yet I watch their faces become greyer than their uniform. Then, as Devlin brings the steps up for another desperate sweep at the glass, I see ice crystals begin to form on the tips of their nostrils; a light frosting glimmers on their lips. Their eyelashes glitter.

Behind us there is screaming, but I don't steal my gaze away. If there is no more that I can do for these poor people, I can at least do this; I can bear witness to their murder. Whatever goes on unseen behind me, I have to trust that others are working this hard to give *us* a chance to get out of here.

Devlin launches the steps against the glass again, and is rewarded with a tiny crack that looks more like a miniature spider's web than a fault in the glass. But the force of the rebound causes the steps to fly out of his hands, ripping away strips of his skin, where his fingers had held on to the frozen metal and losing us precious seconds.

I lift my own hands in front of my eyes. Droplets of moisture are forming into crystals there too. I wonder how many seconds we have left. Devlin scrambles for the steps again, even though the pain in his hands must be considerable. Grey has found something to use too, a packing crate which he uses to launch at the glass in the half beat between Devlin's strikes.

Standing dead centre in front of the cracked glass, I'm forced to step back a little, to let the two men time their alternate strikes. I count the blows in my head as they land, aware that I'm also ticking off the seconds of our lives. Ten, eleven, twelve… will this glass never give way?

On the other side of the door they have stopped fighting for their lives. Where they had crushed against the doors, desperate for release, now they appear to be huddling against one another, linking arms and bodies for warmth and comfort.

They stare at me with glazed eyes and for

all my efforts to hold their attention, keep them alive, I think that a vital light has gone out in each of them. Young men and women, some maybe even younger than I, their lives are over before they have been even half-lived. I try to take in every detail of their faces, every tilt of nose and line of jaw, hold them in my memory as if by the force of sheer will I can sustain them. Soundlessly, they shiver violently, try to wrench their frozen lips apart, to call out for help to me, to one another, to anyone.

Any tear I would cry is frozen in place, a perfect pearl of ice that will not even have the decency to slide off my frigid face, but instead sits there, rigid and unmoving, a travesty of respect. They blink ever more slowly, as if they are doing nothing more than falling asleep, a heartbeat stretching into a lifetime between each blink - between life and death.

They are no longer grey. Gone from their faces is the monotonous shade of a leaden sky; now their skin bears more than a hint of blue. A light dusting of snow coats their faces and uniforms.

And they fall. First one and then another, and another; a macabre avalanche. They pile on top of each other, unfeeling, unknowing.

Beside me, I feel Devlin and Grey redouble their efforts. I'm so cold and so emotionally overwhelmed that I'm not actually sure I care anymore, as if my heart having tremulously reached full capacity, has turned itself off. Numbness seeps from my bones.

It's all so impossible – fighting ELSA – battling a machine that cares nothing for human life. Impossible and pointless. We will fail because ELSA is stronger than us, more ruthless... Except that Willow needs me. Her face, so sweet and true, fills my vision and I know that for Willow's sake alone, I will battle ELSA until my dying breath.

With the back of my hands, I rip the frozen crystals from the tip of my nose. The crack in the glass is wider now, extending from one side to the other. And yet the glass still holds.

Devlin pushes the ladders to the glass and leans his full weight against it. I'm thankful that his body is protected from the frozen metal by his clothing. Grey does the same with the packing case. There is a sharp splintering sound and finally the glass gives way, shattering into harmless little fragments. We climb into the freezer.

Each body I touch is rigid; flesh frozen and solid. There is no life left to save here. Other than our own, if we're not too late for that too. I reach for just one more person, hope a thin quivering bird in my chest. But I know by the stiffness of the body that she's dead even before I turn her over.

Maybe only fifteen or sixteen years old, she

was pretty - slight of limb and with long, dark hair that I suspect would curl around her face, in life. Now it sticks to her uniform like it's been fused there. I hold her frozen corpse to me, rubbing her arms with my own stiffening hands, breathing my cold breath onto her face in the hope that I can find just the smallest flicker of life in her blue eyes. But they are cloudy, lifeless, the colour all but bled from them by the cold.

Devlin wrenches me to my feet. "They're gone. We can't help them now. But we can't let them die in vain." He pulls me back towards the smashed door. I look for Grey and find that he's still on the other side of me, clutching my other arm, dragging me through to the other side.

I am so cold. And yet it's not so bad, I think. There is a soothing numbness to this cold, a chance to forget how we have spectacularly failed. "Tudie, walk!" Devlin shouts at my side, which surprises me, for aren't I already walking?

But when I look down I realise that I'm not moving my legs at all. Instead, Devlin and Grey are dragging me forward between them. I force my feet to the ground, take my own weight and a lurching step forward. Together, we stagger to the exit.

The building is almost empty. Only a few people remain inside, trying to keep the doors open. For us. Whilst we have been otherwise occupied, they have been busy. They've attached ropes to both doors which pass through the ever narrowing gap. On the other side, I can barely make out the lines of people hauling on the doors, only just managing to keep them open.

"Hurry!" the Shadowers urge as they abandon their posts and slip narrowly through to the outside.

"You go first, then Tudie, then me," Devlin says to Grey as we approach. The gap is even narrower now and continuing to close. It's logical that Grey, the biggest of us three should go first.

Grey looks at me and when I nod, he doesn't waste time arguing. He slides his body sideways through the gap and emerges safely on the other side. He holds his hand out to me through the gap, but I hesitate before I take it. There's still just enough room for me to get through, but when it's Devlin's turn he will be trapped. And with the temperature continuing to drop, his fate will be sealed. I can't bear the thought of losing him.

I hesitate. I'm about to insist that he takes my turn, when Devlin shoves me hard and fast into the gap. Grey pulls and Devlin pushes and for a moment that seems suspended in time, I am caught between two worlds – a bright freedom with Grey and a frozen wasteland with Devlin.

As if I am unable to decide which world I want, I remain there whilst the doors close a little tighter on me, squeeze a little more breath from my lungs – and then I am hauled free.

With the obstruction I posed gone, the doors close a little more. I can only just see Devlin through the gap. With a start, I recognise the way he's looking at me, as if memorising my face. We lock eyes and in that one moment, in that instant, all my denials fade away. I have loved him almost from the first time we spoke, from when he tried to hide his real self under a bluff, gruff exterior. And now it's too late to do anything about it!

As if he understands what goes through my thoughts, he shakes his head and steps away from the door in resignation. The gap is too narrow for him to get through.

It's then I do something so instinctive, I don't even think about it. I force myself into that gap between the doors once more. And I reach out to him. Narrower and tighter than before, I feel as if my head will explode with the pressure from the doors, but I remain in place. From outside I hear the gasps of dismay that come from the people there. I only hope my act will encourage them to pull even harder on the ropes.

"If you don't get through here right now, then neither will I!" I say, knowing I mean every word, that it's not a bluff. The pressure on my spine, my internal organs is immense. I'm almost surprised that I don't spew intestines out of my mouth instead of words.

Devlin shakes his head at me and tries to push me back through, so I say the only thing which might galvanise him into action. "I love you, Devlin. I can't leave you behind." The doors are squeezing me so tightly now that the words come out breathlessly. My heart constricts and I can't tell whether its pressure or emotion. Or both.

So I do the only thing I can; I grab at him and pull him towards me, towards the gap. Inch by inch, I work my way towards the outside as Devlin matches my stance and takes up each inch of space I free for him. I prise myself out of the gap and him into it, as if he has only taken my place.

But our soft bodies are no match for the heavy doors. They close a fraction more, almost imperceptibly, and Devlin's eyes bulge. His breathing becomes more rapid and shallow. Unless I get him out quickly, any minute now I will hear his bones snapping.

"Pull harder on the doors!" I scream as I haul on his arm, trying to dislodge him. Perhaps they manage to find another minuscule scrap of effort and apply it, because the gap widens ever so slightly. Enough for someone to wedge one of the smaller crates in it.

It *has* to be enough. I haul on Devlin to the sound of splintering and I'm no longer sure if it's the crate the tremendous racket is coming from, or Devlin, but suddenly and all at once, he's free. We fall down together in a heap of arms and legs.

But as if I have given too much of myself in

my admission to him, we are suddenly awkward with one another. I stand, refusing to meet his gaze. I have no idea what he thinks of me or my feelings but this isn't the time to find out. There will be time later for declarations of love or embarrassed rebuttals. Instead I look for Grey.

He's just behind me. A young woman stands next to him and from the way she gazes up at him, I can tell what's in her heart. And I am relieved beyond words. Her face is open, at once scared and yet strangely expectant, as if she has waited her whole life for this one moment. And who am I to say she hasn't? But although her gaze is so focused on him, it is me who Grey turns towards.

Without him saying a single word, I know everything there is to know, in that one glance. I know that he loves me. But not with the kind of love he shares with the woman at his side, the kind of love I feel for Devlin. His love for me is like mine for him, and for Willow. I wonder if he can read my eyes and expression as well as I can his. Grey opens his mouth but I speak first. "Later!"

There are people everywhere. More than came out of this one place. People flood towards us from every direction, from buildings all around. I wonder how far this mass exodus can extend. All I know is that we don't have the time to stand around waiting to find out, because right now, I'm sure that ELSA is making her own plans.

I look towards Devlin.

His face is strange. Unreadable. "We need to be away from here. Away from the machines and the cameras. We need open ground," he says.

The shortest way to open ground has got to be the direction from which we came. But this time we will have to walk. There will be no automated trucks to ride on, no chance to travel more quickly. "I'll catch up with you in a moment," I say to Devlin and hang back.

I see a brief confusion on his face and then a hard clarity which sets his features in stone. Perhaps he believes that I gave my declaration of love in desperation. And I did. But not in the way I'm sure he thinks.

I wait until Grey shakes the young woman loose, urging her forward into the march towards safety. She leaves reluctantly, with a long lingering look at him and a short wary one at me. I fall in at his side. "Who is she?" I ask.

"Piety," he says simply, not bothering to deny what I already know. I'm grateful to him for that.

"She loves you," I say. He doesn't deny it. "And you love her." I am only a little saddened by the thought of what we might have meant to each other, but now never will.

"Yes." He turns his face towards me as we walk. I see sorrow and remorse but I also see how she makes him feel, how his eyes are alight in a way they never were for me. "I thought I'd never see you again. That this was my life now..."

I am wounded that he thought so little of me that he hadn't believed I would come for him. But not dismayed about his new love, I realise. "We had a wonderful love, Grey. But it's gone. We are different people now. Both of us." In case he thinks this is a reproach, I carry on. "I love someone too. I hope you can be happy for me, like I am happy for you."

Grey smiles. "Of course I'm happy for you, Tudie. Never imagined this is how things would turn out between us though."

I think about that, matching my strides to his. "Fighting ELSA to the death?" I laugh a little too harshly and stem it quickly before it overtakes me. "They wouldn't have done, not if we were still in the dome. But I guess this is what comes with freedom, Grey, the ability to choose your own path in life."

"Your path is with him now, at the front of this." His mouth smiles, but I think that his eyes are just a little sad. At least I hope so. I don't want to think that what we had was so disposable that he won't ever think back on it. One day. When we are all old and done.

I take hold of his arm, hold him back whilst the rest of the crowd surges forward and away from us. I have to stand on tiptoe to reach his lips but the kiss I bestow upon him has no passion.

It's a goodbye kiss and we both know it. "You'll always be important to me," I tell him.

He smiles and this time it reaches his eyes. "That's good, because you'll always have a place in my heart too." He takes my hand from his arm and squeezes it gently. "Now go to him! Find him and stay by his side." He lets me go and I am running, charging through the crowd to be at the front with Devlin once more. I don't need to look back to know that Grey is searching the crowd for his woman too.

By the time I catch up with Devlin, several minutes have passed. I'm too out of breath to speak. It's another ten minutes or so before he breaks the uneasy silence between us. "I've sent people off to every building we pass. Word is spreading. Soon the whole place will be empty. When we are on open ground there will be little time to talk. People will be looking for their families but we will need to make a plan fast."

"I meant what I said back there," I say, trotting at his side. Wishing he would slow down a little, whilst knowing full well that he can't.

"You don't need to keep up the pretence, I'm out now. But thank you for spurring me on."

I manage to snort derisively if rather breathlessly. "You are the most obstinate, stubborn, stupid man I have ever encountered!" I pull in a big breath. "And if you really don't know how much I love every bone in your body, then you are insensitive and unobservant too!"

I am swept off my feet before I even know what's happening. I feel his arms encircle me, his lips find mine. "I have loved you since the very first moment I laid eyes upon you, Fortitude Smith!" His kiss is sweet, his tight embrace reassuring. People surge past us, but I no longer care.

He pulls himself away. "I want to have a long and happy life with you, Tudie. But we have to fight first." He tries to push me gently into the moving mass. "Stay with the women. Please. I need to know you are safe."

As an Alpha I am roughly level in height with him. I use this to my advantage. "And I need to know you are safe. Besides, we've worked well as a team up until now. And we have a vested interest in keeping each other alive." I hold his gaze until I feel him relent.

Linking hands, we push forward to the front again. Ahead of us, the crowd has stopped moving. Have we reached the open ground so quickly? I am sure that we had travelled further than this, into the centre of the sector.

When we finally emerge at the front we find out why the crowd has halted. Assignment vehicles stretch in a straight line directly across our path.

And there are at least twenty of them.

CHAPTER 23

Although I have never seen even one assignment vehicle before, I know that this is what they are. Besides, what else can they possibly be? Black, with every part seemingly made of the same material, they look like large metal boxes placed on top of two series of wheels, and on each side some sort of loop connecting the front wheels to the back ones.

There is no movement either from the crowd or from the vehicles. All is still. Silent. Waiting. It's an unnatural hiatus. I feel it in every cell of my body. I dare not move for fear that if I do, I will trigger something that for now lies dormant, begin a chain of events from which there will be no return.

But haven't I already done that? Certainly there will be no return for the man who was crushed like a bug. Or for those who froze to death. How then can there be a return for me, for Devlin, for *any of us*?

I hadn't noticed it previously, but each vehicle has a display board, just below its roof.

In unison, all of the boards light up. Under different circumstances, the red lights might have been a spectacular sight to behold; under these circumstances, they are simply malevolent. The lights transform into words. *Return to your work. Immediately.*

As if the order is a catalyst, the crowd surges forward. Devlin and I are pushed towards two of the vehicles, so that we have one on either side. Destiny bounds at my heels.

Flaps open at the front of the metal boxes and there are suddenly explosions everywhere, great clumps of earth flying from the ground and landing a giant's throw away. My ears are ringing, and although that sound is maddeningly loud, all other noise seems to have been dimmed. Devlin is clutching my hand, dragging me forward to that gap between the vehicles and I push my legs onwards, trusting his judgement explicitly.

Only once do I look back, when another set of explosions ring out. It's then that I realise those flying lumps are not just dirt and grass – they are human body parts, arms and legs. Heads and torsos. I'm so horrified I almost stop in my tracks, until Devlin pulls me onwards.

We throw ourselves into the gap between two of the vehicles. Destiny is scared, panting hard, but he stays at my side, trusting me above all else. I hope I can live up to his trust. I have no idea what Devlin plans to do, or even if he has a plan at all. Up close, I can see that the vehicle has those same holes it's firing through at the front, on each of the sides too.

"We're safe here because if they fire sideways, they'll hit each other," Devlin shouts at me. "ELSA won't risk that." I think he means it to be reassuring, but the thought of her knowing exactly where we are, has the opposite effect.

I look back at what remains of the crowd. People are running in every direction. Some make it to safety, or at least disappear out of my line of sight with all of their body parts still intact. Others are less lucky.

There is so much noise. And a strange smell fills the air too. I can't identify what it is, and superstitiously I think that if I ever learn to identify its source, I will be a different person to the one I am now.

People are still running towards us. I guess they see that there is a way through. Some brave souls run in front of the vehicles and are not shot down. Perhaps there is an optimum range? Perhaps up close, you are safer than further away? "We have to stay close to them," I yell at Devlin.

He doesn't respond. He seems to be searching the metal for something. I've no idea what. "I'm going around to the back. Stay here," he says. He's standing on top of the belt that encircles the wheels. His head is inches below the open boxes at the front and the closed ones at this side. The risks are more than obvious. The vehicle is still firing, still killing.

Rather than answer him, I climb up beside him and pull Destiny up too. Wherever Devlin goes, we're going. He doesn't waste time in arguing with me. We shuffle along the one side of the metal. There's just enough room for Destiny's narrow flank. Even though I am focusing on what I'm doing, I can't help but notice the swarms of people who are similarly clambering over the other vehicles.

Many have died today. But it appears that rather than subdue and oppress the remaining people, this act of warfare has inflamed them, released in them the desire for revenge, for freedom. Whatever the cost.

Some have things in their hands, tools, levers, perhaps just whatever they were holding when the call for freedom came, but they are using them as weapons now, beating down on the once smooth metal. Some of the vehicles, including the one we are on, are trying to move, to turn in other directions, but their movements are hampered both by their close proximity to one another and by the sheer volume of bodies clinging to them.

We are juddered and shaken by the vehicle's movements but we cling on, and although we continue to move around it, our steps are more cautious and tentative than before. I look back to check on Destiny but he seems more sure footed than me. Perhaps having four feet is an advantage over having two.

Devlin and I clamber to the back of the vehicle. If indeed it is the back. It looks more or less the same as the other three sides, except that it has a panel which looks like it might open to reveal what's inside.

Of course! This is an assignment vehicle. It has to open up to be able to take its load from one place to another. There is no handle on the door, no scanner, button or other method by which to open it. There is merely a rim where the large door sits inside the rest of the panel. "How do you open it?" I shout.

There is still so much noise. Even though the explosions have stopped, there is much screaming and I think that under that noise there is the sound of people crying. I choose not to think of whom they grieve. Grey and his new love, Piety, are out there somewhere. I can only hope that both of them are safe.

Nine too was somewhere within the crowd, the young boy who has lived such a miserable life, through no fault of his own. It's too cruel to think that fate might have been even harsher to him, might have taken his life, when there was a chance that it was just about to begin. I think about all the people I have met, the ones I have a name for and those I don't. The middle-aged Shadower woman with the haunted eyes, the man ELSA forced to amputate his own hands, Gideon, Brean and all the others.

Selfishly, I hope that those who have died are unknown to me. That they are not people I have put faces to, names to. I hope that they were all just faceless strangers and will forever remain that way. But I know now that fate is never that kind. With his bloodied fingers, Devlin pulls at the metal rim. It doesn't give way.

I feel a body clamber up next to mine and glance across. It's Nine! I am so overwhelmed with relief to see him that I almost let go of the side and hug him to me. He hands Devlin something. It's a long metal bar. "Good to see you, Nine," Devlin says, taking the bar and pushing it into the rim.

Nine just grins back, but I think I see his face colour a little at the implied concern. Devlin pushes down hard on the bar. Nothing happens. Then suddenly there is a screech of rending metal and a cheer. I look towards the sounds. One of the vehicles is lying on its side, wheels still spinning uselessly underneath. It seems the people have gained a small victory. But immediately, flaps open on its other sides and where is it not facing another vehicle, it begins its fire assault once more.

A woman, thin and undernourished looking, holds her arms up briefly as if trying to halt the attack heading towards her. The weapons fire and suddenly she is there, still standing, but minus both arms. Blood spurts from both empty sockets and I see the life drain out of her.

If there had been anything in my stomach, I would have ejected it forcibly at the sight. Instead, I am left with a mouthful of bile. I spit it onto the ground and turn my gaze back to Devlin and Nine. They have managed to get the lever further into the rim of the opening. Where the bar is placed, the door is buckled and warped. I watch as they remove the bar and insert it only a little way away from where it was before.

It takes a few moments and a great deal of hauling on their part, but finally that section too begins to warp outwards. They move the bar along.

There's nothing I can do to help but I can't leave either. From beyond where I stand, there are more cheers and more gunfire. I can't tell who's winning and I'm too scared to look. "What's happening out there?" Devlin grunts, still hauling on the bar.

I'm forced to look, in order to answer him. "Some of the vehicles have been toppled onto their sides. I think about eight. And others seem to be trying to form a circle."

Devlin's sharp look tells me everything I need to know about what will happen if they manage to make that manoeuvre. "There are people on top of the moving vehicles though," I say, although I'm not sure if this is actually good or bad.

Devlin buckles another section of door and moves the bar again. "Are there still people on the sides?"

I nod then realise his attention is still fixed on the doorway. "Yes." I look harder. There is nothing else for me to do except inform Devlin. I tell myself I am not looking for one familiar face in particular but I know that I am. You can't love someone, *really* love them, and be indifferent to their welfare. I can't imagine living without Devlin; don't want to imagine it. But Grey was my first love, the first man I kissed, the first person my heart yearned for and I can't just forget that.

I scan the people. First the dead, the ones who are still intact enough to be recognisable. I am flooded with relief when I don't find him there. Then I look at the still living, but I can't see him anywhere. I tell myself that this is okay, that he's just out of my line of vision, but it doesn't help.

Something strange catches my attention. The people clinging to the sides are trying to force something down the holes that the weapons are being discharged from. From this distance I can't tell what they are, but they look like clumps of earth or…

They're body parts, I realise, sickened.

Arms and legs are being stuffed into the weapon holes. I can't figure out the reasoning – then there is a muffled explosion and a vehicle comes to an immediate halt. The red display, which continued to read, *Return to your work*, even as it shot at everyone at sight, goes immediately dark.

"They're blocking up the holes, so they can't shoot. The vehicles are actually blowing themselves up -" There's an ear-splitting scream that makes me jerk my head abruptly in the opposite direction. I can only guess the screamer has fatally mistimed his attack. One of his arms is missing and smoke billows from the empty socket. He falls, writhing, to the ground, and the wheels roll over him, crushing him like a grape. I don't need to look, to know that there is no life left in him.

"I want this one intact!" Devlin grunts.

I don't ask him why. If I have learned anything from being with him, it's trust. He gives a final wrench and I can see that over half of the doorway is now buckled outwards. He places the bar a little differently this time and the entire section lifts and folds out, the metal bending over itself. It's not how the door is meant to be used but it's enough for us to crawl into. The interior is dark, unlit.

"It's just an empty space," Devlin informs us. He uses his arms for leverage and folds his legs into the hole. Regardless of his assurance, my heart is hammering wildly. And doesn't calm even when he reaches out a hand to me. "Get in," he urges. I lift Destiny into the hole then climb through and help Nine in.

The space is much larger than I had thought it would be. There's just enough light shining through the hole we've made, to be able to see that Devlin is feeling his way around the walls, searching for something. "If I can find the access panel -" he stops talking abruptly as his fingers close around something. He pulls and a metal cover comes away in his hands.

Behind the panel there is something that I recognise. It's a screen, although it's currently blank. Beside it are copious amounts of wires, different colours, all snaked and twisted together. Without wasting any time, Devin pulls on the wires.

Instantly I feel the vehicle stop. It's so sudden, I'm almost thrown into Nine, and have to steady myself with my hands outstretched. "This one's inactive now," Devlin says. A dread assails me again. Does that mean we will be moving on to another, to repeat the process? How long can our luck possibly hold out? Which of us will be killed first?

Without bothering to replace the panel, he climbs back outside. Destiny and I follow him. Nine brings up the rear. Outside, everything is suddenly quieter. Or at least there are no more explosions. There are only sounds of human origin. Bizarrely, I think of the other morning, a lifetime ago, when I had walked into the dining area of the dome and thought it noisy. The day when I had first met Willow, when my whole life had turned a corner, had I only realised it.

The vehicles are all still, all silent. It seems the humans have won the war, or if not the war, then at least the battle. People walk around dazed, others search the dead, perhaps for loved ones. Some help the wounded. And yet every face I see looks the same. Etched with grief and shock, it's as if we have lost humanity's greatest individuality - our sense of self.

A lone figure stands out from the crowd. Taller and with a better physique than those around him, it is Grey. He is safe. I watch him find Piety and surround her in his embrace. I am genuinely happy for them, but I look quickly away. I am not yet emotionally distanced enough from Grey, for this not to feel like prying.

Devlin climbs on top of one of the overturned vehicles. "Many of you will have lost friends, lost family today. And with you, I grieve their loss. But if their deaths are not to be in vain, if they are to mean something, to pave the way for a brighter future, then we must not stop now." He gives them a moment to think about that. "There are other sectors - there may be other assignment vehicles, time will tell - but all of them are controlled from one place. From ELSA itself."

I hear their murmured agreement, feel the people come to stand closer to me, looking up at Devlin as I do. But I wonder if any of them are as chilled as I am when he issues his next statement.

"It's time to bring the war to ELSA. To take the war to the dome."

CHAPTER 24

Through a lengthy process of elimination, we manage to get the vehicle moving again without regaining its killing mode, reconnecting one wire at a time to the electronic panel. It's not a neat job. Disconnected wires trail from the cavity beside the panel but we're not bothered about the aesthetics.

"Will you come with us?" I direct the question to both of them, Grey and Piety.

Grey doesn't even need to look at Piety before he gives his answer. "No we'll stay here. Piety's family is here, somewhere." He casts his gaze around but it fails to settle anywhere. "I'm not like you, Tudie. I don't think I can rip people who I was friends with, from the dome, make them change their lives, even if it is for the good of others."

I know he doesn't mean his words to be as condemning as they sound. But he's right in his own way. We're not alike, we never really were. He smiles sadly at me. "Maybe one day I will see my family again, when all of this is over. But for now, my place is here." He hesitates and when he speaks again, it is to Devlin. "How will we know if you have won? Or if ELSA has?"

Devlin doesn't even flinch. "You'll know."

I guess it has to be enough, we have no more to offer. I say an emotional farewell to Brean and the other Shadowers, but when it comes to Nine, I try to persuade him to come with us. For some reason I feel it's safer to keep him with me, than to trust to fate alone.

He pulls away from me. "My mother and father are dead but the Shadowers are my family, I can't leave them."

I understand how he feels. Family are not always those to whom we are connected by blood. Sometimes there are ties which bind the heart regardless of bloodlines and genetics.

Devlin, Destiny, Gideon and I will be travelling together. This is how we originally set out from Gideon's village, so I guess it's apt that this is how we will be returning. Although this time we're hitching a ride on a former Assignment vehicle.

Steering is rudimentary and there are no subtleties of movement, but we manage to aim the thing in vaguely the right direction. Since the vehicle requires no rest and no food or drink, unlike the horses we travelled out on, we should be back at the village in a much shorter time than it took us to reach this Gamma sector. And before any of the crowd we leave behind get close to the dome.

"What's next?" I ask Devlin. "Why are we going back to Gideon's village? I thought we needed to head for the dome?" Although the suggestion had terrified me, it *was* what he'd said.

"If we have to go there like this, that's what we'll do. But I'm hoping that we can go better prepared, than in a vehicle we're only limping along in."

I'm disinclined to ask his reasoning. He's been right so far. Whatever plans he's thinking through have a greater chance of being right than being wrong. Or so I choose to believe. I divide some of the food we gathered from Delta Sector and hand everyone their portion, putting Destiny's on the floor for him.

The delicacies are even better than I remember but my enjoyment of them is tempered with the memories of the dead worker. Devlin and Gideon sigh in appreciation as they taste their first mouthfuls. "Now I know why you Alphas believe you are so superior to the rest of us, dining on this fancy food," Devlin says.

I know he means it as a joke, but there's more than a grain of truth in there too. "We don't eat like this most of the time, only when ELSA wants to treat us for some reason. Most of the time we have boring food. Steak or chicken and lots of vegetables..." I stop when I realise how I sound.

Most of the people they know, have *ever* known, are actually starving slowly to death. And here I am, complaining that I didn't get enough treats! I bend my head to hide my embarrassment and pretend to be engrossed in patting Destiny, who lies on his good side, enjoying the adoration.

"You don't have to explain yourself to us," Gideon says kindly. "You lived a different life just because of the fate of your birth. But no one else has done as much as you to bring change to our world, Tudie. You should be holding your head up, not worrying what people think."

But I *am* worried. I'm worried that Devlin will stop loving me, that he will realise I'm shallow, that he will see that we are from such different backgrounds that we cannot possibly make it work.

Devlin doesn't smile. "Gideon's right." He touches one wire to another and we lurch slightly to the left. "We'll take turns steering. I'll take the first shift. You two should sleep." Angle of our travel adjusted, he drops the wire and we continue on our new straight path.

We're travelling with the hole Devlin and Nine made in the door facing forwards. It's the only way we can see outside. I'm not sure if this means that the vehicle is going backwards or whether it was designed to travel equally well in both directions, but either way, this is the only way we can be sure of not smashing into every tree and bush in our path.

"Let me take the first shift," Gideon suggests.

"No. It's best if you take it as we get closer," Devlin responds. Although neither of them say it, it's clear that I will be of little use. I don't take it as an insult. They're merely being pragmatic. I lie on the hard floor. It's not comfortable, but exhaustion means that sleep will probably claim me, regardless of my unyielding bed. I close my eyes and try to let my body relax. Destiny is at my side and I curl one hand into his soft fur for reassurance. But thoughts of ELSA won't let me rest.

Behind my eyelids I see her rows and rows of terminals, her workstations, her digital display boards on almost every wall, her ever-present, omniscient nature. In the dome, ELSA sees everything, *controls* everything. I think about how hard the people in Gamma Sector fought to be free. Will the people in the dome, the Alphas, the ones who have had the very best of everything, will they fight just as hard to *guard* ELSA, to protect and sustain their way of life?

Faces flit in front of my eyes. Joy, the girl I worked with for so long, my friend – will she turn against me when she realises what I intend to do? Will other people I worked with rail against me? Will Grey's former colleagues? His *family*?

It's almost inconceivable that they would. And yet... I think about the reaction of Willow's parents to her banishment. It occurs to me too, that devastated as Grey's family were by what happened to him and his removal from their lives, none of them offered to come with me, none of them pledged to find him, to bring him back. They let me do it. Alone. Knowing full well, that it might prove to be an impossible task.

Was that the mark of a true Alpha after all? Was I merely a misfit there? I think about my father. I can't imagine that he would have stood by and let an injustice be done. But in truth I have nothing to judge the accuracy of that belief on. Life in the dome, is after all, controlled, regulated. There *are no* injustices. ELSA reserves those for everyone *outside*. And that is what must change. Finally with that thought, my eyes close.

When I awake, Gideon informs me that we are almost back at his village. Devlin is asleep beside me, his body just inches from mine, his face so close. I want so desperately to kiss him awake but out of respect for Gideon, I don't. I let him sleep as long as possible.

The assignment vehicle brings fear and apprehension to the faces of the villagers until they see us inside, controlling its movements. Gideon disconnects the wire which powers the vehicle and it grinds to a halt in the middle of the village.

Everyone is talking at once. Scores of voices all asking the same thing in different ways. *What happened?* I leave the two men to give the explanations. There is only one person I am interested in speaking to.

Willow throws herself into my arms. "I knew you'd come back safe."

I think of how close I came that that not being a reality, but say nothing. She's a child. She doesn't need to know the horror of war. That at least, I hope to spare her.

I let her lead me away from the throng. We sit in the house and await the arrival of Devlin and Gideon. Willow treats Destiny to scraps of food and I watch them together. There's an ease between them as if they were raised together. And yet both of them were waifs, who by rights would never have met. Except for me bringing them together.

Perhaps this isn't a good omen as such, but I choose to take it as one nonetheless. Maybe if I can just believe, everything will work out.

It's not long before Gideon and Devlin find us. But it's not me Devlin seeks. "I want to show you something," he says to Willow. The three of us follow him back outside and to the assignment vehicle. He lifts Willow inside, then Destiny; Gideon and I climb back in on our own.

"Do you think you could figure this out?" Devlin waves a hand at the electronic board and loose wiring. "You'd have to be careful because this thing can kill people -"

Willow interrupts him. "Can you pull all the other pieces of metal around it off?"

"Yes. But I don't think there're any more wires than are already here."

Willow approaches the wires and points. "You see that bit there?" Now that she's pointed it out, I can see that there is something slightly different about the edge, where it's concealed under another piece of metal wall. "I think that under there is another screen. I might be able to make it work."

Devlin pulls on the metal and it tears away with a deep rending noise. "Why would there be screens inside here?" I ask. ELSA didn't need them to know what the vehicle was doing, after all.

It's Devlin who answers. "These vehicles were designed to be driven by men originally, from one sector to another, delivering and collecting things. I guess over time, after ELSA was created, it modified the existing vehicles for its own use. Easier and quicker than having new ones made, I guess."

Willow's fingers flit over the dark screens and then she looks at the wiring. "Which ones did you connect to make it move?" she asks.

Devlin shows her. "Did you figure out which ones it used to hurt people too?" she asks sensibly.

"The red and the blue there. There might be more but when I touched them to that bit there," he points to a section of the disconnected electronic board, "they set off the weapons again." He looks at me then at Willow. "I figured those were probably the weapon controls because they looked the newest and the vehicles wouldn't have had weapons in the original design."

Willow nods as if she completely agrees with his assessment. Without further consideration she picks up a yellow wire and attaches it to a segment of the electronic board. I hold my breath in fear and anticipation, but nothing happens.

She doesn't disconnect the original wire but instead delicately plucks a purple one from the snagged mess of wire and connects it too to the exposed board. Immediately the screens flicker into life. But there is no picture on either screen, just a flickering mass of dots. I don't know whether to be relieved or disappointed.

"Hmm interesting," Willow says. She picks up another wire, connects it and the screens at once stabilise into a pure white glow. She turns to Gideon. "Can you get me a chair please? This is going to take a while."

I hover. "Can I help in any way?"

Willow smiles. "If I actually knew what I was doing, I could instruct you and you could help. But it doesn't work like that. My brain I mean. I have to just kind of let things happen inside my head. It's like my head tells my hands the answer, what to do, without me even really knowing what that is."

I guess it's the closest explanation I'll ever get to what genius is. "Do you want me to stay or to leave you alone?"

She looks at me almost bashfully. "I don't want you to go. But I can work better alone."

I kiss her on the top of her head and leave. Destiny seems disinclined to follow me, so I leave him guarding Willow. For some reason the thought of them together is comforting. Devlin and I walk slowly back to Gideon's house. "What is it you hope she can do?" I ask.

"I honestly don't know, Tudie. Maybe only give us an indication how much information the vehicles sent back to ELSA before they were destroyed. Whether there are more vehicles heading towards us. Anything she can find out can only help us."

"You think there are more assignment vehicles?" the idea is terrifying.

"Who knows? But back there we faced more than I thought there could be. What's to say that was all of them? There could be hundreds!"

We are silent for a long time. Outside, the village buzzes with talk about what we have achieved. There's an air of suppressed excitement, and it communicates itself to us, even through the walls. But it does nothing to dispel the horrible feeling I have that we've underestimated ELSA. That our victory so far has been a fluke, a mere stroke of luck. That now ELSA knows our whereabouts, our strategies and our plans, as well as our strengths and our weaknesses, she will be better equipped to deal expediently with us.

And the future of humanity lies in the hands of a seven year old.

CHAPTER 25

"I've done it!" Willow is quieter about her great achievement than I would have expected. Regardless of her superior mental capabilities, she's only seven after all. I had expected her to be at least a little ebullient about it.

I stand up from the chair where I've been dozing and reach across to Devlin, shaking him gently. He comes awake much faster than I did. "Well? Could you get anything to work?" he asks her anxiously.

"More than I thought I would. It'll be easier to explain if you come and see." We follow her to the vehicle. Inside it is light, the illumination coming from little lamps at the ceiling and from the screens which appear to be fully working. There is a picture on one of the screens. I recognise it as the multi-coloured prism that revolved on my work screen when it wasn't in use.

"Can you tell if there are other assignment vehicles like this, headed towards us? Or anywhere else?" Devlin says.

"Yes, I can." Willow lightly touches the

screen and instantly a keyboard is displayed. She types slowly but although I watch her fingers and the screen, I cannot tell what she has typed. "It's coded," she says, "but I figured it out." The screen flashes and I assume what must be the answer appears. Willow studies it for only a moment. "There are other vehicles, headed for a Gamma Sector and for here. But we can send a command to stop them."

I look at her sharply. *Is that really possible?* "How?" I ask.

"The same way I asked the question." She turns away from the screen and gives me her full attention. "I hacked into ELSA's mainframe, the central core of her. She kind of knows I'm there, but she's so confident in her abilities, she doesn't seem to really understand what I can do."

I feel like it's me who is seven and Willow who is the adult. "She knows you're there and she's not doing anything about it?" I can't imagine how Willow can be right about that.

"She can't do much other than close that part of her intelligence down and if she does that, well…" Willow trails off.

"If she does that, she's compromising herself just as much as she would be, by leaving you alone!" Devlin says, his voice filled with awe.

"Well maybe not as much as leaving me alone, but I would just hack into other areas, other levels of her."

"So if you stop the other vehicles, won't she just start them up again?" I ask.

Willow nods. "She'll try to, but I can make them disable their communications link before she reactivates them."

"Are you sure?" I try to not sound sceptical but there are hundreds of lives depending on us. Hell, the whole of the human race is depending on us!

"Yes, I think so."

I wonder if Willow has any idea of how much is at stake. But it's not a burden I'm happy about placing on the shoulders of a young child, even one who is clearly a genius.

"Do you want me to do it?" she asks.

"Yes, do it now." It's Devlin who gives the command. I wonder if he realises the enormity of the task he has put upon Willow. But of course he does! Isn't he the very one who fully understood what it was that ELSA was doing, when all I saw was a life that was controlled to the point of boredom?

I watch Willow hit keys in combinations that have no meaning to me. Her fingers work increasingly quickly as if she is either becoming more conversant with typing or with deciphering the code. Or perhaps both.

Her face is tight with concentration but there's a light which seems to shine from her eyes. Perhaps it's just a reflection of the bright screen in front of her, but I choose to think of it as her will. She pokes a pink tongue out from between her lips, but otherwise there is no sign of whether she, or ELSA, is winning. Finally I can stand the stress of the silence no longer. "What's happening?" I ask.

She ignores me for a count of two heartbeats. "She's trying...to...override...me... but," her voice is peppered with short silences, her attention elsewhere. "But I've *got* her!" Her fingers fly over a few more keys and she presses the last one with a flourish. When she turns back to us, her cheeks are rosy, glowing.

"What just happened?" Devlin asks.

"I gave the command to stop the vehicles moving. It kind of woke ELSA up again to the fact that I was still there. I could feel her nosing about inside her brain, looking for me, so I used that too. I pretended I was her to the vehicles, told them there was interference in the central core and that they should blow all communication links so that the interloper could not access them."

"Did they do it?" I asked. It almost seems too easy.

"Yes. She tried to override my instruction, but I had got there first and since they didn't have any reasoning facilities installed, they were literally just machines that took orders, they did what I had already ordered."

"So they can't be restarted?" Devlin asks.

"Not electronically," Willow confirms.

I reach forward and swing Willow up into the air. "You've done it, you *brilliant* girl!" Her cheeks glow even pinker at the compliment. "What now?" I ask Devlin.

He's quiet, his attention still on the screen. "Willow, what else can you get into?" Recognising that this perhaps isn't the time to completely celebrate, I put Willow down on the chair in front of the screen once more.

"What do you want me to get into?"

"I don't know. That's the problem. Do you think you can take a look around inside her intelligence and see what you find?" he says.

Willow doesn't answer, she just places her hands back on the screen and types. She types for what seems like a long time, but perhaps measured in seconds, is only a minute or two. When she removes her hands from the screen, the prism appears again. But it is different to how I have seen it before.

Now although it still has colour, it appears to be separated internally into sections. There are lines which stretch from one side to another, lines which bisect *those* lines and others which seem to link one area randomly with another. "What is that?" I say.

Willow looks at me in surprise. "That's ELSA."

Devlin and I stare at one another before I

manage to find the words I want. "That's ELSA?"

Willow shrugs. "Well a diagrammatic representation of her to be more accurate. I remember seeing this at my 'ssessment."

"Assessment," I correct automatically, as I had done during our very first conversation. The incorrectly spoken word is so incongruous here that my mind seems to split in two. On one side of my internal vision I see Willow as I had perceived her to be, an average seven-year-old Alpha girl; on the other, I see her how she actually is, a child genius.

"Can you explain more?" Devlin says.

Willow runs her fingers above the lines, not actually touching the screen, which I'm guessing would cause it to change and the keyboard to display. "Those are the separate areas of her. Memory, history, files, how much medicine is stocked, how many people need more protein in their diets – anything and everything she does all the time, every day, those are all there. They're like separate bits of her, because they can all function and operate at once, independently, and yet they're also all connected."

I think about the sheer number of people in the dome, how they all take orders and supply information all of the time, and how ELSA reacts instantly to each one. Everything Willow has said makes complete sense. But one thing strikes me more deeply than the others. "You said memory.

Did you mean ELSA's own memories?"

Willow doesn't answer straight away. She places her hands on the screen. The prism disappears and she begins to type on the keyboard represented there instead. She types a long time, and this time there is more concentration on her face. The light which shines from her eyes now seems to be a fierce determination.

"She's fighting you harder isn't she?" I hazard a guess.

"Yes. She's starting to realise what I can do."

I want to cheer Willow on, to tell her that she can beat ELSA, but the truth is that I'm not entirely sure she can. Besides, putting that amount of pressure on her, can surely only be detrimental to the cause.

Finally Willow withdraws her hands from the screen and the turning prism appears again. There is something different about it this time and I can't immediately tell what it is. Then I see it, a little section which appears to glow more brightly than the rest.

"I've unlocked the main compartment to that part. You know how the dome is, a huge place with lots of other places inside, where people eat and work and sleep – and then places within those places, other rooms for other things or where different people belong?"

I nod my understanding. "Well ELSA's like that. There are all these pieces of her, and other pieces inside those, and then when you get that far, you find that there are other, even smaller bits of her... I don't know how far it goes but she seems to just go on and on. It's like she gets smaller and smaller inside of herself but doesn't actually ever end, just gets too small to see..."

I think it's probably the best explanation I could ever get from something that's so far beyond my level of comprehension. I wonder if in all this, Willow has become distracted from what I asked her. "Did you find out about her memories? What they're about?"

She looks at Devlin then back at me. "You remember I said that it's all separate but all connected?"

"Yes," Devlin and I answer together.

"Well there are memories of when she was first made, what her original instructions were, what she did, how she carried out her operations. Then there are memories of everyone who has ever lived since ELSA's creation, memories of their jobs, their lives, how they fit with her and one another. There are memories too of all the work that's been done since ELSA was made, every plateful of food eaten. Everything."

"You can get all of that?" I ask.

"Yes," she says simply.

And suddenly the two questions I want answers for are on the tip of my tongue. But I don't speak them out loud. Whatever answers are revealed to me, I want them more directly from ELSA, and I want to be standing right in front of her when I hear them.

"When do we leave for the dome?" I say.

CHAPTER 26

The dome is as huge as I remember it, yet somehow less significant within the landscape it sits in. Before, on the few occasions I was outside of it, I thought it dominated the land around it. Now I feel as if it tries to hide there, to sink itself away from my view.

"I never saw it from outside," Willow breathes next to me, her voice filled with awe.

"It's just a building," I say. "You've already conquered ELSA and that's the difficult bit." I'm scared that the sheer scale of the place will make her feel insignificant, convince her that she's not up to the task ahead.

How much ELSA is aware of our plans is unknowable. During the journey we have kept her busy, preoccupied. Devlin had the brainwave of setting ELSA huge problems to solve, one after another, so that she was bombarded with them.

Neither Devlin nor I asked Willow what questions she set for the computer, or how she kept ELSA focused on them, against her will. Even though he and I are the adults and Willow the child, it was clear that whatever Willow could think up would be ten times more complex than he and I could devise together. "Can you get her to open the door?" I ask Willow now.

By the time I have started to climb out of the vehicle, the dome doors are already sliding open. Clearly whatever damage I did to them when I left, has been speedily repaired. I reach back to help Willow out of the small opening in the assignment vehicle but she hasn't moved from her chair by the screen.

"I have to stay here, Tudie. If I stop now, ELSA will regain full control of herself."

Of course! I realise she's absolutely right. It's the major flaw in our plan. "Will you be okay with just Destiny to look after you?" I ask.

She smiles at me. "I'll be fine."

I hate leaving her behind but there's no choice. Devlin and I walk through ELSA's huge main doors.

Everyone who sees us stops and stares. Devlin is so obviously not Alpha, with his shorter stature and different build to the men here, and I whilst clearly physically Alpha, I am so far removed from how I should be dressed and presented, that we draw attention from everyone. "This way," I say, walking as fast as I can without running.

My heart is hammering. Everything is so calm, too calm. Then again there is no machinery here to lift and squash the life out of us. Perhaps there is no real way that ELSA can defend herself inside the dome.

Just as I have that thought, I see immediately that we are wrong. A strange red line appears ahead of us on the floor. It moves towards us, filling the corridor with its luminous glow, from one side to the other.

For a moment I think that it's harmless, just a clever show of lighting. And then it reaches a small group of people standing watching us. In an instant they are gone, vaporised from the feet up. But not quickly enough that I don't hear their screams or see the agonised looks on their faces.

"Quick, back!" Devlin has my hand and he's pulling me away from the line, back the way we came.

"But it's the only way to her main frame area!" I say.

"We're going to run at the line, jump it clear to the other side," he says through gasps.

I turn my head as I run. The height of the line has got to be at least three feet and extends down to the floor. Although it has come no further since we ran from it, neither has it reduced or dissipated. It remains, glowing, active. "If we don't get clear over we'll die!" I say.

"If we hadn't got out of the first building where the man got crushed we would have died. If we hadn't got out of the freezing store room when we did, we would have died. If we hadn't fought back against the assignment vehicles then we would have died..." Devlin says. "But we did. And we're still alive."

We've reached the entrance again. But instead of going through the doors to the outside, we turn, clasp each other's hand and we run – back towards the red beam.

I throw myself forward and up into the air just a fraction before the beam gets me. The run-up has given us speed and momentum, I can only hope that it will be enough.

I'm still wondering as my feet touch solid ground once more. I am millimetres away from the line, standing with my heels almost touching it. For a moment I rock, unable to regain my balance and I think that I will surely fall into that fatal space, but then with a hard pull, Devlin wrenches me to safety. I laugh shakily. "Thought I was done for then."

He doesn't laugh back. "Let's get this over with."

He pushes on the door but it doesn't open. I move in front of him slightly. "I don't know if this will work, but I don't know how else we can get in." I hold my wrist up to the scanner.

Hello Tudie, the display reads as the door slides open. The greeting is too wrong, too informal, and I know that it's Willow who has opened the door for me. I'm relieved she knows we're still okay after the red beam tried to kill us. Perhaps it was something she couldn't stop or perhaps the fact that it did not extend the entire length of the corridor, but stopped where it did, was down to her efforts to save us.

I expect there to be lots of people in the room, but there's only one man. He approaches us immediately. "You don't have access for this level," he begins before he takes a really good look at us, how different we appear.

Before I can stop him, Devlin has the man by the throat, pressing him up against the wall. "If I throw you out of here, you'll die. There's some sort of beam across the floor which will change you into a puff of smoke in an instant, so I'm not going to do that. But you lift one finger to stop either of us, that's exactly what I'll do. Am I making myself clear?"

The Alpha man, although taller and broader than Devlin, bows his head, and Devlin lets him go. I turn my attention to ELSA. Rows and rows of things which look like metal cabinets, fitted with flashing lights, fill the room. I walk past them, looking for the terminal the workers use to access communication with the super computer.

I find it in the middle of the room, surrounded by the cabinets. I lift my fingers to the keyboard. *Hello ELSA. I have some questions for you*, I type.

"Hello Fortitude Smith," ELSA says out loud. The sound makes me jump. I have never heard ELSA speak, never knew she had that capability. "There is no need for you to type your questions, I can hear you and respond with speech."

Although ELSA has used her normal formality with my name, there is something familiar about her voice. The screen displays the revolving prism. "Willow, is that you?" I ask, in awe of the girl's capabilities.

"The child you call Willow has modified my receptors, so that I can hear and make speech and has lent me the modulations of her voice. But the answers are all my own," ELSA says.

I take a breath before I ask my first question. "Why did my mother die in childbirth?"

ELSA doesn't even pause. "Your mother died, Fortitude Smith because she was like you."

It's not an answer I expect or can do anything with. "She was like me? What do you mean?"

"She asked questions. She thought about things."

"Things you didn't want her to think about?"

"Yes."

"What specifically didn't you want her to think about?"

"You."

"Me?" I don't understand.

"Your mother refused to have the Intervention that all pregnancies must have."

"Intervention?"

ELSA whirrs for a moment but does not speak. When her voice starts up again, it's almost reluctant I think, as if Willow is forcing the computer to answer against its will. "Intervention is where foetuses get corrected of any congenital abnormalities."

"But it's more than that, isn't it, ELSA?" I demand.

There is more whirring before the answer comes. "Intervention is where the foetus is modified to ensure that it fits Alpha specifications."

"You mean how Alphas look and how they think?"

"Yes. And of course, life expectancy."

This fact is given away so easily, I'm sure that ELSA can have no idea how it jolts me. "So that's why there are no old people in the dome."

"Optimal life ends at natural age sixty to seventy. Therefore it is common sense to end life when individuals have declined from peak status but before further deterioration."

I hadn't thought it could be possible to be shocked any more than I already was before we entered this room, and yet I am. "And my mother knew this?"

"Not knew. But she suspected many things. That was why she tried to prevent my Intervention with you."

"Because she didn't want you tampering with my genes so that I would die when I was no longer at my peak!"

"Yes, that and other gene modifications that are done at Intervention."

"Like intelligence levels?"

"Yes."

"Willow slipped through your net didn't she?"

There is a hesitation. Perhaps Willow is monitoring the conversation and is surprised at the mention of her name. Devlin's hand reaches for mine. I haven't heard him come up, but suddenly I feel him there, at my side. I turn my head to look for the worker he threatened. I find him, ashen faced, standing just a little behind us. Clearly the revelations pouring forth from ELSA are news to him too.

"Yes. Willow's intelligence was not picked up at Intervention. It was a rare oversight. She was shipped out as quickly as possible once her level of intelligence was realised."

Devlin squeezes my hand. "You said that Tudie's mother refused to have the Intervention in her pregnancy. Does that mean that Tudie's genes are unaltered?"

"Fortitude Smith is an unaltered Alpha,"

ELSA confirms.

"So she will live as long as her body naturally dictates?" he says.

I look open mouthed at him. I never picked up on this detail at all.

"Fortitude Smith will live until her natural decline. There is no pre-programmed date for her demise in her DNA."

"And Willow?" I'm too scared to ask.

"The child you call Willow is currently accessing memory banks to find the way to reverse her DNA programming." ELSA's speech is slower than before, as if she is being stretched over the various tasks she is simultaneously performing.

"Willow, I hope you can hear me. Work directly on reversing that time thing inside of you. It's important."

"I'm nearly done, Tudie." This time I know it's not just Willow's voice that ELSA utters, but her words too.

"You murdered my mother for protecting me!" I say to ELSA.

"Not murdered, Fortitude Smith. That is too dramatic. I merely allowed her to die when she could have been saved."

"And my father?"

"Your father was an accident. Unplanned. He had not yet begun his decline."

"So you had nothing to do with his death?"

"It is one of my functions, to care for the people in the dome. Unnecessary death is against my core objectives."

"Your objectives really are to care for the people in the dome?" I am surprised after everything I have learned.

"Yes, Fortitude Smith. It was the reason for my creation. My creative fathers wanted me to ensure that humankind became as perfect as it could be. That no wars or natural disease could threaten the future of humanity. This is why I was created. This is my mission."

"But you have done the absolute opposite, ELSA. You have turned the humans in the dome into machines, with not a shred of their humanity left intact."

"My mission is to safeguard human life within the dome and to create and oversee communities outside, that are separated into various industries so that overall harmony and accord can be achieved."

"But that's not what you did, ELSA!"

"I co-ordinated food deliveries and consignments to all areas -"

I cut across her words. "You starved the people outside and punished them when they tried to defend themselves!"

"My mission is to prevent war."

"No ELSA, your actions created war. They have made people divide themselves and finally they have caused your downfall!" I speak directly to Willow once more, through ELSA. "Have you reversed the timeframe inside you, Willow?"

Her words come back through the computer. "Yes Tudie, I'm fine. I'll live to an old age, just like you."

"Can we change it in anyone else? Will we need ELSA to do it?"

In my head I see Willow's smile. "I'm already most of the way through reversing it in the dome's population. It's like a little ticking clock installed inside everyone. In about sixty seconds, everyone will live as long as nature intends for them. Not how long ELSA has decided."

I let her get on with her important work.

"What will you do to me, Fortitude Smith?" ELSA asks. The voice she uses sounds almost forlorn. Almost infinitely sad. But it is Willow's voice she has been modelled on, and emotions are surely only a human trait.

"I want you to reveal yourself to me, ELSA," I say. Directly in front of the terminal, a section of flooring slides away and something rises from the depths below.

The computer is even more beautiful in reality than her image on the screen ever was. Filled with bright luminous colour, she revolves slowly, so that each colour is displayed on its own, before merging with another in an ever-changing spectacle.

I look directly at her physical form as I speak. "They made a mistake ELSA, the people who made you. I think they tried to make a better, purer world when they created you." I speak from instinct, from the part of my brain which knows without ever being told.

"But they were human, with human flaws and human reasoning. And so what they created was fundamentally flawed. You are a computer - rational, devoid of emotion – how could you ever even *start* to reconcile what would be best for the human race, with what is practical and balanced and rational?"

I reach forward, gently easing my hand in between her swirling mass, remembering how Willow told me this could be done. "It isn't your fault, ELSA." My fingers find what they seek and as they close around the hard block which is her core, I say one last thing to her.

"You weren't to blame for what you did. We did this to ourselves." I pull on the core of her, the innermost thing that is ELSA. It comes away too easily in my hand and I stumble backwards.

Devlin catches me before I fall. "Now it's time for humanity to go it alone again," I say.

CHAPTER 27

The dome is dark. Most of the lights have gone out inside and only emergency lighting dimly illuminates the corridors. That too will fail soon I expect; it flickers on and off, each time taking longer to come back on than the time before.

We sit in the assignment vehicle and watch people emerge from the only home they have ever known. For the most part they look scared, panicked. This is not a choice they made for themselves.

In order not to feel too guilty about it, I remind myself that they never actually made *any* choices for themselves, therefore this is just one more.

In time Willow's parents and brother emerge. "Do you want to go to them?" I ask.

Willow is stroking Destiny and barely looks at the people who raised her. "Family is who you make it," she says. She doesn't smile. I think I know exactly what she means though. Devlin, Willow and Destiny are my family now. I chose them and they chose me and that's just fine by me.

I wait until Grey's family emerge before I leave my new family for a moment. They are overjoyed to see me but their eyes search around and beyond me for their son. Before they ask the question, I supply the answer. "He's fine."

"Where is he?" his mother says.

I try to smile as naturally as I can. What they are about to hear will surprise them but it will help to know that I'm fine about it all. "He's with the woman he loves." There's no disguising the shock on the faces that stare back at me. "Her name is Piety and you'll love her too," I add.

"But you and Grey –"

I interrupt their questions. "Me and Grey were in the times of the dome. Those times are gone now. For all of us." It's the easiest explanation I can offer.

"And you, Tudie? Do you have someone else to love?" his mother asks, her eyes showing her genuine concern for me. I nod.

"Would you like to be with Grey and Piety? I can get you there." They take up the offer immediately. I lead them over to where my family awaits. "This is Willow. She's about the smartest person in the whole world. She's done something to this vehicle so that it will take you to where Grey is. You don't need to do anything. Just climb inside and enjoy the scenery."

"How do we send it back to fetch you?" Grey's father asks.

"You don't," I say. "This is a final journey for this thing. It belongs to the old world, not the new one where all people are equal. "Once it's taken you to Grey it will stop working and it'll never move again. That's how it has to be." I kiss them farewell.

"What will you do? Where will you go?" Grey's mother asks.

"I'll go home with my family," I say. I see the looks of confusion on their faces but I don't deign to offer an explanation. I step back and let them be on their way. Willow waves to them and I laugh and join in.

"We could have gone with them and stopped off at Delta Sector," Willow says. "It would have been easy enough to have arranged."

"Yes, I know," I say. "But we have one more thing to do before we get back." I open my right palm.

Inside it, rests ELSA's core.

***

We walk for a long time, until we are completely alone and far away from any sectors, or the dome. Devlin points groups onwards to different sectors, trying to even out how many new people will arrive at any one place.

I don't think about how the sectors will cope. They just will. They have to. After all, we're all the same now. There's no operational dome, no ELSA and no assignments. I have to trust fully in humanity now. And although it's flawed, it's all of us.

When I feel we are remote enough, Devlin and I use stones and our hands to dig a deep hole. It's not wide and it's not long, but it's deep enough that it will never accidentally be discovered.

I drop ELSA into the hole. "It really wasn't your fault," I tell it, even though she can no longer hear me, no longer sense anything. She is finished, done.

"We're human. We make mistakes. One of them was creating you," I say. I throw a handful of dirt over ELSA's core and watch as Devlin pushes the rest of the earth back into the hole, filling it up and trampling it down, so that no one would ever know it was there.

I feel wretched. The dome was in darkness as we left it. Empty and no longer functioning. I feel like I have killed a human instead of a machine. Devlin puts his arm around me. "You're right. Humans make mistakes. But this isn't one of them, Tudie."

I nod. I know he's right. Possibly the only person capable of rebuilding ELSA, or something like her, is the little girl at my side. I wonder if that same thought crosses Devlin's and Willow's minds too.

We stand looking at the filled hole for some time. I am both scared and complacent about the future. There's nothing I can do to manage it, to make it other than what it's destined to be.

"Making mistakes is what's good about being human after all. As long as we learn from them," Willow says.

It's such a profound statement that I don't feel I need to add to it.

"Let's go home," I say instead.

Author's Note: I hope you loved Future Imperfect. Please leave a review and take a look at my other books. Future Perfect will be out soon.

BOOKS BY THIS AUTHOR

The Owners Volume 1: Alone

Loni is terrified. Her very, very worst fears have come to Life. Her Eyon Hatchling, her "Little" is about to be taken from her. Once he is connected to his work machine, Loni knows exactly what will happen to him. He will be gone. Changed. Different. And she can't let that happen.

Not now, not EVER!

Not that Little is prepared to let that happen either! Different to other Eyons, he loves his pet human, Loni, with every feather on his body. And if that means leaving his egg-mother and his home and all he has ever known behind, then that is exactly what he will have to do. And if it means protecting Loni from the brutal never-ending wars, which rage in the distant villages of humans, well then, he will do that too.

Far across the land, San knows that things aren't quite as they ought to be. Comfortable and secure as his life as a pet is, he is convinced that there is something else, some truth that he doesn't yet know...something...darker. And he isn't alone in thinking that either.

And if humans had a different history to what was communally believed, could they also have a different destiny?

When the dreaded appearance of a work machine forces the 14 year old Human, Loni and her Eyon Owner, Little, to leave their home, they have no idea that far away, someone else, haunted by nightmares and enthralled by the mystery of an old medallion, has simultaneously been compelled to embark on a quest, which will inexorably draw all three together and thrust them into a world of danger where nothing is quite as it seems.

The Owners; Alone, Volume 1, is the first in a series of books, specifically aimed at teenagers and young adults. It is a beautifully simple tale of the necessity of human identity, woven intricately into a struggle between what is right and what is more right, between one kind of love and another. It centres on the concept of what it means to be human, with all the emotional and physical frailties this entails and subtly examines how humanity can so easily be lost and at what cost to the soul.

Jigsaw Girl

Jigsaw Girl: When fundamental pieces are missing, how do you put yourself together again?

"Do you think we'll get another dog?" he says.
I'm so shocked I stop in my tracks. "After Shadow?" Breath catches painfully in my chest and I have to force myself not to scream. "Is that what you would have done if I'd died, Charlie? Ask Mum and Dad to give you another sister?"

It's cruel and unfair, especially as the tone it's delivered in is acidic. None of this is Charlie's fault and he's only nine after all. But he can't be allowed to think that life – any life – is so easily replaceable. That like changing a lightbulb, the light of one life can ever replace the light of another, extinguished one. It doesn't work like that.

Not for me anyway.

But what if the end, wasn't the end at all? What if

it was really only the beginning?
Because that's where my beginning started. At the end.

Synopsis: Nothing about fifteen-year-old Scarlett's new life is average.

Tormented by the recent trauma and guilt of being rescued from a house fire when the fireman who rescued her died in the process, she travels a dangerous path of self-harm and alcohol abuse and becomes enmeshed with the darker side of life.

Fuelled by alcohol and guilt and unable to vent her feelings of inadequacy for the sacrifice the fireman made, she's thrust further into despair when her family starts to fall apart around her... and there is nothing for her to hold on to.

When the world seems to turn away from her, one boy shows a keen interest in her, professing his love and swearing they will never part.

But is Matt Jones, Scarlett's salvation, or will he be her final damnation?

Split Decision

Two boys. One chance.

How was Natalie to know that the decision she was about to make between two potential dates, would forever be a pivotal point in her life? That it would mark the time where childhood innocence ended?

How could she even imagine that the wrong decision would send her life spiralling into the stuff of nightmares from where she might not come out alive?

Life takes a cruel twist of fate when Natalie, a completely average [almost] 16 year old, is forced to make a split-second decision...a decision that will change her future and forever alter her perception of trust, love and the realities of life. A contemporary coming of age thriller.

Family: Life

One pair of primate conservationists desperate for a child. One perfect solution.

Primatologists Vlas and Barbara Lingorsky are fully aware of the importance of their work as research scientists in the Rwandan jungle. And of the danger it puts them in.

When poachers kill an infant gorilla, Barbara

is forced into consideration of her biological clock and the memory of the loss of her own child. With Barbara now unable to bear a child naturally, events seem to take on a momentum of their own. It's not too long before her longing for a family overflows into her everyday life, and the perfect solution presents itself...

Printed in Great Britain
by Amazon